A PORTRAIT OF PARADISE

A PORTRAIT OF PARADISE

IYORWUESE HAGHER

Published by J Merrill Publishing, Inc.
2323 W 5th Ave., Suite 120
Columbus, OH 43204
www.JMerrill.pub

Library of Congress Control Number: 2026907285

Paperback ISBN: 978-1-961475-65-6
Hardcover ISBN: 978-1-961475-66-3
eBook ISBN: 978-1-961475-67-0

Book Title: A Portrait of Paradise
Author: Iyorwuese Hagher

Printed in the United States of America
[First Edition]

For Ngiahiin, my Life.

CONTENTS

1

TIME OF QUEEN AISHA

In the beginning was the Monarch butterfly. It flapped its wings and caused a political tsunami in Sofalia. The butterfly was Queen Aisha, a self-styled monarch who lived in her own universe. She was petite, elegant, and beautiful. She lived beneath the bridge of the busiest highway in the high-brow district of the Republic of Sofalia. Sometimes she raised her left hand as a makeshift vanity mirror, tracing the contours of her face with her right, murmuring and nodding in approval at her own beauty. Her inexplicable self-assurance carried the stamp of royalty.

Sofalia, a former British colony in West Africa, staggered from independence into constitutional crises, coups, and a civil war. It claimed to be a democracy, though the word was more boast than truth. Its white, green, and red flag waved on the world stage as the "Land of the Smiling and the Contented": white for peace, red for the sacrifice of the founding fathers, and green for fertile land. Beneath that land, nature had scattered diamonds, gold, bauxite, and oil — as if jokingly hiding treasures across the provinces.

Deeper still lay crude oil, black gold — the curse that set tribes against each other. North Atlantic powers sought to recolonize

Sofalia through its rapacious elite, who enslaved their own citizens. The elite grew rich while ordinary Sofalians became some of the poorest in the world.

The nation called itself the "Land of the Smiling and the Contented," but while the powerful smiled, the powerless bent in grief, waiting for God — or gods — to rescue them.

Queen Aisha lived alone. Her possessions were pans, pots, and rags — props and furniture of her reign. Her bed was corrugated metal, blown loose during a Harmattan storm and delivered, as if by providence, to her palace. She arranged rags upon it, her royal couch. Her pots and pans lay scattered, her insignia of rule. For every queen must have a palace, and hers was under the bridge of Elhadj Kaalu Kabani Way in Calanana, capital of Sofalia.

On the other side of town, in the Abosko and Maidadi districts, the Ogas lived in their homes. The Ogas fenced themselves into fortresses with electrified barriers, cameras, private water supplies, solar lighting, and imported entertainment. Each compound was an island of privilege arrogantly pushing back against the poverty outside.

The highway — built with foreign loans — snaked across Calanana's hills, its asphalt dark and oily. Its smell was less noble: corpses of cats, dogs, even cows, crushed by speeding cars, mingled with the stench of open defecation. Litigation over sanitation dragged between the Federal Government and the Opposition-controlled city council. While the judiciary delayed, the city rotted.

Civilian President Dr. Kima Kila boasted of the highway as his party's greatest achievement. But he never revealed the terms of the IMF and World Bank loans. Rumor said repayment was endless. Foreign contractors had already seized oil blocks. Millions in monthly repayments flowed through the Ministry of Finance before circling into Swiss, British, French, and American banks.

German, American, Chinese, and French companies divided the road, bridges, solar lights, and gutters among them. Sofalia was a neoliberal haven where elites thrived as agents of neo-imperialism.

With no white colonizers left to blame, the elite themselves drove Sofalia into ruin. Inflation soared. Shoppers needed a wheelbarrow of Sodolar notes to buy a bag of groceries: soap, cooking oil, bread, yam tubers. Tomatoes vanished from menus when genetically modified seed monopolies priced peasants out. Famine spread; yet banks posted obscene profits. The stock exchange boomed — a bubble waiting to burst. Paradise for the elite; hell for the poor.

Bandits flourished, taxing farmers and kidnapping schoolgirls. They carried girls from dormitories into forests, violating them with impunity and demanding ransom. Parents wept; governments ignored them. Rumors of a military coup filled the air, a dark hope embraced by the oppressed.

Meanwhile, Queen Aisha remained at her bridge, her universe. Invisible to the traffic linking Maidadi and Abosko, the richest districts, she sat with her back to the bridge wall. Shoulder blades hunched, palm cradling her chin, she sat for hours unmoving, her face locked in fierce internal debate.

Sometimes anger flashed. Sometimes happiness. Then maniacal laughter. Then screeching outbursts. Her moods shifted without warning. Beneath the thunder of the highway, her reign began — her moods the wings that stir Sofalia's storm.

She lived in blissful indifference to everything. Absent-minded and vacant, even when she moved or walked away from her perch, she seemed elsewhere.

She earned the sobriquet Queen of Sofalia partly for her deliberate elegance and self-assured gait, partly for her contempt toward the political class. She spoke with ex-cathedra authority, as though her words issued from a throne.

Often, after long spells of statue-like idleness she called meditation, she would burst into her signature splenetic cry:

"These bastards... these bastards!"

Then she would glare at the world, offended at the intrusion into her supposed deep thoughts — thoughts she claimed were solutions to Sofalia's daunting challenges.

Onlookers often laughed in disbelief when she recounted her near engagement to Senator Kanyi or declared herself the designated overseer of Paradise Church, which she insisted her parents had founded. Other onlookers swore by the high heavens that what the mad woman was saying was true — nothing but the truth.

2

ENTER THE ATSAN

There were others, too. Like Queen Aisha, they were the Atsan — a vernacular term for the poor, unemployed, and down-and-outs, the great unwashed. Past administrations' reform agendas had bypassed them, leaving them economically crippled. Even the multi-point agendas of recent years ignored them.

Thus, they slipped off the radar of human development, into invisibility. They were free at last — free from Sodolar devaluations, fuel hikes, and electricity costs. Anonymous now, they existed outside the National Identification Project, the Health Insurance Scheme, and the Universal Basic Education Scheme. Forgotten. Invisible. They lived on the rim of national consciousness in a land where the ruling ideology was everybody for themselves in pursuit of collective greed.

Nobody cared whether the Atsan ate, slept, or died under the bridge of Elhadj Kaalu Kabani Way. They, in turn, stopped caring whether Sofalia existed at all. They lived moment to moment, inhaling the sights, sounds, and smells of Calanana.

They, too, heard the rumors of a coup and silently celebrated. Whether it succeeded or failed mattered little. The word *coup* itself became their mantra of faith. Only a few remembered the last attempt.

That coup, like most failed ones, ended in blood. Major Julius Ugat led it. Court-martialed with his men, he faced the firing squad in his village square.

The first volley tore through his head and torso. He opened his mouth wide and cried:

"Zombies, I curse you! We came to save Sofalia, but you rejected salvation. May the land know no peace, prosperity, or unity!"

"Squad, shoot!" barked the sergeant. Another hail of Kalashnikov fire riddled his body.

His family wept in silence, too afraid to voice grief. His grandfather, a one-legged WWII veteran, muttered that at least his grandson died courageously. But the military returned that night, killed the surviving family, exhumed Ugat's corpse, drenched it in petrol, and burned it. They would not risk his grave becoming a shrine.

The Atsan were schooled in gutters and sewers. They calculated daily statistics from the garbage bins of Maidadi and Abosko: alcohol consumed, meats eaten, cosmetics worn, medicines taken. All data was in the trash. They became professional scavengers.

Calanana had two dams producing enough potable water for all. But most citizens queued at dry taps, brawling while waiting for supply that never came. Instead, the water was diverted to golf courses, spas, and private pools to rival Dubai, London, or New York.

The Ogas' dogs snarled at the Atsan, but the poor had weightier concerns — what to eat for a single daily meal.

Life was cruel, but solidarity made it bearable. Poverty loves company. The Atsan shared the same absence of education, the same exile from rural homes. Unemployed, underemployed, unemployable — they migrated to Calanana, lured by visions of paradise.

The journey to the capital cost them family, friends, and dignity. But reaching the bridgehead, the Land of the Free, Smiling, and Contented, was their necessary sacrifice.

The dogs could bark but never bite. They, too, were enslaved — pampered by the Ogas' doctors and dentists but chained to guard wealth stolen from Sofalia. Meanwhile, their masters rode armored convoys to banks, where managers petted their dogs as they rearranged dollars and precious stones in vaults.

Dogs lived in the bedrooms of their mistresses. They lounged and slept everywhere, convinced they were family, since their food arrived with the groceries. Called "good boys" and "good girls," they shared their masters' prison: tall fences, electrified wires, CCTV, armed guards.

Perhaps through some animal intelligence, the dogs recognized their kinship with the Atsan — fellow members of the abused and exploited class. They barked on cue, baring teeth, but when the Atsan drew near, they tucked their tails in guilty retreat, pleading for understanding: forgive us — this is only for show. Then they whimpered and retreated into their prisons.

The Atsan feared neither dogs nor Ogas. Behind villa walls, the elite hoarded vanity toys: Bugattis, Lamborghinis, Rolls-Royces, Ferraris, Pegasuses, trucks, yachts. Customs officers waved them through without duties.

There were no proper roads for such toys, except the inner-city boulevards of Calanana. On weekends, especially Sundays, the wealthy children turned them into racetracks, driving with kamikaze frenzy. Deaths were common. Survivors were flown abroad in air ambulances; the dead were buried with pomp.

The Atsan watched from embankments with macabre glee. They clapped inwardly when mangled bodies were hauled from wrecks. The Sofalian elite had not only killed the country on many fronts — they had also destroyed the humanity of their fellow citizens. The day Tima, the daredevil son of the Vice-President, flew over the bridge with his power bike and crashed into the embankment, the whole nation held its breath. He was a handsome, soft-spoken boy. He died on the spot. The Atsan watched the accident as it happened. Briefly, they grieved for him; then the grief turned to glee.

Beyond Calanana, life was worse. Roads were cratered with

gullies like open graves. No good highways linked the capital to the provinces — not even the oil-rich South that fed the national economy. Calanana stood cut off, a parasite living off a body it barely acknowledged.

Militias roamed, trading in kidnapping and robbery. The army "weighed in," but their interventions were a sham. Officers colluded, joining the ransom economy.

Sofalia's affairs seemed impossibly complex to outsiders, but inside they were stupidly simple. Everything — politicians, military, chiefs, clergy, militias — was bound in a web of corruption, a net that drags everyone down.

3

<hr>

THE CITY OF CALANANA

The traffic in Calanana was chaotic. Hour-long jams were routine. Women and children hawked nearly everything, running alongside vehicles, shouting and whistling. They sold soft drinks — Coca-Cola, Sprite, Mirinda — biscuits, bottled water, sweets, teas.

They also hawked traditional medicines: herbal brews that promised to cure everything — malaria, high blood pressure, impotence, even HIV/AIDS.

The men carried imitation watches, perfumes, children's books, rat poison, insecticides, toilet paper, mosquito nets, assault knives, tasers, pepper sprays, and horse whips. The whips were wielded by police in four-wheel wagons, sirens blaring, lashing at small-car drivers too slow to clear the road for officials' convoys.

The Ogas smiled with sadistic pleasure as citizens scrambled out of the way. This was power. Convoys of SUVs and bulletproof vehicles paraded not for function but as monuments of loot. Since independence, Sofalia's rulers had become new colonizers, educated in Ivy League schools, their children abroad pursuing "further studies" and, sometimes, drug trades.

The Ogas lived well — obscenely well — measuring class by their cars and private jets. The more extravagant their garages and hangars, the higher their status. They looked down on the Atsan as rubbish, and the Atsan returned the disdain, fueling a toxic cycle of self-loathing.

They lived close enough to shout at each other, but there was no neighbourliness. Loud weekend parties in Maidadi and Abosko disturbed the Atsan, while the Ogas celebrated in fear. If the Atsan couldn't sleep, neither could they.

It was nature's law: the crying baby who keeps her mother awake also loses sleep. So the Ogas partied behind electrified gates, with dogs on patrol and armed police at barricades.

They feared what would happen if the worlds of Ogas and Atsan merged. Such an ignition could trigger national revolt — a rebellion against Ogacracy, a system they claimed was democracy improved, but in truth a fusion of feudalism and aristocracy: government of the powerful, by the powerful, for the powerful.

For the Atsan, living under the bridge was prestigious. The Elhadj Kaalu Kabani Way was an address of honour. Queen Aisha was one of them, their most educated. Rumour claimed she had once held degrees from top universities before discarding them for life beneath the bridge. This only heightened her stature. She had crossed the boundary from "have" to "have-not," a sacrifice that earned her respect. She was their leader, their queen.

Many Atsan had no bridge, only streets. They sheltered in abandoned government projects — unfinished towers left as carcasses after contractors pocketed kickbacks. Succeeding governments disowned them. Sometimes they adapted contracts; more often they launched new ones, because bigger projects meant bigger cuts.

These empty shells lacked water, toilets, and electricity, but they became homes. Squatter shacks mushroomed across Calanana. Visitors, dazzled by hotels and high culture, were shocked to find sprawling slums teeming with abandoned people — listless, precarious, existing but not truly living.

Perhaps for such people Dostoevsky had written: *"I suffer, but still I don't live. I am x in an indeterminate equation. I am a phantom who has lost all beginning and end and even forgotten his name."*

The rural poor envied urban Atsan, who lived precariously yet closer to opportunity. They recycled the Ogas' waste into food, clothing, and livelihood. The risk was exhilarating. Anything could happen at any moment.

They stood for one another — humanity without discrimination, brotherhood without blood. The unemployed, drifting, hungry, addicted, and mentally ill were all one community. Most lacked both physical and psychological well-being, yet solidarity made survival possible.

The government worried about how foreign tourists might perceive this reality. It could cost Sofalia loans, harm the tourist trade. So the Atsan were often harassed, turned away from shopping complexes when they begged.

The Ogas mocked them: how dare such wretches, vigorous as rats, still breed? They strutted in and out of hotels and malls, brimming with superiority.

The Atsan, for their part, stared at the Ogas and tourists with a mixture of fascination and disgust — mocking their gestures, laughter, and eating habits. Yet they held their ground. Like weeds through concrete, the Atsan endured.

4

—————

INVASION

The senator's visit to Kepe Village felt like an invasion. Six armed guards rode in the pilot car, its siren shrieking louder than fire trucks and ambulances. Rifles pointed outward, menacing villagers who emerged from dingy hovels like a colony of rodents, drawn toward the Apu's palace.

The senator usually travelled in convoys of at least twenty-five vehicles; during election season, never less than fifty. Today was the worst. The pilot car — a Toyota Tacoma pickup — mounted sirens and floodlights. Behind it came a Mercedes-Benz Sprinter ambulance packed with trauma doctors and nurses.

A green Toyota Tundra with more guards followed. Then the decoy car: a Cadillac Escalade carrying the senator's double.

Next rolled the silver-and-gold Bugatti La Voiture Noire. The senator himself drove this toy. Princess Amenika, home from Italy, sat beside him.

Amenika was rumoured to live well abroad, though few knew how. She was bleached white. Her tired eyes shadowed beneath mascara-heavy brows and killer lashes. She grimly flashed between gazing at her phone and fluttering glances at the senator. Her voluptuous figure seemed sculpted for spectacle: breasts jostling against the dashboard, wasp waist, surgically raised behind pressing against her seat.

Behind the Bugatti rolled a Mercedes G-Wagon stuffed with guards, then another ambulance, then a stretch limousine overflowing with thugs, dancers, and ululating women. Fifteen black bulletproof Lexus LX 600s brought additional officials.

The convoy's arrival at the Apu's palace triggered commotion. Villagers crowded the grounds to witness the spectacle. Bugles sounded; guards marched to attention.

Princess Amenika stepped from the Bugatti. A gasp escaped the crowd, followed by applause. Lightly dressed women clapped as if sharing her glory. She smiled and waved, basking in her celebrated return, honoured in the company of Senator Kanyi Mulaake — bachelor billionaire, most eligible man in Sofalia.

Rumour painted him as drug dealer, gunrunner, fraudster. Some whispered of time served in Miami-Dade jail. He neither denied nor confirmed, wearing the allegations as a badge of honour. He boasted of scamming gullible Westerners with Ponzi schemes built on the "stolen wealth" of dead African dictators — Abacha, Gaddafi, Mubarak, Mobutu. To him, the scams were reparations for centuries of slavery.

For this, the Atsan hailed him a folk hero. Who else but a genius could outwit the white men who had once enslaved Africa?

Kanyi's obsession began young. Fascinated with computers, he stole his first machine in a daring shack raid. From then, his fingers danced on keyboards, commanding systems to funnel global bank transfers into offshore accounts. The money bought him police protection, judicial innocence, and political allies. Eventually, he purchased a Senate seat. Now he made laws for the land.

If he were French, he would say, *la vie est belle*. Life was indeed splendid.

But his fortune had its roots in hardship. Born in Kepe and raised amid deprivation, his childhood reflected collective suffering. He and other shoeless boys tied rags into footballs on the beaches, swam naked in the Atlantic, and lived on fish — until oil sludge destroyed the industry.

Fortune later lifted him. He moved his family from Kepe's sands to Abosko's marble floors. His parents, once fishermen, now lived in idle comfort, redefining laziness on their son's mysterious wealth. They prayed daily, thanking God for overflow.

On Sundays they dropped thick wads into the offering basket. Invited by the pastor to give thanks, Kanyi's mother pretended humility, murmuring: "It is the Lord's doing, and it is marvellous in our sight." Her lips praised God while her son praised his genius for theft.

                                    5
                            ____

TIME OF SENATOR KANYI

The drummers announced the Princess's arrival. The crowd surged forward as if beckoned by an unseen hand to join the dance. Senator Kanyi, as usual, sat in his Bugatti, phone pressed to his ear, waiting for a signal from his guards. But this time he didn't wait. From the corner of his eye he saw the people pressing forward. Agitation jolted him into action. He stepped out, plump and glistening, shaded by his Oliver Peoples sunglasses as though to bark silently at them: *You miserable scum, don't dare scratch my shimmering Bugatti.*

His guards dismounted instantly, rifles raised, forming a barricade between their master and the villagers. To Kanyi, "my people" was nothing more than a slogan. Yet poverty itself had been weaponised, leaving the crowd helpless. Hunger had taught them to bow before power. Instead of retreating, they stared in admiration at the display of wealth.

A young man shouted, "It's the senator! It is Senator Kanyi!" The crowd erupted — cheers, ululations, bodies pressing closer.

Reluctantly animated, Kanyi ducked back into his Bugatti, withdrew ten bundles of foreign currency, peeled away the wraps, and flung the notes into the air. They rose like locusts, then descended in chaos. The crowd broke into frenzy — men wrestling, women with infants strapped to their backs diving into the melee, hands clawing at green paper.

His guards tightened the cordon around the Bugatti, the convoy looming like a landed spaceship, an alien craft among peasants.

From the edges of the crowd, Aishatu watched. She had come early to the palace with her trays of rice, beans, stew, and recycled soda bottles filled with her mother's marinated herbal concoctions — medicine, she claimed, for every ailment from malaria to impotence. The Princess's return had drowned her marketplace in noise and spectacle.

When Amenika emerged from the glittering car, Aishatu's lips tightened. Weariness and bitterness lined her face. She glanced at her own ragged dress, the precarious life of hawking to survive, and then at the princess — shimmering, pampered, idolised. *Poverty is bad,* she muttered. *Very bad.*

But she scolded herself. She was not jealous of the princess. Hadn't gossip said that Amenika's Italian livelihood was prostitution? Why envy a whore? She reminded herself that her own mother had sold fish to the palace, had even been present when Amenika was born. They had known her as ebony black. What miracle transformed that child into this pale woman? Everyone whispered about the skin creams that burned and peeled, requiring endless petroleum jelly to hide the damage.

Aishatu sneered again. Why envy a woman who was sick in her very skin? Why envy her boyfriend, this senator everyone knew as a Yahoo Boy, a scammer who preyed on gullible foreigners? Why envy his so-called title, won not by votes but by blood and bribery?

Her mind replayed the scandal: Senator Adurah's family kidnapped, millions drawn from Sofalia's reserves to pay ransom, officials denying, spinning, lying. His wife released only after he resigned, humiliated. And then Kanyi — smiling, congratulating him for "family values," while filing his own papers to inherit the seat. He called it democracy. Everyone else knew it was intimidation, thuggery, a compromised party machine.

Yet here he was: now in his second term, unopposed, throwing dollar notes like a god spraying rain on mortals. The people fought for scraps, and Amenika waved like a queen beside him.

From her place at the margin, Aishatu's throat tightened. The demons whispered jealousy, but she silenced them. She reminded herself again: she was not jealous. But when the crowd scrambled after notes, she remained still, clutching her sodas of bitter herbs, her eyes full of acid.

Aishatu reflected on Amenika. She stripped her of her false beauty — the fake nails, painted eyelids, blue contact lenses, surgically enhanced figure, and blonde wig — and saw only a pitiful, irremediably miserable soul, haunted by a racial death wish and the lowest self-esteem, to be pitied rather than admired. She swore and hissed silently at the princess, *For where?* — keeping at the crowd's edge lest she trip and fall.

Aishatu walked away sorrowfully. She swore to herself that if the load she was carrying in her womb was a girl, she would ensure that she remained the best at everything she did. Her daughter would receive the best education in the world and escape her mother and grandmother's fate — their descent into poverty and servitude.

While Aishatu and her mother lived on the outskirts of the village, in their family's single-room allotment built on stilts at the back of Calanana Lagoon, her daughter would go places and enjoy luxury. She would travel worldwide and be known for her Midas touch. Yes, she would be among the wealthiest women in the world. Poverty was terrible; a good education was the surest way through its haze. Where she and her mother drifted through the valleys of life like dewy shadows, her daughter would have a life. A real life.

And if the load in her womb were a boy — he would not be like the senator: the dubious Kanyi, the scammer-in-chief, the perpetual woman-wrapper, the part-time Christian, the half-idol worshipper, the killer, the liar, the pompous and hollow Kanyi. No, her son would be authentic, honest, and adept at everything he set his hands to. He would be as wise as King Solomon, and kings and presidents would queue to listen to his wisdom. He would be a man of peace, with moderate desires and healthy appetites. Her son... no, it had to be a girl-child, she concluded, smiling delicately.

It was in this state of denied bitterness that Aishatu noticed a stream of warm fluid had filled her pants and was slowly trickling down her thighs and legs. Recently, her mother had warned her that if this happened, her water would break, and she should rush home slowly, lest she give birth on the roadside.

She wondered, as she hurried home, whether, if it were the chief's daughter whose water had broken, how many cars and even helicopters would ferry her to the best hospital. And at the hospital, how many doctors and nurses would spring into emergency action, rushing about to make her deliver with ease. Yet she reassured herself that she did not envy the Princess's fake life with her counterfeit friends, as she made haste slowly with pain in her lower waist — the sticky flow dammed in her underwear, flowing down her thighs and legs, finally reaching her flip-flop slippers.

A swarm of blue-bottle flies buzzed and mischievously licked her behind, while the village dogs — smooth brown mongrels — watched her longingly, escorting her aimlessly, undecided whether to bark or charge at her. After a few yards, they turned away, convinced she was not worth even their bark.

6

THE CROWN DRAWS THE LINE

The king gathered his cabinet of lesser chiefs in the palace's reception chamber. Three raised thrones sat atop the pedestal in the traditional council hall. The central throne was the most prominent — its armrests intricately carved in the shape of lions, mouths snarling and teeth bared as if ready to attack. A lion's skin covered the base of the king's throne. Senator Kanyi and his entourage sat in soft, cushioned chairs upholstered in bright colours, facing the pedestal.

At a signal, a long line of aged men — some thirty or forty in number, very orderly — filed into the chamber. They were brightly dressed in expensive damask, lace, and silk. Their robes, resembling cassocks, bore a likeness to those of Catholic bishops. Around their necks they wore beads of various colours and sizes. The number, colour, and quantity of beads signified their rank in the traditional hierarchy. The chiefs wore different fabrics woven into hats, adorned with bird feathers, raffia, and silk tassels.

Their arms and wrists were decorated with coral beads of different sizes. Each chief held a graceful walking stick of thick mahogany, with a brass leopard head carved at its crown. The sticks served as a fashion statement, enhancing sartorial elegance rather than orthopaedic necessity.

There was a burst of sound — horns, drums, and a high-pitched bugle announced the king's arrival. He was tall and gaunt, with a hungry look on his face. He walked regally and managed a feeble smile at his chiefs. He waved a long horsetail before taking his exalted seat. The court jester heralded this gesture with a loud shout and called on the king's ancestors to take their seats as well. The villagers sitting at the far side of the hall nodded with awe and clapped.

The king beckoned his august visitor to leave his cushioned chair and take the vacant throne at his right hand, reserved for distinguished visitors — the one with carved snakes on the armrests. With the senator seated, all was calm — an uncanny silence. Thoughtful and uncanny. This was suddenly broken by the voice of the master of ceremonies, better known as the MC.

"Testing, testing, testing... testing the microphone," followed by clearing of his throat. Then he boomed an ear-piercing oratory, recounting the great deeds of the king's ancestors, even to the tenth generation. This was quickly followed by the introduction of the king's retinue of high-ranking chiefs. That done, the MC turned to the visitors.

"Your Royal Majesty, today is an unusual day. We are blessed with an august visitor. Your Majesty, we have your subject, your son, the distinguished Senator Kanyi Mulaake, before you..."

At that moment, the queen entered with her daughter. Princess Amenika had vanished from the senator's entourage only to reappear with her mother, who fully embodied the role of a protective mother hen in the kingdom. The queen was dressed in flowing lace and damask, her neck adorned with coral beads that reached up to her throat. Her arms and hands glowed with silver and gold bangles while her fingers sparkled with diamond rings and rubies. Her ample figure showcased an extravagant display of surplus flesh.

Her face bore an expression of arrogance, boredom, and distraction. It shimmered with layers of makeup that seemed to crack at the corners of her mouth, where grimace lines battled with the layered foundation and talcum powder. She held a solitary elephant tusk in her palm, which she inadvertently and repeatedly thrust in a piercing motion — in-out-in-out-in — playfully, as if mimicking tantric copulation. The king gave her a look of stern disapproval and wagged his forefinger at her menacingly. She giggled mischievously, laid the tusk beside her, and wrung her hands with offended dignity.

The princess wore a flowing white bridal robe. Her unusually long neck was adorned with five white necklaces, matched by white earrings — all fourteen of them, seven in each earlobe, like knobs on an electronic appliance. A huge handbag sat on her left arm, much more like a small box. She held it in her lap delicately.

She appeared exhilarated and amused at the gathering. Henna adornments decorated her hands and palms. Two white and silver Android phones were grasped in her right hand as though life itself was inside. Momentarily, her eyes met the senator's, and a small smile flickered toward him, which he caught with a wink and playfully returned.

The master of ceremonies continued: "Our distinguished guest is none other than our most eminent son, the most accomplished son, the noonday sunlight of Kepe, the business magnate, the ICT expert and guru, and the burden of the Western world. The one who gives orders and the bank vaults are opened, the hope of Kepe, a political consultant, the Doctor of Laws Honoris Causa, Doctor of Medicine Honoris Causa, Doctor of Pedagogy Honoris Causa, Doctor of Business Administration Honoris Causa, Doctor of Doctorates Honoris Causa — all from the Kanyi Mulaake Virtual University Global."

For some strange reason, the chiefs began clapping, and a vacuous burst of laughter filled the chamber. From the corner of his eye, the king saw the queen make a savage upward thrust of her ivory stick and again gave her a stiff frown of disapproval. She paid him no attention and savagely thrust the ivory tusk in and out, then smiled at her daughter.

The MC went on: "It is my double pleasure to call on the senator to do the needful by addressing His Royal Majesty, the Paramount King of the Kepe Kingdom, His Royal Majesty Desmond Agbo Ahenga Tondo, the Apu of Kepe."

The bugle sounded at the mention of the king's name, and the algaita, the drums, and the cymbals flourished. Then the MC recounted the outstanding achievements of the king's ancestors, one of whom, he said, was a fire-eater who had sold five hundred thousand slaves to the Portuguese during his reign. The chiefs looked at each other uneasily.

The senator stood up. What had started as an impulsive ride from Calanana was rearing its head, and the senator rose to address His Majesty. The main reason for this excursion to the palace of the Kingdom of Kepe needed clarification. The princess's presence added to the complication. Everyone was apprehensive, nourished by the secret wish that perhaps the senator had come to formally express the desire to tie the nuptial knot with the princess. But the senator's address made no mention of her.

"Your Majesty," he began, "the King of Kepe, I greet you. Firstly, let me introduce the members of my entourage. I am here with five chairpersons from the Senate. The first is Senator Dr. Richards Ihame, Chairman of the Senate Committee on Internal Affairs and Chieftaincy."

"Next to him is Senator Bala Azzein, Chairman of the Anti-Corruption Committee."

"The next is Senator Ibn Siaka Jonstons, Chairman of the Oil and Gas Committee."

"The Iron Lady of the Senate, Senator Fola Kay-Stevens, follows him." She stood and took a bow.

"And last but not least, Senator Oparah Momoh, Chairman of the Agriculture Committee."

"Your Majesty, we are here on the first leg of our constituency briefing. As they say, charity begins at home. This is my home; you are one of the country's most respected monarchs. You paid your dues fighting to keep this country united during our unfortunate civil war. The country needs your wisdom now. We are at a crossroads.

The Senate of the Federation is in the process of amending the Sofalian Constitution. It demands that we first take oral memoranda from our royal fathers and then from our constituents. This is why we are here in your domain." The chiefs looked at one another. A few nodded in approval; others smirked in disbelief; the rest remained silent.

The master of ceremonies requested an ovation.

Princess Amenika had been the senator's girlfriend since his first year in the Senate. She had attached herself to him by sending gifts — expensive wristwatches, Italian shoes, and perfumes. They met by chance during the senator's private visit to Milan. He encountered her at the spa of the Palazzo Parigi Hotel, alongside an elderly white man, presumably her husband or boyfriend. She knew him from social media and had harboured a long crush on him. She followed him into the restaurant and approached him.

"Hello, Senator." Kanyi was not expecting anyone to meet him. When he turned to her, her face lit up with glee.

"Senator, I am Princess Amenika; we have been friends on Instagram."

"Oh, Princess, what a pleasant surprise. And yes, I remember you."

She looked directly into his eyes with a lingering smile.

"Yes, I remember you and the many gifts," Kanyi said, chuckling at her oily smile and puppyish friendliness. She was an easy catch for him.

"No, Senator, don't mention it. It's the least I can do to make your job a little less stressful. I know you don't need them. But when I discovered you were also from Kepe, I felt God had answered my prayers — so all the other girls should keep off. God does not provide the frog's food on top of trees. He puts it within the frog's reach. Similarly, it is also with us. You belong to me... God has buttered my bread Himself." Kanyi met her gaze with quiet inner amusement.

The senator was not at a loss for what to say. Her body language openly signalled him. He smiled a dangerous smile, determined to uncover her so-called royal blood and to ravish her. He invited her into his hotel suite.

A love affair was kindled. There was never any mention of marriage or engagement; they always remained in a muted state of becoming, possibly even marrying someday, yet neither of them ever brought it up. The princess toyed with the idea of having a baby for him, of being his Baby Mama. But she knew deep down that he belonged to everybody. The senator, on the other hand, treated their love affair as an intermission to more meaningful ones.

Kanyi knew that the Kepe Clan operated under a strict caste system and that he, a commoner, could not marry into royalty unless granted special permission by the king. The king's representatives would first cleanse the commoner's scent through costly ceremonies and rituals. He harboured a deep loathing for the so-called traditional rulers: foolish figures who inherited power from a long line of slave traders, demanding more unearned wealth and privilege.

He silently swore to himself that he must gather like-minded individuals to abolish the outdated institution of traditional chiefs. The US Republican democracy that Sofalia was plagiarising did not recognise traditional rulers. Kanyi found the idea of an aristocracy based on birth within his tribe deeply disturbing and objectionable. Yes, he could afford the princess, but why limit himself when all the other fish were in the river? She was fun — plenty of fun — but that was all. He had too much dignity to marry the princess.

The princess had forced her way into his itinerary during the trip to Kepe, hoping that the royal presence of her mother the queen and her father the king would indirectly persuade Kanyi to address the matter of marital introductions. She naively believed that her visit with the senators to her home might result in a media scoop, where they could announce their engagement and make it a fact.

She was furious that Senator Kanyi did not even acknowledge her presence, let alone address the important matter of publicising their love affair or at least informing her parents that she was not the one shamelessly throwing herself at him — that they both shared the shamelessness. She had her plans and watched two camera operators from the Daily Star rise to take positions to record the seemingly insignificant matter of the constitutional review. She was bitter that the marital review agenda had been ignored by her parents and her lover, the senator.

Her father, the king, adjusted his turban and called for his royal interpreter. A short, stocky figure, sweating profusely, emerged from behind where the chiefs sat and positioned himself before the senators. He was dressed in a sweat-soaked white kaftan; on his head sat a red cap too tight for his skull, and beneath its frayed edges, tufts of grey hair betrayed his age as somewhere in the mid-fifties.

The kaftan tightly hugged his pot belly. He had a thick mouth and protruding, tobacco-stained teeth. The king pushed his lace turban away from his mouth and began his speech in Kepe while the interpreter struggled to keep pace in English.

"Distinguished Senator Kanyi and most esteemed senators, friends of my celebrated son. I welcome you to Kepe, the ancestral home of our people. When I considered your august assembly in my mind a moment ago, before the senator's speech, I wondered whether the senator had finally decided to do what is necessary — to reveal and make known his long-standing relationship with my daughter, Princess Amenika, whom the press will not leave alone."

He laughed at his joke, which fell flat. The queen cast him a reproachful look; the princess smiled approvingly at her father, who paid no attention to either of them. The audience perceived it as a crude and inept ex-cathedra attempt to secure a son-in-law. The chiefs and visitors lowered their heads, smiling in embarrassment.

Undeterred, the king said: "But then, our young people of today are different. The West has made marriage obsolete, even objectionable. I therefore welcome the delegation, including my dearest daughter, Princess Amenika, to the Royal Palace of the Kepe Kingdom." Everybody clapped. The princess pouted her lips in a magisterial taunt at Senator Kanyi, who bit his lips in mock annoyance. The king raised his staff of office, and silence ensued.

"Distinguished Senators, you have brought a heavy agenda to my kingdom. The constitutional matter you seek the royal fathers to address is neither here nor there. You, the politicians, have damaged the land. The military killed Sofalia, and today, you, the politicians, have become the undertakers to bury her. With the stroke of a pen, you have erased common sense and reduced us to ornaments — jobless and powerless."

"This country belonged to us. Yes, we have been accused — the royal fathers — of selling Africa's workforce into slavery. I submit to you that you are ignorant and ingrates. Do you know the white man? Do you know that our royal fathers fought the Gatling gun with their bare hands for over three hundred years? We faced the devious white slave traders and stopped them from carrying all of us away as slaves. You know nothing. We entered white men's parliaments and, using our juju, turned other white men against the slave traders." The chiefs gasped and clapped in support; the senators resigned themselves in silent disbelief.

"When you call figures like William Wilberforce abolitionists, our ancestors had been abolitionists before them but lacked the means to enforce it. Then, after the slave trade was abolished, we faced even more ruthless and greedy white parasites in the scramble for Africa and colonisation. Our ancestors, the kings of Sofalia, used diplomacy to retain power, leaving the white colonisers strutting around like cocks, thumping their chests and collecting taxes here and there — and we the chiefs ate much of the taxes, wiped our mouths clean, and ruled our subjects as things had always been."

"We, the traditional rulers of Sofalia, governed in our own way. We had our police force, our judiciary, and even our prisons. After independence, you, the politicians, and the men in khaki sidelined the landlords and took control of the Sofalian estate. Sadly, your so-called constitution declared us persona non grata. We felt humiliated. We no longer had our native authority — our police, our traditional courts, our subjects. You encouraged the subjects to rebel and to start calling themselves citizens. Then you initiated this thing called human rights and equality. This is how you went overboard and embraced tribalism and corruption." The senators shifted in their seats at the king's mockery of human rights.

He paused and looked at his team — the lesser chiefs, who punctuated the long-winded speech with applause and supportive noises. He watched with relish the faces of the six senators wincing with fatigue from his hour-long tirade.

"You, the politicians, have destroyed the country. This nation has no true politicians anymore. You are organised criminals. After the army left, the country reeked of corruption and bribery. Then you spread it among civil servants and even poor schoolteachers. Our affliction is systemic and endemic. Sofalia, a cesspool of corruption, has begun its journey toward failure."

"Politicians must learn about the leadership of a complex multi-national, multi-ethnic, multi-cultural entity called Sofalia. And now, for reasons best known to yourselves, you want to change the constitution, and you want us, the owners, to submit our verbal memoranda." He looked suspiciously at the interpreter, then swept him away with his horsetail. He resumed addressing the senators directly in English. His voice began to rise. The interpreter, in anger and disbelief at the royal displeasure, desperately tried to regain authority by switching to interpret the king's address into the Kepe language. The senators looked at each other nervously, wondering what would follow.

"It is too late. This Sofalia will follow Lebanon unless you return it to us — the rightful owners of this country who possess the pedigree, sagacity, capacity, and ability."

He paused once more and glared at the senators. The lesser chiefs were overjoyed. "Give them, tell them, give it to them," they chorused, clapping at each word from their paramount ruler. Meanwhile, the senators sat pensive and silent beneath the weight of the royal indictment.

"You have stolen everything," he resumed. "Sofalia belongs to us, the traditional kings. This is the reality you are trying to change unsuccessfully through your constitutions. You cannot change an unpleasant reality without building a newer or better model. Just take a look at Lebanon. That was a country. Lebanese politicians watched rising inflation and the free fall of their currency, leading to a colossal human tragedy. A Sofalian disaster is a disaster in slow motion. Prices have spiralled out of control.

"Like Lebanon, Sofalia has been betrayed by her politicians. We would not have faced this stupidity if the traditional rulers were in charge. We are fighting tribal and religious wars, and politicians are behind all the banditry, theft, and distress. What have you done? Why have you stolen the country, and where have you taken it?"

The king shouted at the senators while the interpreter struggled to translate into the Kepe language, jumping and waving his hands, dramatising every accusation and insult. When the king demanded, "Where have you stolen Sofalia and taken it away?" the interpreter pointed at each of the visiting senators in a menacing, accusatory manner.

The king finished his speech by shouting into the microphone: "We, the royal fathers, reject your grandstanding and your pretence that you want constitutional change. We refuse to be the grist for the mill of corruption and anti-people policies. Thank you." He sat down majestically on his throne and glared at his visitors with admonitory anger.

Kanyi was in a difficult position. How was he supposed to respond to these vile accusations from a greedy, parasitic traditional oligarchy that had enslaved the people and treated them as private property? How could he later explain to his colleagues the savagery and disrespect they had endured? When the interpreter pointed at him and demanded to know where they had stolen and carried the country, Kanyi stood — sweat-drenched, forcing a smile — and paused before he spoke.

"Your Majesty, we thank you for granting us an audience. So, what message should we deliver to the Senate's plenary session regarding the constitutional amendment?"

Although Senator Kanyi was speaking through the interpreter, the king — three worry lines deeply furrowed across his forehead — raised his staff and stomped it firmly on the stage beside Kanyi. Kanyi was compelled to look into the king's squinted, small eyes. The king was foaming at the edges of his mouth.

"Amend your constitution, do the right thing, and return the country you have taken from us — the rightful owners and traditional rulers."

An eerie silence filled the room. Then the king rose to his feet. The bugle sounded, the algaita called out, and the drums roared into life. The king burst into triumphant, raucous laughter, shaking his long horsetail at each senator before slowly turning to leave the hall, leaving his visitors in awe and to their own devices. The meeting was concluded. Amenika was visibly distraught — her mobile phone fell to the ground. She was furious at the sudden end of the proceedings and the refusal of both her parents and her lover to do the right thing: to bind her to Kanyi with an official engagement.

7

MEASURE OF A QUEEN

Queen Aisha did not socialise with the Atsan. Though they considered her one of their own, she saw herself as above their station. She was the Queen. Her impenetrable palace lay beneath the bridge, marked by her fierce disapproval of intrusion. She resembled a rabid dog in its lair — ferocious, unapproachable. She answered to no one, and no one answered to her. The Underbridge Palace simply existed, sheltering her from rain and blazing sun. A roof, clothes on her back — these were all she required.

Queen Aisha had three moods: sadness, happiness, and anger. These spirits lived inside her, switching like traffic lights in her mind. In cheerful phases, she organised the Atsan, teaching them English and Sofalian history. They respected her — not for her beauty or her skin, but for her knowledge.

She had no remembered friends, no family who drew near. If she had kin, they kept their distance — or she from them. In sorrow, she whispered mantras. In anger, she became unbearable: every human an enemy to be stoned or struck, every object a weapon.

The Atsan were colour-blind. They scavenged narcotics from the Ogas' children, smoked strange plants, inhaled fumes from soak pits.

They shared their highs with Queen Aisha in reckless, tragic solidarity.

When she woke cheerful, Queen Aisha never stopped talking. In bad moods she returned to her den beneath the bridge, ranting at humanity: their betrayals, jealousies, stresses, madness. Humanity itself was madness; she alone was sane, and so she commanded respect. She could gaze for hours at traffic, then turn to her mirror, reassure herself she was the most beautiful woman in Sofalia, and resume her small domestic rituals.

Sometimes she ventured into town at night for food. Restaurants and mosques provided bins or shared meals during Ramadan or Christmas. Sofalians, devout by law — every citizen bound to one faith or the other — could not bear to let even a mad queen starve. Yet both religions, foreign imports, had bred enmity as lucrative as trade itself. Hatred and religion fed politicians, warlords, and terrorists.

One day, in a cheerful mood, Queen Aisha strolled along the pedestrian pavement, smiling as brightly as sunlight breaking through clouds. She walked a mile along the bridge, turned around, and then walked another mile on the opposite side. She spoke loudly to the Republic of Sofalia, waving at drivers who slowed down to stare. They saw a slender, curvy woman, her hair matted in clumps around her face like a mane. She wore nothing at all.

Men in cars devoured her nakedness with their eyes, raping her unconsciously in their minds. Her body seduced, but her words cut deeper. She hurled insults, gestures sharp, voice relentless.

Shame washed over them. They realised they had violated a madwoman in thought. It was not consensual. She offered not her body but her words — harsh truths to Sofalia.

She declared the bridge her palace, her life her own to do with as she pleased, even to end it that day.

Women in tinted cars averted their eyes. They envied her athletic body, the beauty they chased with creams, gyms, and spas. Why should God grant it to a beggar, a madwoman? They dared not say so aloud. They muttered instead: what kind of country has no mental health policy? "It's a pity," they sighed. Only a pity.

Then Queen Aisha's mood shifted. She realised people stared not at her face or words but at her midriff. With a trembling hand, she covered herself. Veins throbbed at her temples; the sun burned her pale skin.

Rage overtook her. Why was she unclothed, when she owned Sofalia's finest clothes at her castle? Breathless, she ran back to her lair, found the sack of garments untouched. She spilled them onto the ground and began counting.

She did not wear them. They were her treasure, her wealth — like coins in vaults or cattle in fields. She counted them daily for reassurance. Each day she scavenged new clothes from the bins of wealthy districts, adding to her hoard — a ritual of sovereignty over scraps. She was a collector. That was her choice.

She could do without clothes. Shouldn't a woman of her calibre be judged not by the texture of her garments but by the texture of her morality, her stubborn ethics? Yet she sighed, laughed in resignation at the ignorance of Sofalia's people — mad judges who presumed to rule over her. The world has gone wild, she concluded.

Being unclothed was the final stage of her ecstatic freedom. People of true importance needed no clothes; only the insignificant obsessed over trends. They were unstable, superficial, mad.

She hurled her question to the traffic: why should she wear clothes and shoes, enslaved in regalia that shackled hands and feet, enslaved to fashion? These were manacles, not adornments. She sneered at the daughters and mistresses of the Ogas in Maidadi and Abosko — slaves to their wardrobes.

Yet despite her contempt for clothing, Queen Aisha confessed no shame in being a collector. Every Sofalian woman was. She reasoned that if all their barely worn garments were sold in the secondhand market, the proceeds in dollars could erase the national debt.

She set her rags aside and opened another sack. From it she retrieved a gleaming silver mobile phone, salvaged from a trash can in Abosko. It was nearly new — a cracked Apple 30 X ProMax, its screen split top to bottom. Someone had smashed it against marble in rage.

She could imagine the quarrel: *George, see what the other ladies are holding. You went to Dubai and brought me only this miserable Apple? Didn't you see the new Golden Apple G30 Pro Max?* And before George could answer, she saw the lover smash the phone to the floor. That was how Queen Aisha came to possess it. She had reassembled the pieces with rubber bands. Dead as stone, but it was her blissful prop.

To passersby, it was alive. They gawked: how could this underbridge queen afford the latest phone? They never guessed it was useless. To her, though, it was more than a phone. It connected her to her universe — and her universe orbited a single planet: Senator Kanyi Mulaake.

She spoke to him every day. He was her lover — yes, her lover. Life without love was unthinkable. At first, it had been difficult. Her name was Aishatu. The senator hadn't loved her; she was too dark. He imported light-skinned women, trophies collected like currency among his colleagues. But that was another story.

She still called him daily. He never replied — not even a hello. But true love was like that. It left her speechless. Her heart raced whenever she pressed the dead phone to her ear. She believed he heard her. His silence meant her beauty stunned him; her voice lulled him to sleep. Yes, he listened — she was certain. And today was no different.

Turning her back to the traffic, she raised the useless phone and addressed him:

"Hello, it's me again, Senator Mulaake. Yes, your beloved. It's been ages since we last saw each other. My love remains as strong as ever. You are irreplaceable, unforgettable. No, I cannot come to your world of Ogas. You must come to my world of Atsan." She paused, bit her lips, and made a sweeping gesture. "The elephant walking in the forest does not forbid the rat from walking there too." She looked at the traffic passing by, then quietly said: "And you, Senator Kanyi, are the rat."

She continued: "I am Queen of Sofalia. Things will soon improve for the poor citizens. They have suffered enough. No, no, no. Your senate does not exist. Corruption rides you like a horse. You are spineless, gutless, without balls. Yes, without gonads. I am doing you a favour by condescending to marry you — so that my beauty may cloak your bloodstained, thieving body with integrity."

Lowering the phone, she turned back to the street. She caught her reflection in the tinted window of a Range Rover and followed it, furious. Why should the Ogas ride in cars while the Atsan walked?

Sofalia was a bubble — a paradise for the Ogas, a nightmare for the Atsan. And like all bubbles, the Ogacracy would burst. The conflagration was inevitable. She consoled herself with this certainty, and raised her fist in triumphant salute.

8

TIME OF AISHATU

How time has flown. It feels like yesterday — yet it has been fifteen years since her husband went to Calanana Lagoon to fish, and his canoe drifted into the dangerous waters of the Atlantic Ocean. Her husband, Anyam, a brave, strong, loving fisherman, disappeared on that fateful day without a trace.

After the death of Anyam, Mama Aishatu refused to be consoled. She was not just distraught; her husband's death was a wound in her heart — visceral, tangible, very deep inside her. She yearned to die. She had nothing to live for except the unborn baby Aishatu carried within her, whose very existence felt like a miracle of resurrection.

She believed her purpose on earth was to come here and endure torment and sorrow. She thought she had had her fair share of life — it was mostly anguish. But this was her lot on this earth. She had paid her dues and now deserved to die.

The pain was unrelenting. It was numbing, sometimes throbbing and aching. She moved about as if she were a ghost, muttering to herself and calling out her husband's name at odd intervals. She refused to accept that her husband was dead and was caught many times trying to drown herself.

She said she knew her husband was still alive but was simply held hostage by underwater mermaids — the Mami Wata spirit, with her serpent hair and jewelled eyes. She was determined to enter the spirit world beneath the sea, confront the Mami Wata face-to-face, and demand her husband return to Kepe village to fulfil his duties. She dismissed all pleas that this was a sad and pointless misadventure, asserting she had nothing to lose.

At night, when it rained and she heard the lagoon's water lapping against the banks of her house, the pain felt even more profound — in the lagoon's scents, she detected the aroma of returning fishermen with their daily catches. When she finally managed to sleep, it wasn't just rest; it was an escape into the depths of the Atlantic Ocean, where another world thrived with life. She would explore the towns of this new world, searching for Anyam. If she ever found him and they chose not to return to Kepe, ignorant earthlings would claim she had drowned.

She knew her husband was somewhere beneath the ocean. Night after night, she searched that other world without success. Yet she refused to lose hope. Hope meant everything, and everything depended on hope. Human beings live and thrive on hope; without it, life becomes unbearable.

In her destitute state, she laughed at those who had rescued her from drowning. "Leave me alone. If you understood that neither life nor death can separate me from my husband, you wouldn't be here disturbing my attempts to die."

But she would follow her rescuers back to the village, to her one-room, rat-infested hovel precariously perched on the edge of Calanana Lagoon. The room had a window that let in fresh air and the associated odours from the lagoon. Sewage flowed into the lagoon from the large industrial estates upstream.

Mama Aishatu's one-room hut had a self-contained pit latrine that drained into the lagoon. There were tales of water creatures that devoured people and could control storms that overflowed the banks, carrying folk away to the sea. It was even said that many years ago, the village had been swept away by the wrathful spirit of the lagoon during a stormy night. It was merely a rumour, and rumours only threaten the naive. But if the Mami Wata wanted to take away her husband, then she was ready to challenge her on land or in the sea.

Mama Aishatu had three daughters, with Aishatu being the youngest. Aishatu was only a year old when her father went to sea and never returned. Her older siblings were four and eight years old. These three girls were quite a handful. She struggled to raise the children alone, without a husband or means to support them. This is why she sent Aishatu away — far away. The pain of sending her daughter away was even more profound than the loss of her husband, and would later haunt her far more than his disappearance.

While fate had dealt her a treacherous hand regarding her husband, in her daughter's case she had succumbed to the despair of poverty and dire circumstances, entangled and overwhelmed, feeling as if she were selling her daughter into slavery. But when she heard her pastor, Godswill, recount the story of Joseph in the Bible, she comforted herself with the hope that one day her daughter would also reign as a queen in a foreign land.

Soon after Aishatu left, her other two children died in rapid succession. Movihinze suddenly died at noon on a Saturday after complaining of a headache and fever. She had been vomiting all day — every bit of food she had eaten, then all the water in her body, a foul-smelling, slimy green substance they call bile. She lost much water and blood and lay on the floor, hugging the ground with her bare hand, over which spattered blood and bile painted a deadly mosaic of the horrific loneliness of death.

She had no money to take her to the pharmacy to buy Nivaquine for her malaria fever. Movihinze died. The other, Aseka, was struck by a hit-and-run truck loaded with mahogany timber while returning from across the street, where she had gone to fetch water from the village well.

Her only hope was her daughter, Aishatu. She had been encouraged to send Aishatu away to be raised by a wealthy woman in Kambia, a distant city that could take a whole day to reach by lorry. Although she had never been there, she knelt every night before bed, praying for her daughter's safety and success.

She regretted collecting money from the men who took her away. It smacked of slavery. She wept over what she had done — what no mother should do: selling her daughter into slavery and accepting money too. Abominable treachery. That perfectly described her. Yes, she was dreadful and treacherous.

She did not contact the woman to whom her nine-year-old daughter had been sent as a house helper. All she knew was that the men had paid her a small amount. It made her guilt worse. Aishatu had cried, fought, and clawed at the two men who took her away. Her cries echoed through the streets. The villagers watched helplessly, determined to mind their business. The abductors tied her hands and feet, carried her on their shoulders, and forced a dirty piece of cloth into her mouth, delivering her to her new duties as house help and babysitter for the wealthy Ghanaian woman, Kofo-Aidoo, a trader in Kente cloth.

The day Aishatu left, Mama Aishatu wept and refused to be comforted. She blamed herself for selling her daughter into slavery due to poverty. She kept telling herself she had no choice — the poor often had none — and that she was making a better decision for her daughter, who would grow up in a rich woman's house. Through this, she hoped her daughter might also become rich someday, perhaps return to Kepe, and save her impoverished mother.

She believed she had heart disease, so she apprenticed herself to the village herbalist, who provided her with free herbal juices for her ailing heart. She was advised to go to hospital but could not afford to pay for the registration card, let alone for consultation and prescription.

She was even afraid that her wounded heart's condition was so severe that she might need surgery. Her herbalist told her he was willing to help with the surgery whenever she was ready to give him a chance. She told herself she would consider his offer only when she was about to commit suicide but was too cowardly to do it herself. The herbalist believed that practising on living humans would make him a good surgeon-herbalist. He knew that nobody would hold him guilty of malpractice even if Mama Aishatu failed to survive the surgery. She had no one to lay a complaint to the police.

Mama Aishatu was in for a surprise on a fateful night. It was a great shock when someone knocked on her door unexpectedly. She shifted restlessly on her thin, straw-filled mattress, unable to sleep. Then she heard the voice — Aishatu, now a tall, fourteen-year-old girl, knocking on her door in the middle of the night. Even in her semi-conscious state, her beloved daughter's voice was unmistakable. "Mammy, it's me, Aishatu. Open for me." The persistent voice sounded like music to her ears but also brought unbounded terror and foreboding.

It was surreal. Perhaps her daughter had died in distant Kambia, and her spirit had travelled across time and space to question why her mother had sold her into slavery. She stepped outside and carefully unlatched the door. The moon cast its silver glow over everything. The slender woman outside resembled her daughter. She looked weak and exhausted, and in the moonlight, the signs of terrible suffering were visible on her face. The cold wind's bite stung her in the moonlit night. She realised she had failed her daughter, and woefully so.

But even before she could search her mind, Aishatu flew into her open arms with whatever strength she had left. The hug became awkward as her daughter's protruding stomach was the first thing she noticed. Both mother and daughter released their embrace. While the mother gazed at her daughter's rounded belly, the daughter looked down, avoiding her mother's gaze. Mama Aishatu regarded the pronounced stomach with apprehension — a puzzling mystery. She realised that something dreadful, humiliating, and unimaginable had happened to both of them. Her daughter's unexpected pregnancy had not been part of the deal, just like her sudden return. *Had the city chewed her up and spat her back out?* she asked herself.

Nonetheless, Mama Aishatu welcomed her daughter home. As soon as she entered the room, Aishatu threw herself onto the only straw-filled bed in the centre. Her mother was delighted to have her back and sought to make her feel at home, despite the pregnancy. She was her daughter.

Even as she took everything in, Aishatu said weakly, "Mammy, I am hungry. I have trekked for four days without food. Do you have anything to eat in the house?"

There was no readily available food, but fortunately there was some pap and milk. Mama Aishatu prepared the pap, adding sugar and their last sachet of Peak Milk. Aishatu took the pap in large gulps before turning back to the middle of the bed and falling asleep. Noticing her swollen, dirty feet, her mother gently washed and massaged them with warm water before joining her daughter on the bed.

She sat at the edge of the bed, sobbing all night. She wept for the sorrows, the melancholy, and the penury that made her life a misery. She also wept for the struggles of her daughter and the visible suffering she had endured at the hands of strangers who possessed power and money but failed to use it to protect a poor, innocent girl. Despite her sorrowful heart and anguished spirit, sleep eventually overcame her.

When Mama Aishatu woke the following morning, Aishatu was still fast asleep. She looked at her legs again and was relieved that the swelling on her feet and ankles had reduced. But her back was partly exposed, and the mother could see scars of welts liberally applied across her back and shoulders — pink, cruel fingers that seemed to claw her anew in the morning light. An involuntary gasp escaped her mouth, and then a tear rolled down her cheek.

It was entirely her fault. There was nothing to be ashamed of in being poor, but everything to be ashamed of in being cruel, insensitive, and sinister. The people who took her daughter away were monsters. Yet they were wealthy, and instead of confronting them, Mama Aishatu chose to leave their fate to God's vengeance. When Aishatu woke, she prepared a lavish breakfast of yam porridge with fresh fish that her mother had bought on credit at dawn.

The daughter ate her fill. Life had taken many things from her — her joy, peace, dignity, and innocence — but it had not taken away the spirit of gratitude instilled in her during childhood. So she looked at her mother and said, "Mom, thank you for the food."

Her mother wanted to congratulate herself out loud for doing a good job, but instead said, "Why? We should thank God instead."

"We thank God, Mammy," the daughter replied.

She leaned back against the pillow and fell back asleep. When she woke later, the day had slipped away, and the muezzin's call to prayer echoed through the area. It signalled dinner time for the family. Aishatu got up and assisted her mother in preparing the garri dinner — ground cassava flour mixed with vegetables.

They ate in silence. After dinner, Aishatu helped her mother clean up and do the dishes. Mama Aishatu then summoned ominous patience, waiting for the accusations, blaming, and shaming to commence. The silence between them thickened, heavier than the meal they had just eaten.

She knew that Aishatu was unyielding in imposing her beliefs on what was fair and what was not, and anxious terror filled her thoughts that her daughter had become a judge over her — and she stood adjudged guilty.

She would have pleaded guilty if it had come to that, but first she waited for her daughter to decide how to approach the sensitive issue. She was not going to worsen the situation by saying too much. She was fully aware that she was facing a complication. But when her daughter remained in foreboding silence, she ventured, with grim calmness, to ask: "Tell me, Aisha, my daughter, who is responsible for this, and what happened to you over these past five years?"

Aishatu stirred and looked up. When she spoke, her voice had a cynical, melancholy note.

"Where should I begin?" she asked, restraining her sorrow, which was quickly fermenting into anger.

"From the beginning, my daughter," her mother answered.

"All right, I will begin from the beginning... but where are my siblings? Where are Movihinze and Aseka? Did you also sell them? Or are they married?" she demanded.

Her head cradled in her hands, Mama Aishatu replied, her voice broken: "They both died." Her eyes looked at the ground, and the palms of her hands opened in a plea.

"What? What happened?" The pain in Aishatu's face was visceral.

"Movihinze died of fever, and Aseka was killed by a hit-and-run driver."

"So, you and I are the only family we have on earth?"

"No, my daughter, you have many uncles and aunts farther in the hinterland."

"I don't know them. They don't know me, and I don't know them."

"Everybody in Sofalia has uncles and aunts in the hinterland."

"Yes, but we have never moved back to the village. Those people live without electricity, without piped water, without hospitals."

"Yes, but they don't buy food. Everything they need is cultivated on the land."

Her daughter's words stung; she had heard the same disdain whispered by city folk.

"I don't know them, Mama. When you are not familiar with others, it is difficult for them to share in your pain or love you." Then she said, "I am so happy I ran away from the people you sold me to and returned home."

Her mother felt the whiplash of her tongue again, and her body winced as her hand reflexed to ward off the imaginary blow to her heart. Aishatu scanned her mother's skinny body with brooding eyes. She was worried about her mother's health. She seemed on the edge of madness, her whole body suffused by unmentionable suffering. Aishatu's deep feelings were an embarrassment to her.

"How is your health, Mammy?" she asked.

"Don't worry yourself; nothing will happen to me. My old heart is still troubling me. But I know God will not allow me to die yet. I will see you and my grandchild in the land of the living. And even if I were to drop dead today, my Pastor, Apostle Godswill, would care for you."

"I don't know him, Mama." Aishatu was on guard. She had known, first-hand, how cold the love of strangers was. Her mother continued:

"They moved here two years ago. He is a very kind, pious man of God, and even kinder is his beautiful wife, Beatrice."

Ignoring her mother's praise of the strangers, Aishatu said matter-of-factly: "Okay, Mama. May God hear your prayers. May God keep death far away."

"Tell me what happened to you, my beautiful daughter." Her mother braced herself for her imminent conviction as a shameless, wicked, and diabolical mother who had sold her daughter into slavery.

As Aishatu began her plaintive narrative, her mother's eyes filled with fear, sorrow, and shame. She questioned whether her spiritual father, Pastor Godswill, his wife, or anybody in Sofalia had a religion to deal with the suffering her family had endured. She had tried to keep busy, hawking petty herbs and concoctions across Kepe daily from dawn to dusk, to expand her life and ward off the traumas that had beset her family. It was better to die than face this unbearable shame — a past action thoughtlessly taken with good intentions to lessen her burden, and now this.

"Five years ago, you sold and threw me into the hands of two horrible men I had never seen or heard of in my life. I was nine. I did not know why you sent me away. You were my only mother, my family, and I had two sisters." Mama Aishatu's face puckered and contorted, and her throat went dry as the sobs and tears took over. Her daughter's words cut through her like merciless whiplashes, drawing hot blood. Aishatu watched her with pity, anger, and something like hatred, then continued her story impassively.

"Snatches of conversations I later heard, in the place you sold me, were that you sent me away because we were so poor, and our father had died, and so you wanted fewer mouths to feed — and I was the mouth to be put away."

"Please forgive me, my daughter. I did not mean to sell you into slavery. They told me the Ghanaian woman was good. She was a Kente-cloth merchant who would train you in her trade, and one day you would be as rich as her."

"But, Mammy, those two human traffickers — you saw how I cried and cried, my hands reaching out to you to rescue me from them, from taking me away from you. But you turned your back on me and clasped your ears. They loved the job — grabbing me and tying my hands and feet, carrying me on their shoulders, and forcing a dirty piece of cloth into my mouth."

"They did that?"

"You should have seen their faces. They were dirty, evil-smelling, wicked souls from hell. They told me that you had sold me to them and that they had paid you."

"They said that? God have mercy — those nitwits lied. They lied to you; they lied about me. No amount of money on earth can make me sell my daughter. It was poverty. Oh my God, have mercy and remove the curse of poverty from us."

"Poverty is bad, Mammy, but to be poor and free — free to move, think, and be in charge of one's destiny — is enormous wealth. It was work, work, and work. I wasn't even allowed time off on Sundays to go to church. All the work I did was without compensation. And then I was raped repeatedly by the madam's son, and there was nobody to report to. When freedom is taken away for any reason, slavery takes over."

"Forgive me, my daughter. How dare they rape you?"

"Forget about that. You want to know how I arrived here with an eight-month pregnancy. But this pregnancy is just the end of the story of what I went through. I went through a whole lot — and I had nobody's shoulder to lean on."

"I know, my daughter. I knew your training would be hard."

"What training? Let me tell you my story," she began.

"The day we left Kepe with those dreadful fellows — your nitwits — we trekked for over fifteen miles. I was hungry, tired, and afraid, and my feet were aching terribly. When we came to Adobe Junction, we stopped to eat. They ate, but try as they did to force me to eat, I refused to touch any food or drink. Your nitwits were likely trying to poison me.

"I knew I was being carried away, probably to be killed as a ritual sacrifice for juju. I decided in my heart that I was not going to my death in a docile and stupid manner like a sheep. I planned to escape at the earliest opportunity. I believed I could dart away, especially after they untied my hands and feet, and I walked between the two evil men.

"They must have read my mind, for the one coming behind me — Mr. Twiddle — pulled out a sharp knife and threatened to slash my neck if I attempted to escape. Even as they ate, he ensured I could see the knife. The idea of ending up a corpse by the side of the road — a putrid, decomposing corpse whose entrails would be gobbled by vultures and dogs — mellowed me down. My escape plan was suspended until we reached the dreaded destination, where I was convinced they would carry me to a shrine and slaughter me on some blood-drenched altar.

"The two wicked men told me fantastic stories about where I was going and how lucky I was to be trained as a Kente cloth merchant by the Ghanaian lady, Mama Kofo-Aidoo. I didn't believe them.

"After eating, they paid for seats at the back of a pick-up truck carrying palm oil to the hinterland. The driver warned that the vehicle was not meant to transport human beings and that we were there at our own risk. He also warned that due to his merchandise, he had to negotiate around the many potholes to avoid spilling his precious palm oil. He could not guarantee the time of our arrival and advised that we leave the timing to the Almighty God. I rested between the two men, and we had a bumpy eleven-hour ride to Kambia. It took several days of scrubbing before I could get the palm oil out of my hair.

"It was far into the night when we arrived at Mama Kofo-Aidoo's house. Every living thing was sleeping except my captors, the driver, and me. We drove into the night, and the driver dropped us on the main road before proceeding on his unending journey to the interior. We walked another two miles before we arrived at the Kofo household — a one-storey building in the centre of town.

"My captors announced themselves at the gatehouse, and we were promptly ushered in. The commotion must have woken the household. The sound of loud scraping continued, accompanied by the whirl of a rotor and the thud of a generator engine roaring to life. Lights sprang up everywhere.

"The main entrance to the living room stood on the right side of the building. We entered in silence. The curtains parted with a crank and a whoosh, and my captors moved into the spacious living room, which doubled as a factory floor with sewing machines and bales of Kente cloth piled around.

"Madam Kofo-Aidoo, a stocky, stout woman in her fifties, emerged from upstairs, accompanied by a fawning, gaunt gentleman of about sixty. His face was clean-shaven, his head too — bald as a vulture, and he looked like one: long, wrinkled neck, sharp-beaked nose, and a small, lipless mouth. A thin slit under the nose was all he had for a mouth to eat and speak.

"He could have passed for someone in his forties, except that his sunken cheeks, furrowed forehead, and crow's-feet around the edges of his sad, bulging eyes denied him that estimation.

"He asked, unable to bear the silence any longer and without faith that he would be answered: 'Did they bring the girl?'

"He was instantly ignored and disregarded by the Madam. She was disturbed by whatever activity she had been engaged in upon our arrival. She tied a loose wrapper over her massive chest and walked as if she were pushing a trolley.

"She stood in the middle of the room while my captors huddled together, squeezing me between them in my palm oil-soaked clothes. There we stood as if we were farm produce — sacks of soybeans, palm kernels, or cocoa beans — and Madam stood over us impassively.

"Her small eyes squinting in her proud face, where a lone gold tooth smiled wistfully, she was determined not to laugh at our calamitous palm oil-drenched outfits. Madam Kofo constrained her laughter, but a chuckle escaped her lips. Finally, she fixed her eye on me with a mixture of exasperation, curiosity, and poignancy.

"'So, this is my Nanny?'

"'Certainly, Madam,' Twiddle answered, curtsying.

"'What is her name?' Madam graciously asked.

"'What is your name?' Dumbo dug his elbow into my back, pushing me forward.

"'Aishatu,' I said. The woman and Twiddle expressed displeasure and, facing me, yelled, 'We can't hear you!'

"At this point I realised that tiredness, hunger, and thirst had stolen my voice. I was not afraid. I believed that these rich people prosper by kidnapping young girls and making rituals — converting them into money-vomiting corpses. I was not scared. I was not going to be led to slaughter like some sheep. At the thought of my imminent demise at the hands of this murderous horde, I found myself crying. Crying requires no effort.

"Madam Kofo walked towards me and softly held my hands.

"'Why are you crying?' she asked, bewildered, with as much tenderness as she could muster.

"I responded emphatically: 'I am hungry.' Alarmed, she turned to the terrible duo. They both shouted simultaneously: 'She refused to eat.'

"Her money, her authority, and her imposing persona unnerved your nitwits. Madam Kofo-Aidoo asked them if everything was well. They replied that all was very well, and that although I cried a lot, I was as strong as a horse and would be an asset to her.

"She then paid them, and they collected the money effusively, retreating backward as if afraid something terrible would happen if they turned their backs. They could both have become pillars of salt — I thought it and wished it.

"Without letting go of my hand, Madam Kofo-Aidoo took me into her kitchen, and luckily, the kitchen was alive with breakfast boiling in the pots and frying pans. My favourite — rice and beans mixed with cow offal — made my stomach rumble. She handed me to the cook and mumbled something in their language, Twi, as I would later learn."

"Yes — the rich woman is Twi, from Ghana. You remembered correctly. My only friend in Kepe was the Ghanaian lady, the cook to the king. She used to buy fish from us," her mother added, her voice warm with empathy.

Her mother was seeing Aishatu in a new light. In all considerations, Aishatu was a mature young woman at fourteen, ripened enough to hold strong views about everybody and everything — not to mention that she was an expectant mother. Even in appearance she could have passed for eighteen: tall, raw-boned, composed. Yet she was merely a child.

How could anyone have entered the sanctity of her garden to violate the young tendril? It must have been the familial bonds that provided Mama Aishatu with a soft landing — a way to escape her daughter's justified recriminations.

Aishatu cooked some more native rice and served it to her mother, accompanied by palm oil and pepper sauce. Mother and daughter ate in silence. Each tried to reconstruct how life had dealt with them and how they might salvage what remained, or navigate the twists and turns ahead. Aishatu's eyelids grew heavy with sleep, and her eyes pleaded with her mother as she rolled onto the mattress and slept — exhausted from the burdens of her young life, the heavy meal, and their long conversation.

The early morning solemnity was broken by a burst of roosters competing to make the loudest wake-up call. In the village, the first cockcrow at five in the morning signalled couples to finish any remaining activities from the night before. The cockcrow at dawn, an hour later, served as a wake-up call for all creatures in the village — big and small — to leave their beds, mats, mattresses, holes, pens, and perches and start their day. Only the sick and lazy remained asleep after the second cockcrow. Thus, Mama Aishatu and Aishatu woke up, exchanging glances as if they did not quite understand how they had ended up sharing the same bed.

Cognition brought them memories — memories too deep and too bitter to wallow in the blame game. There it was, a finger of fate: mother and daughter in the same room where Aishatu was born fourteen years prior. Whatever had transpired was in the past. But the past had to be unravelled and understood in its deepest roots, so that the mistakes of the past would not be repeated. And cognition would lead to transcendence.

Despite her condition, Aishatu sprang from the mattress like a spring and, kneeling on the ground as was customary, said:

"Good morning, Mammy. Did you have a good sleep? Did I scream in my dream?"

"No, my beloved daughter. Good morning. You slept soundly."

"Mammy, let me make pap and beans cake for us. Don't you have bean cake mixture?"

"No, I don't. I am sorry — feeding well has been a challenge."

"No, Mammy, I'm sorry I asked. Don't worry, I'll help you sell your wares. I'm still strong; the baby doesn't bother me," Aishatu replied enthusiastically.

Mama Aishatu said, "I would rather hear what happened to you all these years in Kambia. Let's declare today a holiday to welcome my daughter home to her prodigal mother."

"Mammy, don't say things like that about yourself. I am the prodigal daughter, back home and with you, and I am free to think and do as I please. I don't do anything as a forced chore."

Her mother got up and rummaged by the corner of the room, where the kerosene stove sat on a low table, and lit a match to the wick. An acrid smoke filled the room, and Aishatu started to cough. Her mother threw open the door to the street, which let the smoke, as well as the fried onions and pepper, chimney out. But Aishatu continued to cough.

"Mammy, can I open the window?"

"No, Aishatu, don't open the window. Don't let the terrible smell of Calanana Lagoon into our home. I have never opened that window since your father disappeared into the lagoon. I don't trust the lagoon — especially the underwater kingdom."

"Mammy, do you still believe the devils live inside the lagoon, and that Mami Wata, who lives under the sea, took away Daddy?"

"Yes, I do," she answered without hesitation. "The Atlantic Ocean is a wicked body of water. It continues to consume us, the poor. It is the body of water that took our ancestors into slavery. It is the ocean for rich people. They come here to Kepe to swim inside, lie on their stomachs, and offer themselves to the sea — but it vomits them back onto the sand."

"But, Mammy, it also gave us our staple fish diet before the oil spills."

"And how many baskets of fish will they give me to carry away for my husband? Go ahead and open the window, my daughter."

Aishatu pushed and pulled until the rotten hinges almost fell apart, the windowsill hanging precariously, and Calanana Lagoon suddenly stared into their small, dingy shack. The sky outside was windy and stormy. A ragged, angry light — white, blue, and yellow — flickered over the body of water, lighting up the outline of boats of various sizes dotting the surface. It was as if blood had been poured on the water. Within a flash, Aishatu's teeth were knocked together by a loud clap of thunder.

"Aishatu, close that window before those devils come and take us."

As Aishatu precariously rehung the window, the retreating thunder sounded grumbling, threatening, and angry — as if it had unfinished business with them.

"Mammy, let me cook for you." Aishatu returned to the burning stove and started the stew as her mother joined in preparing breakfast.

"I can make different dishes. I did everything in Mama Kofo-Aidoo's household: nanny, cleaner, washerwoman, storekeeper, cook's assistant, steward, and chief cook. And there were days I was the day or night nurse too."

"I can see that, my daughter. You are intelligent and smart."

They prepared a sumptuous breakfast of roasted plantain in less than an hour. After the meal, Aishatu washed the plates, stacked them with the stove, and slipped back into bed with her mother. They declared the day a family holiday.

"Where did we stop yesterday?" she asked her mother, her smile quizzical.

"Your first day at Kambia. You arrived covered in palm oil."

"Oh, yes," she recalled. "I arrived covered in palm oil. Madam

Kofo-Aidoo handed me over to the Ghanaian cook as my immediate boss. She fed me well and showed me a mat to sleep on in the kitchen — that was after the day's labour, when all the other workers had left for their homes.

"The cook gave me some used clothes and said they belonged to the previous nanny, who had left without taking her belongings a month before. She had eloped with one of the madam's customers. She was sixteen.

"My suspicions were aroused when I heard that my predecessor had left without anyone knowing where she went. I felt something was wrong. Deep inside, I felt that her sudden departure was a bad omen, and I needed to be on perpetual guard. Maybe they took you in, fed you well, and bided their time until you reached puberty and were ripe to be plucked for ritual purposes. I was determined to be on permanent alert."

"And Madam Kofo-Aidoo — did she talk to you?" the mother asked, her voice trembling.

"Of course. After I scrubbed thoroughly with the sisal sponge and Dettol soap, she sent for me immediately after breakfast."

At this point, the mother stopped her. "You are tired, my daughter; you need to sleep now. Tomorrow is another day. You are back home."

"Yes, Mom. There's no place like home. At least we have a roof over our heads, and the lagoon still provides us with fish."

"Yes, my daughter. The dreadful lagoon — it feeds with one hand and takes away with the other."

"Mammy, I am eight months gone," she said, changing the subject.

"It seems like seven. But don't worry; your mother understands about giving birth, so it shouldn't be an issue."

"I know."

"Go ahead and sleep. We have our whole future to tell each other stories of what was, what is, and what is to come."

"Yes, Mammy."

They went to bed, both facing the same side, with the mother putting a protective hand over her pregnant daughter's belly as they fell asleep.

9

———————

AN EVENING WITH THE SENATOR

Senator Kanyi looked outside the window of his Bombardier Challenger 350. The air hostess, Anita, had politely carried the red wine glass and platter of small chops back to the "kitchen in the clouds," a magnificent oak wood cabinet with gilded trims. The kitchen was fully stocked with the best global cuisines.

Anita spoke with a Serbian accent, announcing that the plane was about to descend into the Clement Nick Agyo International Airport, Calanana. There was only one passenger — the senator. She wheeled back to storage the golden trolley loaded with victuals: Spanish tapas, Belgian chocolate, Neapolitan pizza, Japanese noodles — all of which the senator had declined.

The senator was returning from a journey to nowhere. He had decided late in the afternoon to ride in his favourite air toy, the private jet, simply to go nowhere. He needed to think, to clear the many situations entangled in his brain like spider webs. He thanked God for blessing him with this beautiful bird, which symbolised success and entry into the upper echelon of society. He asked the French pilot to fly him to conquer the weather and rise above the mountain peaks and clouds. He often took solo rides like this — no friends, relations, attendants, or colleagues.

He wanted to be alone with his thoughts, to rise above the world, to soar into a realm of creativity. It was his sanctuary. Usually, two air hostesses were assigned to serve him — Agatha and Anita. Today, Agatha was off duty and not privy to the flight schedule. He knew how money bent ambitions, especially among the young women who served him, some dreaming of rings, others of allowances. He knew his power over them — young, ambitious women who all wished to be married to him or be his Baby Mama.

He had had a bad day in the Senate. He faced many challenges as Chairman of the Committee on Finance and Appropriations. The opposition bitterly contested the financial and fiscal policies. They called the government corrupt and Senator Kanyi the chief enabler of official corruption in Sofalia. It was a turbulent day as the opposition raised motions countered by the ruling party's senators, who in turn raised countermotions.

The underlying theme was that the Sofalian Republic, modelled after the US, had failed. That the economy was dead and could not be revived. The Central Bank had become an ATM, ready to provide muted dollars for the executives and a few senators. Imagine. That was too close. Too close. There were calls for the constitution to be amended to remove the immunity clause for the executives and for the Governor of the Central Bank to be fired and handed over to the police for prosecution. Yes, there were seditious calls for the president to be impeached. It was a dangerous day for democracy.

Democracy, as far as he could tell — especially from the US model — was a civilised way of transferring power to the most capable, powerful, and creative citizens. Here in Sofalia, democracy was quite simple. It was Ogacracy. All it required was to win an election by any means necessary. The ends justified and sanctified the means. And then, with power, one could control the national treasuries. Military coups were outdated. Sofalian Ogacracy was *government of the powerful, for the powerful, by the powerful.*

Democracy might have its discontents — the nay-sayers and grumblers — but majority rule remained the best form of power transfer without shedding blood. But imagine these ignorant and idealistic senators upsetting the apple cart on a Monday morning with such dangerous motions. It was bad for him, especially.

He surveyed the cabin as the plane descended gently, smoothly, and silently onto the runway. That exhilarating feeling of flying into a shoal of stars returned to his mind. He grasped the plane's armrest involuntarily and tried to steady himself as the crackling microphone announced: "Welcome, Honourable and Distinguished Senator of the Republic, to the Clement Nick Agyo International Airport."

Anita, the air hostess, smiled her most charming smile at him. The cockpit door opened, and the captain and co-pilot came out. The plane's door was opened, and Anita swiftly put the retractable stairs in place. Kanyi patted his black leather handbag. It was always at hand whenever he travelled. Inside: his asthma spray, two bundles of crisp hundred-dollar bills totalling four hundred thousand dollars, and a fully loaded P226 double-action pistol.

From his window seat, he saw that his orderly and special assistant were gathered at the foot of the plane. He felt refreshed in his soul. It was a moment to withdraw and think strategically — like the Prophet's *Hijra* or Jesus' retreat to the mountain.

He took his time stepping off the plane, reminding himself that solo flights were not about shared power but power projection. As he looked outside, he noticed his orderly and special assistant had been joined by his SA (Media), his constituency party chairman, the party's Woman Leader, and a professional videographer. His welcoming party also featured a group of Creole dancers.

The senator was angry. For a moment, he believed that the prebendal chain made corruption unavoidable. Before stepping down the stairs, he quickly handed the pilots ten thousand dollars and saw them smiling joyfully. He waved to the welcoming crowd as the drummers and dancers blocked his way. The orderly angrily chased them away and cleared a path for the senator to enter the VVIP section of the private wing of the airport.

The welcome band rushed to arrange the senator's convoy while the senator established his presence among other VVIP users of the private terminal. It was evening, and his colleague, the Senate

Chairman of Oil and Gas, Senator Ibn Siaka Jonstons, was there. He stood up, and they hugged, thumping each other's backs.

"How now?" he asked.

"Splendid. Are you also travelling out?"

"No, returning."

"We were in the Senate this evening. Then I went home, cleaned, took a bite, and now I am going to Geneva. I don't know why we did not vote you the Senate president."

"Me, Senate President? Have you also joined the conspirators? Oh, you are off for the OPEC meeting."

"Exactly, but *na wao*, you must be a magician. Where would you be returning from?"

"Don't ask. I left before the evening session ended. I feel sad about the things the opposition was bringing up."

"Did you? I was mad. Didn't you hear I shouted at them?"

"Is it because we are running the most lenient democracy in the world that they open their mouths and vomit on the hallowed red carpet of the hallowed Assembly?"

"Precisely. They now talk of corruption and even point their leprous fingers. Nobody recalls previous administrations leading us here."

"The SP is very weak. If I were the presiding officer, I would brand all of them as unruly radicals."

"Yes, my brother, *na wao*, he is weak."

"That is who he is: pathetic and weak."

The orderly entered, and they quickly reverted to talking in low tones. Kanyi looked at the orderly and motioned with his eyes: *"Make una get set. I'm coming now now,"* he gestured with a wave of his hand.

Returning to his colleague, he continued:

"Chairman, I wish you a great journey and success at the meeting. Get to know the members and let them help us."

"Sure, Chairman Approp. I will see you when I am back. Take care of things."

They parted with absurd, conspiratorial laughter.

"Yes, you bet." Kanyi nodded almost imperceptibly.

Senator Kanyi shook hands with the airport ground staff and handed each a hundred-dollar bill. They formed a guard of honour to receive their share of the monumental plunder the Calanana elite imposed on their country. The tips they earned while working at the private airport were shared among their colleagues within the establishment. The Ogas in charge owned the nation, but *the forest where the elephant reigned could not deny the rats their right to foliage.*

The workers exchanged banter and prayed to their various gods, hoping to make the senator richer so they too could benefit as wealth trickled down from the nest of corruption. They watched in silent admiration the sirens and flashing lights of the senator's convoy driving out of the airport.

Kanyi sat in his bulletproof limo, sandwiched between a small convoy of twenty-five cars, each blaring sirens in striking dissimilarity. The police escort, wielding kobokos, chased smaller taxis and private citizens from the road, even though it was a multi-lane street. The streets were dark and dreary.

The solar lights, installed with great fanfare by the previous administration, were cannibalised, leaving the steel arms waving — a terrible symbol: *the leprous fingers of corruption.*

The beggars on the streets — those who were neither in wheelchairs nor crawling on their stomachs — stood at attention, vicariously engaged in the paradise of Calanana's Ogas. These men had appropriated the nation.

Senator Kanyi's convoy sped into the exclusive Abosko District and stopped before his sprawling home's heavily fortified southern gate. The security cameras and lights flickered to life, and the ornate gates, adorned with fierce gold lion carvings, swung open. The police officers in the convoy leapt out, striding into the area as if they were late for a lover's arms.

The senator's mansion was on the most pristine and exclusive side of Abosko in Calanana. Its colonial Spanish architecture was impressive. He lived in the main triplex while his aged parents, who had been uprooted from Kepe, resided in the attached duplex guesthouse. This arrangement made the parents part of the good life and also safely sheltered them from the greedy arms of kidnappers.

The palatial home spanned two hectares. Its allure came from its architecture and ornate furnishings: luxurious marble swimming pool and poolside pavilion, expansive patios, and lush, perfectly manicured lawns. The grounds featured a private helipad for exclusive meetings with foreign business partners and state dignitaries, including the highest officials.

The interior walls were all crafted from Crema Marfil marble. The space was decorated with paintings by renowned artists, including Yisa Akinboye, Ver Sen, and Picasso. The doors were constructed from premium steel, standing ten feet high, with high-quality wooden finishes. All fixtures were sourced from Europe's finest artisans.

The mansion's banquet hall featured theatrical lights, an electronic podium, and a capacity for three thousand guests. Anyone entering his banquet hall could not help gasping and entertaining presidential or gubernatorial ambitions for the young senator, even though he had never hinted at such. The banquet room was equipped with an anteroom for thirty people.

The senator's educational qualifications were unclear and unverifiable under oath. He obscured this deficiency by acquiring numerous books, especially biographies of prominent statesmen. Externally, no one could deny his love for books; only upon closer inspection did it become apparent that this affection was superficial. He possessed an impressive collection of biographies — Mandela, Clinton, Bush, Nasser, Hitler, Franco, Machiavelli, Stalin, Idi Amin, Sekou Touré. Among these were titles on mafia leaders and underworld kingpins.

His magnificent library housed fifteen thousand books displayed in glass panels on elegant walnut shelves. His massive reading table was made from the finest mahogany, and he sat in an automatic reclining, back-massaging desk chair. Aside from official documents, with the imposing Senate crest facing forward, the table was otherwise empty. Only three books rested on the surface: *The Art of*

War, *The 48 Laws of Power*, and *The Prince*. These served more for show than for reading. The senator spoke polished English, but was never truly literate. The entire library functioned as a façade, unsettling his visitors and compelling them to regard him more seriously.

The kitchen, adjacent to the banquet hall, was the ultimate culinary pleasure. It featured a massive temperature-controlled wine room with a vintage global collection, opening onto the Olympic-sized swimming pool. Stores of prepared food were held in storage for the entire mansion, and all visitors were fed. Kanyi's directive to his South African Afrikaner and Togolese chefs was to ensure that everyone arriving at the villa had enough food to eat, regardless of the time of day. His mother insisted on this when his parents came to live in the mansion.

His kitchen was symbolically situated between the living room and the banquet hall — the centres of political circulation. It spelt luxury, modernity, money, and the ability to meet all the senator's expectations. There were over ten cooks. The air-conditioned kitchen, noted for its cosiness, came with state-of-the-art appliances: bright induction hobs and smart ovens.

The senator finally reached his residence. The sirens silenced. The strobe lights were no longer necessary for ego-boosting and were turned off. Sitting in the front seat with the driver, the orderly jumped down quickly and saluted. He grabbed the senator's side of the door to open it but shut it again promptly: the senator was on the phone. It was an important call. The orderly heard him answer, "Yes, C-in-C—". He was speaking with the president.

There was a flurry of movement around the compound. The mansion staff was on high alert. Oga had returned.

The gateman quietly called the chief security officer, who had gone to town for business:

"Hello, the Black Scorpion has landed."

The pager answered, "Hello, the message was understood. I'll be back in a second. Over."

The gigantic dining hall was being set up, and more than ten cooks were standing there, waiting to serve Oga and his guests.

Kanyi opened the car's door and adjusted his long, flowing Agbada before entering his living room. About fifteen people stood up involuntarily to attention.

The senator could not have been less happy. *These people,* he thought, and scanned the smiling faces. He forced a smile to his face, hiding the pounding of anger swelling in his heart.

He felt unhappy and fearful of the future, especially after the president had spoken to him on the phone. It meant he had to attend another secret caucus meeting with the president that night, after midnight, when the city was asleep.

He saw the speaker from his Provincial House of Deputies. The rest were a mixture of people seeking favours: fathers needing letters of introduction for themselves or their children, prominent men fallen on hard times and seeking money for their needs, and others simply wanting to keep in touch.

Huddled in one corner were his thugs and social media team. They were his hit squad and cyber-army. Both teams were functional in browbeating his enemies, distracting his detractors, blackmailing his opponents, and haranguing his political rivals. Each member of his social media team had an iPhone, and each was on a generous salary way above the national minimum wage. It was expensive, but the peddling of mischief against his political enemies and the endless promotion of his brand more than compensated.

He was thrilled by artificial intelligence. Fiction was more factual than reality. Nothing was real anymore except perhaps human imagination. Everything else was an imitation. Even the creation of man in God's image was God's imagination of the perfect man. Still, the clay hid an imperfection. In the Garden, the imperfection was revealed where man's insatiable greed for glamour was exposed — a fatal flaw even in God's own creation.

"Una don chop?" he asked the chief henchman of the thugs, inquiring whether they had been served.

"Yes, Oga. We chop beleful."

Kanyi was happy to hear they had been served. He left the living room and took the secret elevator to his third-floor penthouse and main bedroom. It was an oasis of indescribable elegance and comfort — his retreat, mental resetting kit, and paradise.

The plush, thick carpets were cream and beige, and the rug was royal purple. The ceiling lighting was kaleidoscopic, and the walls were a blend of emerald, ruby, and sapphire.

He opened the door to his walk-in deluxe wardrobe, which featured extensive lighting, mirrors, and cabinets. The wardrobe displayed outfits from Bond Street, London, and Avenue des Champs-Élysées, Paris. The suits, shirts, and shoes were sourced from various locations and displayed uniformly. Only a few had been worn.

The senator pressed a switch on the wall, revealing another room that displayed his extensive collection of wristwatches: Vacheron Constantin Tour de l'Île, Lange & Söhne Grand Complication, Franck Muller Aeternitas Mega 4, Patek Philippe chronograph, Rolex Albino Daytona, among others. The collection seemed endless; it was not merely an exhibition — it was extraordinary.

The senator surveyed his entire collection, felt satisfied, and entered his luxurious bathroom. This was his most private retreat, where he was alone, naked before his Maker, the way he was born. Except he was born with nothing, in a slum in Kepe village, the son of an Ikaw fisherman. But now, here he was in his bathroom — his mini spa, with toasty towels, a life-size mirror — elegantly spaced, with room to move about, naked, and not be ashamed or hemmed in.

Kanyi spent only fifty minutes in the bedroom before taking another secret lift into the dining hall. He was raised to honour his father and mother and live a long life. He ate dinner with his parents every evening, except when he was engaged in state, business, or other matters, such as pleasure. He was happy to see his parents seated at the table, waiting for his arrival so they could begin dinner together.

He greeted them and genuflected before them in a deep, customary style.

"Good evening, Mama; good evening, Dad. I hope my delay didn't make you too hungry. Dad, please say the grace."

"Welcome, my pikin. Baba, please say a prayer for the food." His mother, not to be outdone, added her voice since her husband was hard of hearing and seemed not to have heard the prayer request.

"Okay, let's pray," Papa Mulaake Adedem pronounced —

Our Father in Heaven, the Only God, the all-seeing God.
We thank our father.
For bringing our son back from the Sofalian jungle.
From that pit of hell, the Sofalian Assembly.
Thank you for this paradise prepared for us,
Our cup overflows
Our enemies are shaking.
They are pissing in their pants
They are nothing but toothless lions
Our son, the Daniel of his time.
He shall dwell among them.
He will not be like them.
He will take a larger share of everything.
You will be blessed by those who bless him.
Put a mighty curse on those who curse him.
Lord, we invite You, our guest.
At this table, bless the food.
Bless the water and the wine.
In Jesus' Name.

Kanyi and his mother said aloud, "Amen," and the stewards, chefs, and all those dressed in white, pushing metallic trolleys, descended on them *like surgeons entering the theatre of power.*

Kanyi was famished and ate ravenously for a while, devouring a plate of Fish Pepper Soup, the Chicken Casserole, and the Herder's Pie. A lady, also in white, pulled away from the servants — she was the senator's dietitian, Dr. Mabel Gado. She brought a piece of paper in her hand. On the paper, she had written that 750 calories had been consumed, and she handed it to the senator with a smile.

"I haven't eaten the whole day, and you want to kill me with this calorie count. Have I eaten 750 calories already?" the senator asked with a scowl.

"Yes, sir. Let's follow the science." She gently rubbed his shoulders and said, "You are doing so well."

The dietician retreated to her place. She had been employed when Senator Kanyi went for his quarterly medical check-up at Mt. Sinai in the US. His doctor, Dr. Einstein, of the Nuclear Medicine Department, had reviewed his medical condition and detected an early onset of pre-diabetes and excessive cholesterol. He had therefore recommended that the senator lose a significant amount of weight. That meant reducing carbs and alcoholic beverages, as well as monitoring his blood glucose levels.

Nearly all members of the National Assembly had potbellies, which they nourished with oversized, flowing garments that concealed their distended bellies.

That was why Dr. Gado, a clinical dietician from the University of Sofalia, joined the senator as his personal staff member. The senator was concerned about his appearance and did not want to jeopardise his reputation as the best-dressed and most handsome senator in Sofalia. That was another way of saying he was the most eligible bachelor in the country.

Mabel accepted the twenty-thousand-dollar monthly pay offer, which was ten times her university salary.

The senator had a secret crush on her and restrained himself with traditional wisdom: *"A crocodile does not eat fish that live in the same water with it."*

The dietitian carefully documented her research on the effects of African Topesia flour and roasted goat meat on the glycemic index and its impact on the blood plasma of large mammals in the Sofalian Senate. Her two peer-reviewed articles had already been accepted — one in an online journal, another in *Clinical Medicine* in India.

She glanced at the senator, who was indulging himself with great delight. He was *her specimen.*

Mama Kanyi had barely touched her food. Her husband devoured a massive serving of Pounded Yam with Grasscutter Bush

Meat in Egusi Soup. He sampled the assorted platter of snails imported from Nigeria and *Giwan Ruwa* fish from the River Lafa, one of Sofalia's main rivers. He was that kind of man: the more he ate, the thinner he became. He had an excellent constitution, while his wife, Mama Kanyi, and their son tended to be overweight.

Kanyi eyed the plate of salad before him, as recommended by his dietitian, with dread. *This was grass.* He bit his tongue to avoid blurting it out — he didn't want to be seen as bush, uneducated, uncouth, or uncultured.

He saw his mother also merely toying with her food.

"Mama, why? You hardly ate this evening," Kanyi asked his mother.

"No, my pikin', I no dey hungry."

"Why aren't you hungry?" her husband asked with a hint of sarcasm. She glared at him and smirked. Caring for their son had created a deep rift between husband and wife over everything.

Even though Kanyi's father, Mulaake Adedem, did not have much education, he had finished Primary Seven at St. Savior's Primary School in Kepe. Then, Kanyi's grandfather, Adedem Abomtse, an illiterate fisherman who had vowed to give him the best education that money could provide, died suddenly. A black mamba bit him fatally in the groin.

His father, Mulaake, had nobody to turn to. He ran to the Methodist Church, where the pastor took him in as a houseboy and employed him as a teacher in the church's Adult School for its members.

Mulaake Adedem began to adopt the airs of a schoolteacher and started to dress in shorts that stopped above his knees and long white stockings rolled to below the knees, where he securely attached his red and blue pens and other writing materials.

Pastor Mkarna found a wife for himself during an evangelism trip to a distant Creek Province. He was then twenty-eight, and his wife, Deborah Mtomgba, was gifted to the pastor so that she could escape from a spiritual husband tormenting her life. Whenever the spirit took possession of her body, she convulsed and had epileptic fits. The pastor gave the strapping girl tortured by her spiritual husband to Mulaake Adedem — Kanyi's father — as a wife.

At the age of fifteen, Deborah gave birth to a baby girl named Ambura. The child had been given the name Ambura after Grandpa Adedem Abomtse's beloved sister Ambura, who died during childbirth. Mulaake Adedem's Ambura lived out the prophecy of her namesake, and she too died at the age of two after a brief bout of Lassa Fever.

After five years, Kanyi was born. By then, their mother was twenty years old. The grateful mother named him Kanyi, which translates to "The One." Kanyi was *the one who would stay and not die a premature death, the one who would wipe the mother's tears, the one through whom the family name would be perpetuated.*

Sadly, they were never able to have another child. All doctors consulted were unable to find out what was wrong. When she travelled back to Creek Province during the funeral of her mother, she learned that her envious spiritual husband from the sea had claimed the first girl-child as his biological child.

She spoke Pidgin, the English language of the oppressed. It was the British who inspired the language to evolve more than three centuries ago when they invaded West Africa for slaves. It was the language that the interpreters and native intermediaries developed to communicate with other tribes and the white man. It was like the traditional language of Sofalia — an amalgamated potpourri of five hundred languages jostling together to create meaning.

Mama Kanyi refused to be deterred and spoke fluent Pidgin, while her husband and son spoke the language of class and suppression — grammar.

Recently, her husband was getting on her nerves. He seemed to be enjoying their son's home and the pathetic films he had been watching on the television, which was, more than anything, a cesspool of perversion. *Knacking* — street slang for sex — a very private activity of man and woman, was openly displayed with shameless perversion. That was not right. Her husband, unfortunately, she observed, was enjoying this perversion, especially of the young female bodies on display. Mama Kanyi found her husband's inclinations morally reprehensible and deeply unsettling.

Even the female newscasters were not innocent, with their wigs and heavily made-up faces, often accompanied by talcum powder and blood-red lipstick. They spread their lasciviousness and wantonness more than the rumours they called news. This was why she wanted her husband to return with her to their village and live lives of contentment. Their son's house was a prison for her. She came to conclude that bringing them to Sofalia was a benign form of kidnapping. What her husband saw as luxury, she saw as pathetic misery.

She cleared her throat: *"Kanyi, we fit to return to Kepe village, our home?"*

"You have started," her husband told her in a whisper.

"I no start nothing. This is not our home. I no get happiness for here, lai lai."

"Mama, is the TV in the guest chalet not working?" her son asked.

"Which TV? Na so so knack knack knack."

"Is that what makes you sad? I will have them change the Television to Local channels. Is there any other issue?"

"There are plenty, plenty things. I don't see my chicken farm, snail and vegetable farm, or palm oil business."

"But you don't need those things. God has blessed us, Mama; no more suffering. You are not an ordinary woman again."

"Wanda! Na you sabi! Why I no ordinary?" she asked.

"No, Mama, it is not like that. God has blessed us and taken us out of *Egypt,* the land of poverty and slavery."

"My pikin, you dey speak like a child. Abeg, no spoil God's name."

Kanyi was not used to arguing with his mother, who had become tetchy recently for no apparent reason other than his mansion. He would not risk her anger, which he knew too well could lead to hollering, hysteria, and embarrassing the guests.

He felt sad that his parents' hearts were left behind in the thatched huts they called home in Kepe, despite his luxurious grand residence in Calanana.

"Na true, you say this prisoner wey I become, why I no cook with my hands, no visit my friends, no go dance masquerade dance at the festival, and no take bath on the ocean side. This is not being rich, my son. You poor well well."

The husband and son started laughing at her. Sensing she was about to explode, Kanyi's father gave him the evil eye, hastily beat a retreat, and tried to calm her.

"It is enough, Mama Kanyi. It is enough. Our son, the senator, also needs to talk to other people waiting for him," he said, half joking and half serious.

"Which people? Dem pass me? Na dem bonam?"

"No, Mama. They did not give birth to me — your only pikin. Please, I have heard you. A helicopter will take you home this Saturday. You will stay for three hours, meet your friends, and then be taken back by the police, who will provide you with a security escort."

"I no agree. No, be me. I no be prisoner. I wan enter bus for garage. Calanana to Kepe na small money."

"You don't understand, Mama. All the bandits in this country, all the kidnappers, all the insurgents, are looking for you to kidnap. Your ransom will break me. They will ask for billions of dollars."

"Na dat one worry you? Let them kidnap me. No be another prison dem go carry me go?"

Kanyi cackled mirthlessly. "Mama, God will not bless me if I allow my mother to be kidnapped. They will torture, maim, or even kill you even after the ransom is paid."

"That one worry you? Blessed Virgin Mary. Lef them kidnap me. Dem no fit do me harm."

"So, Mama, what do you want?" Kanyi asked in exasperation.

"My son, na rape de worry you? Let me be raped — no be other woman pikin of Sofalia dem dey rape? Wetin' you no kill all the kidnappers? Wetin una dey do for dat Senate house? Na only to share money?"

These words of his mother went through his heart. The suggestion that perhaps the senators do nothing except share the people's money was deeply troubling. Ever since he joined politics, his mother had been his reality check. She was frank and brutal. He needed at least one lone voice to bring him away from the surreal and dizzy world of politics and the intoxication that politics brings. It was an *instant transformer from rags to turbans*. It made the impossible possible; it elevated, dominated, and brought life and death. Politics intoxicated, aroused, and quenched desires. Money and power belonged to the realm of politics.

Kanyi's mind wandered again to the source of his stupendous wealth. His investments in the Western education system concentrated on the essentials: the English language, mastering its accents, phonology, inflections, and cadences, which opened all gates to Western hearts; technology; and Information Systems, which opened Western bank vaults.

Like the Africans who sold their best workforce to the West as slaves, the West was willingly reversing its wealth with a measure of joy, relief, and apprehension. The West was more than obligingly willing to transfer its wealth. Bank vaults could be scoured, and cryptocurrency provided a risk-free environment. Neither Western institutions, legal systems, nor law enforcement could touch his loot. He had entered the Western mind, its veins and arteries, matching their greed with his even greater greed. It was risk-free.

He had entered the essence of the Western mind: greed. The main business of the West was greed. The main business of Senator Kanyi was also greed. This was the human essence. He had agreed with the Western Philosopher Ayn Rand on the virtue of human greed. He enjoyed listening to the audio of her books. The source of all human inventions had been greed to satisfy, the quest to dominate, and to be in control. This was the rock from which all politicians were hewn.

He boasted that *Artificial Intelligence was African Intelligence*, in the DNA of people like Kanyi, born in poverty but now living like the kings and queens of the West. These people spent their lives idly enjoying the pillage amassed from all over the world by their greedy pirates and buccaneers. With AI, it didn't matter how high

Westerners were in society; they always heeded the dog whistle of greed expressed in their language and accents.

The people in white descended with steel trolleys and carried the food — much of it uneaten — to the kitchen, where the people who lived on the streets joyfully ate the leftovers they picked from the large waste bins outside the gates.

"Mama, I have heard you; please go back and sleep. I still need to go out tonight to meet with the president."

"My pikin go in peace. Your little toe no shek, your hair no shekin."

He hugged his mother and hurried back to the living room, where the crowd had increased. But he couldn't possibly see all the guests that night. Did he need them? What for? He didn't need them. They needed him. His chief of protocol brought a long list of people needing monetary assistance with school fees, medical fees, money to pay for farm labour, and to marry wives.

Nobody discussed the provision of tap water, the construction of better schools, and improved health services, nor new policies to make education compulsory and free at all levels. They all wanted personal migration from poverty to riches instantly, and all were greedily basking in the euphoria of instant gratification from the senator. They didn't care how he became fabulously wealthy. It did not matter. It was God who took Kanyi to the earthly Paradise. So, it was pointless to feel envious. They only wanted Kanyi to remember them and *cut a few inches of paradise for them.*

He sat briefly in the living room to receive a whispered consultation from the speaker. The senator had taken an interest in him — including arranging medical checkups for the whole family, paying school fees for the children, purchasing a new car, and providing funds to secure an agricultural loan. Kanyi thought that the followers of Sofalia were the problem. They didn't elect people to provide a better life. They wanted instant gratification. Their needs were forever mounting. The expectations were enormous. They projected their greed onto the Ogas, surrendered their thinking to the Ogas, and even paused their lives in abject abdication, dreaming of living like their Ogas. How could anybody with any modicum of self-respect be a politician without a healthy dose of insanity?

Kanyi had to go. Reaching into his legendary handbag, he thoughtfully ran his finger on the metallic barrel of his pistol. *Bang, bang, bang* could end his life.

Life was a joke; being a politician was a dirty job. *It was a dirty job for the brave, who could end with a bullet in the brain.* But it was the dollars his hands brought out of the bag that he gave the prebendal guests to share.

This thing money... he mused as he watched from the corner of his eye the effect of money on the receivers, whose countenance immediately changed from helpless supplicants to mini-Ogas in their domains. With dollars, he was empowering these followers too — to go to town and shine with the senator's lustre.

Their faces reflected the miraculous transition from helplessness to power and demagoguery.

He reflected on his relationship with his mother. She was the most precious thing in his life. She defined his whole world of love. She was more precious to him than all the money in the world. If he had to choose between losing her and trillions of dollars, he would choose his mother. If he had to choose between her life and becoming the president of Sofalia or even the whole world, Kanyi Mulaake would bid political ambition goodbye and return with his mum to Kepe.

As the senator left his followers sharing money in his living room, he pondered his mother's words that senators do nothing except share money. His convoy had started its journey to the presidential palace, and the sights and sounds of the convoy woke everyone up this late at night in Calanana.

But the senator paid no attention. His mind was focused on urgent solutions to the challenges facing the ruling party, which was now being defended by a restive public, greedy and evil journalists, and a followership that had lost its right to follow and needed to be *uprooted, deleted, and delinked* from the ballot. The party had to promote a seamless democracy, albeit one hinged on kleptocracy, kakistocracy, and oligarchy.

The senator was unfamiliar with the meanings of the words his professor-friend had provided to enrich his English vocabulary: *kleptocracy, kakistocracy,* and *oligarchy.* The school system curriculum must include the Ks and Os.

At the Presidential Palace gates, the senator's convoy suddenly switched off its swirling lights and cut off the loud wail of its siren. Power had met a mighty force and must bow like a dog tucking its tail between its legs to get the patronising pat on the head.

Such was the law of power, where ascension was guaranteed only through self-abnegation and self-immolation. Power was accessed through the destruction of the self before the higher power.

The palace gates opened up and swallowed the senator's convoy. Meanwhile, on the streets, the beggars shouted, *"Thief! Thief! Thief!"* at the senator's convoy until it was out of sight.

10

TIME OF GUNGUN

It was not the first time the Sikorsky S-92 had landed here. Captain Chu, the pilot, quickly contacted his supervisor, Senator Kanyi, in Calanana as soon as the helicopter touched down at the helipad. The helicopter's blades and rotors stopped, and the lights turned off. The grassland swallowed the blackbird whole without a ripple.

A flashlight approached the big bird and stopped behind the helicopter's tail. Heavy footsteps trudged forward; men moved dutifully, carrying precious stones. At a flicker of signal from the aircraft, the torchlight died. Seven men lifted a coffin draped in the Sofalian flag into the helicopter. They saluted and marched away.

Captain Chu stepped out of the aircraft and handed the Commander-in-Chief, Gungun, a briefcase filled with twenty million Sodolars. "Oga told me to give you this," he said.

The Sikorsky S-92 had landed in the jungle, settling in a clearing in the heart of the Sofalian Midlands District — a no man's land. Few could witness a more extraordinary state of collapse than this vast Sofalian savannah, where Islamist insurgents and the Sofalian Liberation Action Power (SLAP) contested territory, raising their flags in claim. Although the Sofalian government proclaimed victory, the declaration was a smokescreen that justified larger army budgets.

The helicopter had circled the savannah at tree-top height before landing at midnight on the outskirts of Umoubo Village. If one had been here a few hours earlier, one would have noticed the young men in military fatigues — the undisputed authority in this fifty-square-mile area — a patch of Binda mountains, Tse Gbagir forests, lakes, and the Lafa River.

"Tell Oga I am still loyal," Gungun said. Captain Chu squinted at the sheet listing the coffin's contents, then turned on his throat-mic and spoke into it.

"May the souls of hundreds of pounds of gold rest in peace."

"Perfect peace, Captain."

"May the soul of rhodium rest in peace."

"Perfect peace, Captain."

"May the soul of twenty pounds of lithium rest in peace."

"Perfect peace, Captain."

A pause. The captain's phone chimed — his boss in Calanana.

"Oga asks why the lithium is small like this."

"Not my fault. Army wahala too much. But Oga talk say global demand is huge — supply is small. Gas pump prices go up. Supply dey down. Trouble be say everyone wan drive battery car for abroad."

Captain Chu, short of words, ended the call with a dry line: "May more lithium rest in pieces."

The C-in-C, undeterred, pushed further:

"Tell Oga to talk to the president. The war against Gungun too hot. Make the new Chief of Army Staff cool down. His battle too much. This war is not a war to end all wars. It is 'you-chop-me-I-chop' war. The army pretends to be capturing and winning; we, the insurgents, kidnap, capture the villagers, and get to mine their minerals. We get a small chop. The army chiefs get their chop. Senator and his friends take the rest because dey be Ogas on top."

Captain Chu had no patience for politics and strolled back to his bird. "Chu here to chop, no politics."

"Tell Oga talk to army chief to take it easy. Business is good; God don bless us with all the world's minerals here."

Chu started the rotors. The Sikorsky lifted off. A gust of dust and grit swirled around Gungun and his ragtag soldiers — SLAP, the Sofalian Liberation Action Power.

Captain Chu knew the coffin needed to be reported in Switzerland — declared diplomatic baggage. Chu chuckled darkly, thinking of how people toiled for the minerals and got nothing but scraps, while men like Gungun grabbed a sliver.

Africa was the world's exhaust pipe, and Sofalia the world's latrine. God had made Africa abundant, then — it seemed — pointed so the rest of the world could keep her in perpetual servitude while her Ogas gorged on toys, private planes, exotic cars, fine wines — total indulgence. The Ogas were blind to nation-building; they were dim-witted, amoral clowns who had stolen the people's dignity and left them drowning. These thoughts flickered through Chu's mind, but politics was not his concern. The senator and his friends paid him well; his job was to pilot the bird — nothing more.

Gungun was unhappy when he opened the briefcase. Twenty million Sodolars — roughly nine thousand dollars — for running expenses and the SLAP boys. He considered it insultingly small. Apart from supervising mining, he ran a private surveillance network that eavesdropped on local businesspeople, politicians, and banks; recorded movements of money, private conversations, and compromising videos — all stored in the IOU bank.

They used the internet to awaken greedy, retired Americans and help them pursue the American Dream. It was a lucrative service; Gungun had gained Kanyi's esteem and became his bodyguard. That was when he diverged from Catholicism and later became the senator's medicine man. He introduced the senator to powerful spiritual forces. The senator always wore amulets beneath his flowing robes and bathed with incense every morning to facilitate election victories, secure innocence in court, and bring him prosperity.

At the top of powers, spiritual force reigned. Convince a man of his own smallness before a spirit, and you had a willing slave.

Gungun recalled buying the *Bente* — a leather band studded with tiny amulets — from a travelling Buzu Arab medicine man. The *Bente* promised bullet-proof protection. Any weapon made by a human hand could not harm him.

That extraordinary resume qualified him to oversee Kanyi's growing empire. Gungun was small in the larger world, a Commander-in-Chief in his patch, leading the Western department of Kanyi's vast, unaccountable wealth. He prayed Kanyi would grow richer so Gungun might win amnesty and retire to a villa — ideally in the South of France, Germany, or, at worst, Belize.

Gungun was concerned that the new army chief had taken his appointment and oath of office too seriously. He hoped the man would soften his ways and realise that soldier-go-soldier-come, but the business of soldiering carried on. This was the man's turn in the army's cycle: to accumulate wealth, feather his nest, look after his family, and prepare for retirement. It was his time to rise above his peers, earn the respect of his ancestors, win his wife's love, gain his children's loyalty, and secure the future gratitude of great-grandchildren who would revere him — not for sanctimoniousness, but for wealth.

This was acceptable corruption. Nobody was stealing from government coffers. Participation meant dipping *eye and finger* into the new wealth — private wealth created from national precious metals, far removed from central banks or treasuries where processed monies were held.

The new army commander had vowed to end the insurgency in his first month in office. The week ahead would be hectic. Gungun knew he could not be killed so easily, but many would suffer collateral damage. Stupid soldiers, who believed the lie that an insurgency could be crushed, might become overzealous and harm or stop Gungun. He would retaliate with ferocity, inhumanity, and military capacity.

Umoubo village was his fortress. Beneath its soil lay the world's richest minerals. It was his home. His late parents' graves stood in front of his deceptively simple village mansion. Inside that house was a vast arsenal: semi-automatic pistols, IMI Uzi sub-machine guns, Ingram MAC-10s, M4A1 rifles, and an arsenal said to hold nearly a million AK-47s. The "simple" house was a fortress, guarded by a hidden population of SLAP fighters in the Binda mountains, less than fifty miles away, nestled in the forested slopes.

Gungun hated politics and politicians. There was nothing concrete in a career built on other people's perceptions. One had to become what others projected. Different faces to different people. Politicians spoke in tongues: one side heard one thing, the other another, and both were seduced. Political promises were blah-blah. Hangovers. Cold turkeys after drugging.

The need for a gun in hand was a reality. Kill or be killed. Kidnapping strangers — innocents who had done no harm — ran against Gungun's Catholic upbringing. But his friend Kanyi had told him that capitalism had no friends. Business companies were considered people, and for businesses to live, to breathe, human rights had to be violated. Kanyi taught him to be unsympathetic, merciless, to kick down those already sagging into dereliction.

The soul of capitalism was to accumulate. If, in the pursuit of capital, a few died, it was tragic but not terrible. If a few thousand were displaced from their lands, or infants and women perished, it was collateral damage. Numbers. Inconsequential numbers. This was the law of nature. The lion did not feel guilty over the rights of the antelope. It tore it up for food.

Kanyi reminded him that the thrones of Europe and the massive cities of the West were built with blood money stolen from Africans and Indians. If Africa could make the West rich, the West could also make Africa rich. That was when Gungun began visiting his Catholic confessor less frequently, until he stopped altogether. He only returned for special occasions — to donate large sums, to collect Holy Water from Jerusalem and mud from the Dead Sea, tokens meant to win affection.

He reasoned that one should not gamble with religion. If the Catholic God was real, then Gungun's insurgency was also real. If the White Garment Church held truth, then Gungun was involved. If traditional cults were genuine, Gungun was there too. Discriminating within religion was dangerous. He admired his role model, Senator Kanyi Mulaake, who took communion every Sunday yet confided how, in the Udoni cult, the deified Akuran had once been swallowed by a cow and emerged unscathed at its rear, suit and bow tie untouched. Was it a miracle? A scam? That, Kanyi said, was the new Sofalia: a patchwork of faiths, all chasing the mighty American dollar.

It was midnight. The Controller of Invisible Forces had hidden the moon behind a thick black blanket. Darkness cloaked Umoubo village. Hundreds of huts — raffia-thatched, grey-mud-walled — stood in concentric circles, eerie as matronly women huddled on the savannah at night. Villagers slept early, their evenings swallowed by darkness.

Strange things happened at night, things unfit for ordinary eyes. Access to Umoubo was only by a potholed laterite road over rocky terrain. Villagers lived as their ancestors had lived for centuries: no electricity, no schools, no health posts, no police. Civilisation's only evidence was young men carrying AK-47s where hoes and cutlasses once were.

Most of these young men were strangers to each other. They had come from far and wide to join Gungun's outlaw government. Umoubo was an ideal hideout — inaccessible, with villagers who were uncivilised and poor, making it easy to control. At night, the gun-toting youths became rowdy, intoxicated on native gin distilled to a lethal hundred percent alcohol, and high on acres of cultivated marijuana, their staple cash crop. Nearly every village woman had been a victim of rape, and families were bound by oaths of silence under the threat of death. In Chembe, atrocities were to be forgotten, never spoken of again. It was the deepest wound of Umoubo, unspoken and unhealed.

But the villagers were uneasy. Low-flying aircraft had begun to pass over Umoubo. Everyone knew it was only a matter of time before the village's secrets spilled into the world. Youths, already unruly, were drinking and smoking heavily. Miners from nearby districts poured in, but Umoubo youths who went to dig rarely returned. Rumours said they were trapped in collapsed shafts, their finds never recorded. Helicopters came by night to lift precious stones. Nobody knew the truth. In Sofalia, everyone lived on *rumour.*

At midnight, bad things happened — and many bad things were happening. Gungun, *son of Imohime, son of Achir Gbagir,* of the Azenga tribe from Umoubo village, was the notorious bandit and warlord who had wrought terror on the land. He had dropped out of school after his junior secondary certificate. His father, a respected public servant, died of a broken heart.

Gungun graduated from petty thefts to robberies, then became an unofficial paid security guard for local politicians. He was radicalised by watching miserable, poverty-stricken politicians steal money meant for development and transform into overnight Ogas.

He was often recruited to snatch electoral materials, rigging elections for his principals. The sham democracy — an ogacracy — was full of powerful men who turned voters into quisling slaves. These Ogas sought office not to serve, but to legitimise theft. Gungun wanted to be an Oga, quickly. The gun was his shortcut. He made Umoubo, his ancestral village, the headquarters of this project. His ambition turned his people into cowering slaves, forced to obey.

At night, bodies were dumped in forests or shallow graves — opponents, or kidnap victims whose families failed to pay ransom in time. Winds sometimes carried the stench of decomposing flesh across the village, and people would pinch their noses shut. In the bush, exotic cars lay hidden under tarps and sand. Jaguars, BMWs, Mercedes-Benzes, Land Cruisers — stolen vehicles disappeared into thatched huts disguised as ordinary mud homes. A wooden mock door and a thatched spear-grass roof concealed immense wealth, swallowed up by invisible hands.

At midnight, everything was whispers: muffled grunts of victims being strangled, sharp claps, tat-tat-tat of AK-47s celebrating another skirmish. Villagers, the poorest, watched helplessly as their son battled the most ruthless army in Africa. The Sofalian military, armed with Pentagon technology, was an overwhelming force. Yet hushed whimpers of money changing hands still freed some kidnap victims — vomited back into the world from these ominous huts.

Strange things happened at midnight. Government officials, politicians, and bureaucrats arrived in SUVs. Their security details prowled as their bosses consulted with the warlord. Some came to negotiate peace. Others sought his help to win elections. Some delivered cash for arms. Umoubo had become Sofalia's kidnapping capital, and Gungun its most dreaded warlord.

The government propaganda machine routinely claimed he had been arrested or killed. Each time, he humiliated them with YouTube videos showing him alive, flanked by his killers with AK-47s. Rumours said he could transform into anything — white man, snake, lamb, rabbit — to escape capture. He was too slippery to hold.

That night, Umoubo's militia headquarters knew they were surrounded.

Akember, Gungun's wife, went out to relieve herself behind their decoy hut. Villagers would often urinate behind their thatched homes at night. She pulled her skirt up and squatted, urine splattering her legs. Then she saw a strange glow — not pigs rummaging, but the flicker of a phone screen glinting on metal. Shadows moved. Helmets. Soldiers. Federal soldiers.

Her body froze. The stream cut off mid-flow. She yanked her skirt down, whispered "Soldiers," and crept backwards into the hut. She groped in darkness, hands stretched like a praying mantis, until her foot touched the mattress. Gungun pulled her to him, crushing her breasts against his chest. His precarious life only sharpened his libido; he wanted her with desperate hunger. She pushed him away.

"Shhh. Don't. Soldiers outside. They've surrounded us."

Gungun sprang like a rabbit sensing an eagle. He knew sudden flight meant certain death. Calmly, he dressed. His undergarment was a leather amulet sewn with human flesh. Around his waist he tied a duiker's horn, containing the flesh of a virgin — a charm for luck. He unwrapped his AK-47 from its hiding place in a clay water pot.

He spat curses. His police and army informants had lied, assuring him Operation Girinya was postponed, the bounty on his head withdrawn. He had bribed them heavily, lobbying for amnesty and a government appointment. Now he wondered if Senator Kanyi himself had betrayed him. Kanyi claimed his share — over twenty million dollars — waited in a foreign bank. But who could be trusted? No one. They were all fraudsters.

He pulled his iPhone apart and slid in a new SIM card.

He had hundreds of unregistered SIM cards and several phones, making him nearly impossible to track. He dialled his lieutenant.

"Hello, Man Bishop. Where are you? Can you hear me?"

Man Bishop was notorious for twisting the Bible to his ends. He bound a King James Bible with a chain and padlock, claiming that once a kidnapped victim held the chained book, he must confess his true net worth. If he lied, the Bible would shake like a fish on a hook. The ransom would be doubled. If the chain shook again, the victim was marked as a liar, marched into the grove, shot, and buried in a shallow grave with others.

From the far end of the village, an excited voice crackled:

"I'm at the T-junction to your mansion. Soldiers surround the village."

By then, Gungun had finished loading his gun and slung a belt of ammunition across his waist.

"I no sleep at the mansion; I sleep inside a village hut with my queen," he said. *"Get the boys. Ambush them. Kill them. I dey clear?"* He cut the call, swapped the SIM card.

Gunfire erupted like thunder, shattering the night. The bandits outnumbered the troops, and their thunder was louder. Gungun pulled his young wife close and whispered:

"I swear on my ancestors who defeated the British, these soldiers will fail. For three years, they have tried to find me. During elections, I am their friend. After, I am their terrorist, hunted like an animal. If anything happens, dig beneath this bed. You will find enough treasure to live forever."

Akember whispered back, "Amen and Amen."

He stepped into the darkness. His escape route wound across ravines and zigzag footpaths like lost streams searching for rivers.

Crawling low, body taut as a bowstring, he slid through the bush, finger on the trigger.

At the far side of the village, troops of Operation Girinya Dance prepared to ransack every hut. Any weapon — even a hoe or cutlass — would be seized. But Gungun knew his men outnumbered them, and his weapons stores were vast: caches from suppliers in the east and south. He was ready.

This was their fifth hunt to kill him. Each time, he was branded militant, terrorist, rustler, robber, kidnapper. The media had condemned him without trial. Yet no one heard his truth: he was their creation. He had helped rig the elections that brought them to power.

He checked his rucksack. Three phones, each with fresh SIMs. He called Bishop again.

"Any casualties?"

"Yes, General Commander. They killed Borogo, his wife, and children."

Poor Borogo. Gungun had fortified him personally with *bente* amulets — bulletproof, grenadeproof, bombproof. Even his family had drunk *Gberkpugh* potion. Yet a bullet had cut them down. Rumours swirled that a white spirit, *Ijov*, had placed Gungun in a spiritual helmet, making him unkillable, able to shift forms at will.

The villagers dared not betray him. They knew his ears were everywhere. Whispers in the dark could reach him as if amplified on rooftops. Calmly, he ordered Bishop:

"Kill them all. No survivors. Burn the vehicles. Seize the ammunition. Send it to the Binda cave."

He moved into the yam fields. Under grass and tarp, he uncovered a sparkling new Chinese Baja motorcycle, full tank. He kick-started it, the engine roaring as dust and smoke rose around him. He sped off into forgotten lands where abandoned Sofalians lived.

At the mountain cave by the river fort, a boat waited. Behind him, black smoke curled from Umoubo — his home burning again. He laughed. His true treasure was hidden, his wife safe, invisible as another poor village woman.

Retribution would come. Not a single soldier would live to tell of tonight. He stepped into the motorised boat. A burly youth pulled at the oars, blanching with fear but determined.

"What is your name, boy?" Gungun asked.

"Thunder, Commander-in-Chief."

"Good name."

"Thank you, sir."

They rowed in silence. On the far bank, another boy waited with a Baja cycle. Gungun pressed money into Thunder's hand. The boy tried to refuse, but a hard stare made him accept. He was grateful yet dared not show it.

Without a word to the second boy, Gungun mounted the motorbike. He twisted the throttle, and the machine roared into the night.

Thunder had been ferrying bandits across the river for months. He had joined raids against the army, carried weapons, and delivered men into ambush. His family was gone. The bandits were his family now.

He had studied International Relations at Calanana Federal University, graduating, but with no job and no hope. Banditry became a desperate investment in an uncertain future, with only one guarantee: war. War was life. He could end anyone's life with the twitch of a finger on a trigger. He was eerily aware his own life might end the same way.

He no longer knew why they fought the government. Why did they kidnap schoolchildren for ransom? Why did they blow up facilities? The war had become *acephalous, faceless, and relentless.*

Thunder's family had been obliterated by the Sofalian Air Force, which carpet-bombed his village and later claimed it was a mistake. In the Senate, any investigation was blocked by Senator Kanyi, who rose to declare it "unintentional collateral damage." Nobody was to blame. For Thunder, the senator's words were a second bombing.

From that day, Thunder's purpose hardened: avenge the deaths of his parents, siblings, relatives, women. Layer upon layer of tragedy had stiffened his resolve. Kill or be killed. Only war gave meaning now.

The international community blamed the government for fighting the bandits. The U.S. president warned Sofalia's president not to fight but to negotiate. He called it "a domestic quarrel to be settled amicably." But the government would not. They unleashed ferocity against Gungun.

And the irony was brutal: the government backed the very man it claimed to hunt. SLAP knew it. Their commander, Gungun, often travelled in disguise to Calanana, meeting foreign envoys and senior officials. With international voices urging negotiation, Gungun grew bolder. SLAP was decisive. They repudiated every attempt at pacification.

11

THE SENATOR'S PORTFOLIO

Senator Kanyi, chairman of Finance and Appropriations, kept the war on the bandits well enough fed that it never quite ended.

Rumour had it the fighting was less about victory than about supply chains: bandits and army units both surfaced now and then with sacks of rough diamonds, lithium, titanium — cargo ferried out by convoys no one asked too many questions about.

When the firefights died down and foreign rations were airdropped, bullets and munitions occasionally got left behind — ammunition that would find its way back into rebel stocks. War, everyone agreed in private, hid many sins.

A foreign paper, the *Cincinnati Albatross*, had called the Sofalian campaign "a deep pond: placid on the surface, toothy and predatory beneath."

The crocodiles beneath the water were not only commanders in uniform but also chiefs, advisers, and some members of the National Assembly. In the Senate, Kanyi was a thunderhead: eloquent, theatrical, and lethal with his tongue. He demanded more budget, more leeway, and more secrecy — for if there was one thing the war needed, he said, it was money.

He owned three private jets, a Sikorsky helicopter, and other helicopters that touched down in places the maps ignored. He was often seen in those borderlands, arranging evacuations or — if the rumour mill spoke true — collecting the day's takings: sacks of ore flown into friendly hangars. Kanyi framed his raids on the treasury as patriotism; his teeth bared when anyone suggested otherwise.

Far from Calanana, at the foot of the Monticules and the Binda Hills, Gungun's mountain cave waited. The hills were green and deceptive; underfoot, mud, diggings, and greed had hollowed the earth. There, amid caves and tunnels, operations continued until "normalcy" returned — whatever that might mean for the men below.

Akember had once been a student of a different kind of hunger. Expelled from the university for joining the Black Axe confraternity, she had come from a household that measured shame in decibels. Her parents were retired civil servants — staunch, churchgoing individuals — and they regarded discipline as a sacred duty. Her father, Adagi Ubwa, was convinced that the koboko, a leather whip, saved souls.

His patience broke when the university scandal was reported in the local papers. He dragged Akember home and brought out the koboko, an old leather whip folded and polished by the family's custom. He lashed out in the tight, hot room where suitcases, shoes, and porcelain crowded the floor — objects that, to him, marked his respectability and which his daughter had thrown into the mud. How could he attend Church service the following Sunday and take communion? He raged internally.

Akember did not plead. She took the blows in a slow, terrible arc — spun by the whip and by the fury behind it — until her skin was read like a ledger. Her skirt rode up; Bruno, the family dog, bunched under the bed and whimpered. When the cane struck for the fifth time, something inside her snapped.

She rolled, reached into her handbag, and produced a pistol she had kept like a poor woman keeps a secret: close to the chest and never to be shown. The room held its breath. The barrel clenched her fingers. She shot once — clean, terrible — and her father's head bowed as if the room itself had folded. His body hit the carpet with the brittle noise of old things breaking. "Die, wicked man," she said, voice low and exacting.

This was not Akember's first kill. The record of the Black Axe clung to her like a second skin: initiation rites, orders obeyed. Kuyila's death — a friend ordered, a pistol unlatched at point-blank range in the university library — had been the first hard line she crossed. Kuyila had laughed with her, unsuspecting, and then the laughter ended with a high, raking sound and a mouth that called, "Jesus!" while life left her under the yellowing lamps. Students scattered; the campus became a theatre of flight.

No one named Akember in the inquiries that followed — not because they did not know, but because fear and complicity wrapped themselves in rumour. She had taken her place in the underworld quickly: efficient, brutal, and useful. Her father's death only opened a second door. She ran in the rain, waved down a motorcycle, and vanished into a city that now wanted her head. The photographs splashed across papers with the bright cruelty of a public execution. Friends dissolved into silence. But she did not care. Now it was kill or be killed.

Agencies and the press pursued her, but she had friends that mattered — those who trafficked in fear. Through channels that smelled of oil and old money she was shepherded to the underworld's gate. Gungun, who collected men like coins, welcomed her. He needed an educated first lady for his court, and she needed a place to belong.

In Umoubo, education meant new kinds of power. Gungun had eyes and ears everywhere; his men buried stolen cars in mud huts and turned stolen trinkets into the architecture of false poverty. He liked Akember's mind as much as her readiness to pull a trigger. With her, he was not only the mountain's brute but also its cleverness. She became, in the bandit's language, First Lady: a woman whose resume read both schoolbooks and blood.

She became his wife by proclamation. He trained her in the trade: kidnappings, armed robberies, the lucrative business of underworld entrepreneurship. Together, their notoriety grew so spectacular that even the government felt threatened, embarrassed after announcing Gungun's death so many times before.

The bandits now held territory where sham democracy — ogacracy — had crumbled. Poverty, lawlessness, and despair filled the vacuum. Powerful politicians, eager for their cut, propped up the disorder. Kidnapping and banditry became investment portfolios in themselves. Provinces slipped, one after another, under bandit rule.

For many abandoned citizens, the bandit takeover almost seemed a relief. An unelected but decisive underworld government replaced the corruption of elected leaders. It was, in its own logic, a bandit-de-tat — a coup by necessity. At the centre: anarchy and fascism; at the periphery: mimicry, lawlessness, the same rot in miniature.

Yet the setting was deceptive. The Binda Hills shimmered like paradise itself. Waterfalls spilled into glassy pools, vines dangled, frogs croaked, and geese glided onto ponds as if alighting on airports of water.

Hippos, crocodiles, pythons, lions, elephants — all lived undisturbed, nature keeping its own balance from ants to elephants.

But paradise was invaded. The beating blades of a Chinook helicopter scattered the geese and bush fowls, their cries tearing the sky. The bird of metal — new from the United States, christened *Girinya* by the army — bore down on the hills. To Gungun, it was death itself descending. He abandoned his Baja motorcycle and sprinted, zigzagging through the rain of bullets.

The pilots had a single order: find and kill. A fifty-million-dollar bounty hung over his head. For years the government had declared him dead, only to be humiliated when he appeared again on YouTube, mocking them, listing collaborators in government and the security services. Now he had to be ended.

But Gungun, in the villagers' telling, was more than mortal. He was rumoured to transform into sparrows, chameleons, iguanas. The helicopter gunners swore their rounds never landed, though they saw him tumble and rise again, a dark figure scrambling into the treeline.

The terrain was treacherous. Sofalian aircraft had been lost here before. Fuel was low, but the mission could not be aborted: three years of Girinya Dance had to conclude. Gungun crawled on his stomach toward the Binda cave, his fortress. He moved like a wounded crocodile, hugging earth, each inch pulled from rage and fear.

He thought bitterly of the Church that had scolded him with laws and prohibitions, of his cousins with degrees but no work. He had chosen a different path: crime, profit, women, and outlaw fame. He told himself he would retire soon with amnesty, perhaps even a political appointment.

But now, betrayal felt like breath on his neck. He cursed the senator who spoke two-faced promises. He cursed the police shielding politician-robbers while mistresses travelled abroad under immunity. He cursed the sky.

Then he saw it: blood on the ground. His body trembled. He had been shot. For years, he believed his skin was iron, armoured by the *Bente* charms, the duiker horn, the potions brewed with virginal blood. How could the bullets pierce him now? Fear overtook him — fear to die, fear to live.

His mind raced: was it betrayal? Who revealed his escape route? Could the gods have failed him? Could even Akember, his youngest and most beloved wife, have given him up?

He crawled deeper into shadow, heavy with thirst, hunger, and dread. His body shook, his eyelids sagged like curtains of night. Then the hallucinations came: Akember, beautiful as ever, laughing at him from the cockpit of the helicopter. Her hair spilled down her waist; her eyes mocked him with every breath.

He wondered whether she had been laughing at him. Dizziness swallowed sight and sound; he fought to stay conscious by sheer will. He felt for the phone at his waist — fingers numb, the device slick with blood — and managed to fumble a call to his second-in-command, the indomitable Barkin Banka.

Barkin Banka's true name was Suleiman Baba. He was mixed-blood — half Kilan, half Swari — raised on a Nyamazenga farm where he learned to fight before he learned much else. Fleeing bands of herdsmen had left him and his dying mother for dead; Gungun had rescued him once, and the two had grown into a brotherhood of crime and vengeance.

Suleiman was the opposite of Gungun in looks: tall, grotesque, a slashing scar tearing the left side of his face — the souvenir of a knife fight when cattle raiders left him for dead in a rice paddy. The scar fed his fury and his legend. He was ruthless, earning the nickname *Sarbin Banka* — "Chief Slaughterer" — and his teeth, chewed black by tobacco and kola, peered from a mouth devoid of mercy. His eyes were small and bloodshot.

He wore a cramped jeans jacket splattered with old blood. The medicine man had dyed it with human gore and promised the cloth would shield him; in the superstition-soaked world they lived in, such talismans mattered. Gungun's hand, slick with his own blood, fumbled the phone. Barkin's voice came like thunder and balm; hearing it steadied Gungun long enough to drift into a fevered, half-religious, half-violent dream of rescue.

In the dream Barkin Banka stood massive at the cave mouth, RPG shouldered like a warrior from an epic, vowing to bring the sky down on the metal bird. Then reality and Barkin's roar collided: the RPG fired, a streak of orange, and the Chinook convulsed into a hellfire blossom in the sky. The helicopter detonated with a thunderclap that drowned everything for a moment; smoke and fire cascaded toward the earth. An eerie silence followed — the kind that swallows the world just before everyone remembers to breathe.

Barkin Banka surveyed his men as they gathered in the cave's mouth, stunned and exultant in the same breath. They had felled the dragon. The boys clustered around him like subjects around a strange new king — part fearful, part worshipful. For a moment the cave felt like the centre of the world: war made them gods, and gods were not to be trifled with. Abede, a new recruit, silently pissed in his fatigues. He was homesick and terrified.

They advanced toward the wreckage. In the sand they found a kicked-off Baja motorcycle, and further on — the rider. It was their boss: Gungun, collapsed and drenched, the life seeping into the earth that had been his refuge. Barkin's scream tore from him, a riotous, animal sound that ricocheted off stone and hill. Men poured like a river around the fallen commander, equal parts terror and devotion.

Suleiman found him and crumpled. Tears ran down his blood-stained jacket. That sight rooted the men to the spot — the immortal chief no longer moved. For a moment terror did what legend could not: it made them human. Barkin gathered himself and barked orders, forcing breath and action back into the group. "Pick him up! To the cave — our healers will do the rest," he snapped, his voice iron. Fearful hands obeyed. Two of the bandits — nurses in their other lives — moved forward with efficiency and authority, putting compresses and bandages on Gungun to stop the bleeding while they bore him back to the hideout.

Far away and high, the Sofalian Air Force lost signal with the Chinook. The pilot and co-pilot's radio went dead. The Commander of the Air Force alerted the Minister of Defence and the National Security Adviser. It was midnight; waking the president would wait. Another billion-dollar aircraft down — the cost in hardware and pride mounting like a toll.

Back in the cave, Barkin Banka paced like a colossus dammed by grief and duty. He had performed the impossible; he had turned the tide of terror into a single mythic victory. His boys looked at him not only as an enforcer but now as a deliverer. He barked another order: secure Gungun, move him into the inner cave where the old medicine people and the modern scavenged medics worked in a panicked choreography. They carried their boss on a jute sling, the men whose births, marriages, and deaths he had dictated now shouldering his cargo like frightened priests.

At the palace and around the capital, the news moved like wildfire. Rumours, denials, and recriminations would roar within hours. For the men in the cave, the world reduced to breath, bandages, and the small machinations that kept life from slipping away. For Gungun, myth and mortality met on the cave floor; whether he would rise again to mock the state or be laid low by the very talismans he trusted remained to be seen. At the flicker of life in

Gungun, he whispered hoarsely, repeatedly: *"I swear by my ancestors, my ancestors."*

The Defence Minister, El-Hadj Asamu Kakusa, arrived without notice at Senator Kanyi's house. It was late. The senator was still poolside, entertaining his Chinese investors — a code name for black-market entrepreneurs — who had come to buy the newest consignment of illegal gold and bauxite supplied by the bandits. When the minister was announced, Kanyi quickly drew him into a side room. This visit was unusual; he half-expected it was about the rumoured coup.

The minister clasped his hand.

"Distinguished, I have sad news."

"What happened?" Kanyi asked with a mask of concern.

"Our boys who took the Chinook to the Binda Hills did not return," the minister answered grimly.

"What! Did they find the bandits?" Kanyi's alarm slipped through.

The minister caught the flicker of terror in his eyes — the senator's face seemed to mirror the nation's unease.

"Distinguished Senator, it is a sad day for Sofalia. We lost the boys and the billion-dollar Chinook. The bandits must have used RPGs and downed the bird."

"This is terrible news," Kanyi said flatly.

"Yes. And just when we discovered Gungun's hideout. We were ready to sack SLAP."

"So why not send the army to overwhelm them tonight?"

"It is too late. The boys are demoralised. They speak of Gungun's witchcraft, as if every soldier sent after him walks into a death sentence."

The senator saw the plea in his face. *What does he really want?*

"Honourable Minister, the president must hear at once."

"Exactly why I am here," Kakusa said, his voice cracking. "Please, Distinguished, be there in the morning when we report for breakfast. Help douse his anger. This is the third fighting plane we've lost this year. The president swore to dismiss the Air Force Commander if it happened again. I'll be disgraced if the son of the chief of my tribe loses his job while I am Defence Minister." His voice trembled. Kanyi, listening, silently wished him sacked for daring to authorise the operation.

"Did you say Binda Mountains?" Kanyi asked absently.

"Yes, exactly. Please, Senator — do I have your word?"

"You have my word. Now go home and rest. Tomorrow will be long."

As soon as the minister left, Kanyi went to his study, pulled out a hidden phone, and dialled. The line clicked immediately.

"Suleiman, what happened?"

"The Air Force people hit Oga, our Commander Gungun. Been trying to reach you."

"How is that even possible?"

"A flying bullet, neck wound. But no die sha. They pump a thousand bullets, no touch am, until that juju bullet. I radioed the Flying Ambulance quick — they carried him alive. He looked at me, Oga, and said with his eyes I should take over. They fit reach Germany now."

The senator seethed. The idiot did not grasp the gravity.

"Suleiman, plenty worries! Listen: leave that location tonight. Cross to the other side of the mountain. Carry everything."

"Yes, Oga. We mine stone worth two billion dollars. Heavy sha."

"Good. Guard it with your life. Please take it to the far side of Binda Hill. Captain Chu will meet you. Move all the gold. Scatter the boys into Calanana — empty buildings, abandoned government projects, half-finished houses. Let them occupy quietly. While they hunt you in the bush, you'll be invisible in the city. If anything happens, you call me immediately."

"Yes, Sir. And Oga Commander?"

"Use the old video. Post on Facebook that he is alive, unhurt, healthy. Take over command — no gap."

Kanyi leaned back, pleased. His air ambulance was already bound for Germany, delivering Gungun to Herst-Schmidt-Kliniken, the finest trauma hospital in the world. One good turn deserves another, he told himself, satisfied. Paradise demanded constant blood, but he was always its banker.

12

FURY OF THE LAGOON

They called her Mama Aishatu, after her youngest daughter, who hawked wares to keep the family afloat. But tonight, Mama Aishatu's heart was heavy. She blamed herself for her daughter's condition: a fourteen-year-old girl — a mere child — carrying an almost nine-month pregnancy without a husband. It was both an aberration and an abomination.

From afar, she saw Aishatu walking like an old, frail woman, her dress soaked, her legs caked in amniotic fluid. Her delivery time had come. Mama Aishatu ran toward her, relieved her of the heavy market wares, and balanced them on her own head. Aishatu's pain was palpable and unbearable. She staggered inside and sprawled on the dirty vinyl carpet.

"Mammy, my waist, my waist — Oh God, Mammy, it is too painful to bear."

"Aishatu, you are doing just fine. Let me hold you. You are a tough woman."

"Mammy, it is the most painful thing on earth... childbirth."

With only her mother as midwife, Aishatu fought to control the stabbing pain. She opened her legs as far as she could. Her mother adjusted the pillows behind her back as the expulsion stage began and the baby's head came into view. Mama Aishatu hastily boiled some water, washed her hands, and knelt between her daughter's open legs.

"Push, Aishatu."

"Mammy, I'm trying, but it's too painful; oh, Mammy, I am dying."

"No, Aishatu, push; you won't die."

"I don't want to be a mother. I want to go to school."

Mama Aishatu coaxed her. She had given birth three times herself — painlessly, a genetic gift from her mother — and had believed her daughter would inherit the same ease. But this was different: a child giving birth to a child.

She whispered promises to herself about naming the baby. "Jesus. Mohammed... even Hitler." Then, correcting herself, she resolved to name him *Barack Obama*.

Aishatu screamed as she thrust the baby's head out. Her mother grasped the small, blood-slicked body, hollering at the world with its tiny mouth, demanding food and life. Mama Aishatu placed the child on Aishatu's chest.

"We made it. Aisha, you are a strong woman. You are a mother now, and I am a proud grandmother," Mama Aishatu exclaimed, her face lit with indescribable joy.

Water and blood pooled on the floor. The newborn latched instinctively to its mother's nipple. Mama Aishatu scooped out the placenta and fetal afterbirth, cleaning the room with antiseptic she had saved for this day, giving the shack the smell of a maternity ward.

Aishatu felt the baby wriggling against her chest, a sweetness she could barely comprehend. She whispered in her mind:

"You will be real. You will not be like Senator Kanyi, nor even a politician, those lying animals. You will be a professor... a banker in America. I will take you away from Kepe."

That night the lagoon was not its usual self. It was dark, unfriendly, brooding, and dangerous — a body of water swollen with vengeance. It tore at the coastline where fishermen and squatters had built their dingy hovels. Shack by shack, the lagoon sucked homes into its torrid current.

Wind, rain, lightning, and thunder lashed Mama Aishatu's shack. The roof ripped away. Rain poured from above. The newborn was thrown from his mother's arms.

"Where is my baby?" Aishatu screamed.

"The house is falling. Aishatu, hold onto me."

"Where are you? Where is my baby?"

"Hold me, my daughter; we will survive this monster storm."

"Mama, where is my baby? I must find my baby."

"Leave the baby. The Mami Wata spirit came to carry him."

An unusual streak of lightning flashed at the mention of the Mami Wata spirit, and a grumbling, grudging thunder rumbled overhead.

Aishatu thrashed through the water, flipping her hands for her baby as the storm crashed in. Her mother's words echoed — *"Leave the baby"* — but she knew this was a spiritual battle. She saw her mother slip under the water. The lagoon raged like a vengeful spirit armed with a basket of grudges, swallowing huts like sugar in hot chocolate.

Aishatu had no time to reflect. Fear numbed her. She cried out tonelessly to Jesus, knowing that any shout would choke her with water. Heaven felt so far away. In seconds, she replayed her short life — sold to slavery, betrayed by her mother, siblings dead. The lagoon folded over her like a dark womb, swallowing its child.

The waves of the Atlantic rose in fury, smashing against the banks and hurling Aishatu into the air like a child in the hands of a capricious father. The lagoon seized her back, dragging her into the dark, its lightning and thunder flashing like the laughter of angry gods.

It was hopeless to resist. If only the whale that swallowed Jonah would swallow her; if only Jesus would rise and hush the storm with a single word. Another violent surge lifted her again, flung her against the sandbank, and left her unconscious. The waves retreated smugly, as though mocking their prey.

Silence followed. The storm that had raged like a predator now flowed with guilty calm, covering its dead. Hundreds who had gone to bed unsuspecting had perished — without confession, without forgiveness, without prayer.

The lagoon, undertaker of the poor, buried its secret and smoothed its banks, pretending innocence.

At dawn, fishermen raised a cry. The village rushed to the shore: no huts, no families, nothing but emptiness. The women wailed, chanting protest songs against the treacherous lagoon that had lulled them into trust only to betray them with rage. They sang: *We no go gree oo, we no go gree. Mami Wata, we no go gree.*

The men whispered among themselves, too fearful to accuse any spirit. They knew the bodies were gone, carried into the deep to feed unseen fish.

The elders who once appeased Mami Wata were long dead. Their children had become Christians, and all they could mutter now was thanksgiving through clenched teeth — because scripture demanded it, even in tragedy.

Then a murmur spread: a body lay twisted on the sandbank, one leg bent at a grotesque angle. The fishermen hesitated, fearful she was part of the evil forces. The women came forward. One knelt, touched her, and exclaimed — she is alive! Her ribs fluttered faintly; her skin was still warm.

The men, shamed into action, lifted the girl — Aishatu, though scarcely recognisable — and carried her to the palace of the Apu of Epeland. She remained unconscious, broken and limp, as they laid her at the gates.

But the guards blocked them. "The king is not awake," they said. "It is against protocol to disturb him before noon."

The villagers erupted. What use was a king who feasted and slept with his wives while his people drowned? The women led the protest, singing mocking songs that ridiculed the monarch who slept while his kingdom perished. They sang: *E don do eeeh, e don do, chief de sleep — him house dey fire.*

Into this uproar came Pastor Godswill with his congregation. He prayed over the girl and offered to take her to the health centre. The villagers relented, relieved to hand her over.

The midwife appeared in her khaki uniform, pushing a trolley loaded with blood transfusion bags. Behind her, another woman cursed her husband as she laboured in childbirth.

The corridors flooded with grief: mourners waited to claim the mangled bodies of the town's football team, killed in a bus crash with a timber trailer.

A bed was cleared. A messenger ran for the senior nurse. And there, on the examination table, lay Aishatu — broken, battered, yet alive — the lone survivor of the lagoon's fury.

13

TIME OF THE MAN OF GOD

Pastor Godswill of the Paradise Reformed Assembly now lived among the Kepe people. He had travelled hundreds of kilometres from Calanana after breaking away from his former ministry, the His-Voice-Must-Be-Obeyed Church of God. His departure came in the wake of the enthronement of the widow of the late General Overseer, Bishop (Dr.) Mrs. Doris Kwaghngu, as head of the Church.

Once, Godswill had been an associate pastor — indeed, the "Armor Bearer" of the late Bishop (Dr.) Harry Ajekwe Kwaghngu. Under Harry's commanding hand, the Church had flourished into more than five hundred presbyteries, a vineyard vast in both souls and revenues. But when Harry died, the mantle fell not on Godswill but on his widow. Already her husband's de facto deputy, Doris was swiftly ordained and enthroned by the President of the College of Apostolic Bishops, the Most Reverend Archbishop (Dr.) David-Praise Ikyaangi. An American university conferred its own blessing: a doctorate in Divinity and Church Administration.

Wealth now cascaded toward her. Though no one could pin down the figure, her late husband's estate was whispered to exceed *two billion dollars*.

Her children, long departed from the vineyard, suddenly demanded their share of the inheritance. They knew, in startling detail, the Church's tithes, offerings, investments, and inflows. They were prodigals without repentance, claimants without labour.

Enter Deacon Ackan Akpabio, Director of Finance. To soothe the children, he provided them with undisclosed amounts. To ease their mother's loneliness, he offered... other services. To Pastor Godswill, this partnership reeked of impropriety. Unlike the late Overseer, who had lived transparently, the widow appeared to feast on the sheep rather than feed them.

From a modest duplex, Doris moved into an elite mansion with a grand banquet hall fit for spiritual theatre: Overseer's Appreciation Dinner; Friends of the Overseer Breakfast; Holy Ghost Dinner for the Next Millionaires; The Overseer and Her Shunamite Amazons.

Godswill had once imagined that when the will of the late Overseer was read, his own elevation would be confirmed. Instead, Harry's testament entrusted leadership to his beloved wife, promising to guide her "from heaven." To Godswill this was baloney from the pit of hell. For it is given unto men once to die, and after that — the judgement.

He did not covet riches or grandiose titles. His eyes were fixed on holiness, heaven, eternity. To him, the widow's romance with the finance man was not merely scandalous — it was symptomatic of the Church's collapse.

When senior pastors confronted Madam Overseer in her banquet hall during preparations for the International Ministers' Fire Conference at Tivoli Hotel, Calanana, she did not deny the rumours. Instead, she spiritualised them:

"If it is God's wish for me to marry him, who are you to stand in God's way?"

One assistant pastor, Afolabi Abayomi, warned that whispers of immorality might swell into scandal. She shot back like a thunderclap:

"If everyone minded their own business instead of playing accuser, there would be no whispers. And if you busied yourselves with evangelism, the world would hear only about Jesus — not Church scandals."

She rose, posture magisterial, eyes aflame:

"If we are here to pray, let us pray. But if we are here to cast stones, then let the innocent among you throw the first stone."

Her gaze scorched the hall. Many pastors lowered their eyes, studied their shoes, fiddled with Bibles. Only a few met her stare, unbowed. Pastor Godswill was among them.

Madam Overseer pressed further:

"We know what's happening in the choir. We know some of you are regulars at hotels. But we keep quiet. Let no one presume to judge."

It was blackmail, an unholy bargain of mutual silence. Some faltered. But Godswill stood firm. Others even insinuated, in hushed rage, that the affair may have predated the founder's death — that perhaps even his passing had been hastened.

"Madam Overseer," Godswill called, still struggling with himself. "There are some of us here who will not be intimidated by your holy bully. The fact is, we are not here to judge you. We are here to help you judge yourself and confess to the murder of an innocent man who had discovered your matrimonial infidelity and wanted to divorce you. He conveniently died, and you and your accomplice are now—"

Madam rose, eyes spitting fire, and yelled:

"I command you, demon, to shut your blaspheming mouth at once. Your mouth is sinning against the Holy Spirit, which is unforgivable. I order you to leave this congregation at once."

"Madam General Overseer, you don't need to tell anyone to leave the nest of iniquity you are building. I obey you and wash my feet of this unholy place."

This sordid degeneration — within Sofalia and within the Vineyard of the Lord — made the nation a near-hopeless basket case.

Godswill determined to make a difference. At fifty-five, he decided it was time to take destiny into his own hands. He had graduated at the top of his class in the Bachelor of Arts Education programme at Sofalia Federal University, applying himself with distinction. His father, a retired headmaster and respected catechist, had shaped him deeply. Just before Godswill left Ukwena Boys' Grammar School, his dying father counselled him: make a difference wherever you go.

The elder died at seventy — perhaps fulfilling the biblical "three score and ten." His real gift was not longevity but the legacy of reverence. His name, however, was a burden. Godswill's birth name was Tsavhemba Anyamtswam — *"witchcraft is supreme, the son of the devouring animal."*

It was not a name to carry into Christendom. Following his father's example, he shortened their family name to Anyam. He was baptised Clement Anyam, distancing himself from the devouring leopard. But at university, restless, he shed Clement as well. The Catholic fellowship seemed to him lukewarm — salt without savour. Instead, he gravitated to the Pentecostal movement, immersing himself in crusades, Bible reading, and fiery worship.

When the Bishop of the Covenant Church of Accra, His Lordship Archbishop Dr. Gregory Kwam Aggrey, arrived to ordain their campus chaplain, Brother Roland Kwame, Tsavhemba sat in the front pew. The Archbishop preached a blazing sermon: *Will You Be in the Number?* — a fire-and-brimstone meditation on the world's end.

When the altar call came, Tsavhemba was the first to rise. The bishop tapped his forehead with holy water, and suddenly he felt himself levitating, then collapsing backward as if God's glory had jolted him like an electric bolt. Hands caught him and laid him down gently on the carpet.

This manifestation marked him. Heaven itself had confirmed him as chosen. A vessel beloved. Set apart to lead lost Sofalians back to Christ.

By the crusade's close, he was speaking in tongues, praying "dangerous prayers," and basking in the aura of destiny. At the farewell dinner, he was honoured to sit near the Archbishop and his radiant wife, Bishop Naomi Aggrey. She had sung like a lark during the crusade, her trembling soprano seeming to guide the choir itself. Her presence was magnetic — an aureole of charisma.

At table, she turned to him with an innocent smile:

"Sorry, what is your name?"

He hesitated, but decided to bear it fully. "Tsavhemba Anyamtswam."

"Wow. What a jawbreaker!"

"Yes, ma'am. They are my traditional names."

"May I know the meaning?" she asked, coaxing gently.

"My first name means *witchcraft is supreme*. The second — my surname — means *the devouring leopard*."

"No, seriously? In this age? Tell me you are kidding."

"I am not kidding, ma'am. These are my names. But I have forsaken all to follow Jesus."

She laughed — unsettling. "Delicious."

Archbishop Aggrey, devouring plantain and bitter-leaf stew, overheard. He drained his wine, suppressed a belch, and fixed Tsavhemba with a stern gaze:

"My son. Surely you are not going to carry that pagan name into the Church?"

The words struck like a blow.

"Your name is a foundational challenge to our faith," the Archbishop pressed. "It mocks the supremacy of Christ. Such names must be dropped. Only then will you be free of ancestral curses clinging to you like iron chains."

That very day, Tsavhemba shed his birth name. He became Godswill. Not Clement, not Anyam — simply Godswill. For God was both Alpha and Omega, beginning and end.

And from that day, he resolved never to settle for an ordinary wife. His spouse must mirror the radiance of Bishop Naomi Aggrey herself — beauty as mantle, charisma as adornment — to accentuate his calling and magnify his destiny as overseer of the Church he was certain to found.

It was a long reverie, but today he had to face a tragedy that had befallen the land. The wicked had done their worst. The angry demons of the sea, the dreaded Mami Wata, had claimed scores of human souls to satisfy her desire for blood.

The villagers had abandoned him to deal with the miraculous rescue of the young woman. This strapping girl had been vomited by the lagoon upon the seashore from the raging, roaring, and foaming mouth of Mami Wata. Yes, he had faith and religion to help him cope with this tragedy. It was not tragedy, he reminded himself: it was pleasing in God's sight, a manifestation of His power even in the horror on the beach.

This was déjà vu. He had seen it in his meditations: a lady with a mark on her body would appear on the shore. She had survived not by her power or might but by the Spirit of God. *A thousand fell by her left side and ten thousand by her right, yet she was not afflicted. For it is written in Mark 5:17: let no sickness nor death trouble her, for she bore on her body the mark of Christ.*

Godswill and the Church assumed all payments for Aishatu's treatment at the health centre until she recovered. At fourteen, Aishatu was now an orphan and homeless. Godswill took her into his own house because she had nowhere else to go. He had authority for this in Matthew 25:36: *"I was hungry, and you gave me something to eat; I was thirsty, and you gave me something to drink; I was a stranger, and you took me in!"*

Her new home was a little paradise compared to the shack she had lived in by the lagoon. God had to be behind this transition. But before she could call it her home, Godswill had to find a way to convince his wife, Beatrice, that this was acceptable. It was a difficult conversation.

Beatrice did not trust any other female around her husband. Even though Godswill had never given her cause to suspect, social media had thrown up too many images of pastors taking advantage of their female flock. Or indeed, too many female flocks had ambushed men of God from pulpits into Delilah's arms. She would not be a besotted, cheated wife.

When Aishatu had fully recovered, a month and a half after her manifestation on the beach, Beatrice confronted her husband:

"Honey, when is this girl going back to her people?"

"My love, she has no people to go back to."

"No, you can't be serious. You mean her father, mother, siblings, aunts, uncles, cousins, nieces — all gone?"

"Her mother was a member of our Church. She lost all her siblings in a series of misfortunes, and then she lost her mother on the day of the storm. The poor child even lost her child, too."

"Poor child, indeed. That is how it starts: pity, empathy, love — and sex. All interchangeable emotions. I don't trust even your religion to deal with these emotions. I cannot live with a tragedy waiting to happen under my roof. She is too beautiful. This is temptation, my husband."

"First Lady, my love, be calm. You raise your voice as if I have already committed some terrible sin. She is just a child."

"In the eyes of manly libido, there is no child in the female world. After all, she has given birth. There is nothing to hinder her again. I would prefer you took her back to her people or the village chief. He can marry her for all I care."

"Yes, but she also told us of the circumstances — she was sold into slavery, severely abused, tortured, and raped. She returned home only to meet this terrible fate."

"I know it is bad luck. Please, don't bring her bad luck to this house. You don't know if the devil saved her."

"I reject what you say in Jesus' Name. I saw it all. She was saved because of the mark she bears on her body."

"Have you been inspecting her body already and found your famous mark?"

"No, my First Lady, my love, calm down," Godswill said very calmly. "I have prayed and fasted about this matter."

At this, she looked at him with a long, quizzical gaze and softened. She looked down at the floor. Godswill pressed gently:

"Please, First Lady, God has given us a child."

"My husband, the Church business is full of charlatans. I am sorry. It was hard."

"I understand, my wife. Maybe God will glorify us because of how we treat her. If we treat her as our child, God might surprise us with His grace."

"Don't worry about yourself. I will clothe her the same way I dress. She is a beautiful thing."

"One more thing, my love. The doctor said that even though she is beautiful and physically unmarked, she has suffered profoundly and has gaping wounds in her mind which only time will heal. Even though she looks calm, timid, withdrawn, and always smiling, her mind is knotted, fragile, unpredictable. He calls it 'manic depression.' She does not know she is sick."

"Stop there, honey. Are you sure you shouldn't just take her back and leave her where you found her? Do you mean she is mad?"

"My wife, the term 'madness' is not polite to describe mental health challenges. Besides, we are all a bit mad. Even the best of us is given to bouts of madness, and it requires the grace of God to be saved."

"I take back what I just said," Beatrice replied.

Holding his wife to his chest, he whispered:

"Sorry, no offense meant, and no offense taken, darling. God is testing us to see if we can nurture the flock. She is the lost one — the one our Lord in His glory called the lost sheep for whom the Shepherd left the ninety-nine and went back through the thick bushes, the wild forest, stomping on serpents and scorpions, searching the wild and attacked by wild animals. The Shepherd found her hungry, confused, and abandoned on the cliff overlooking the deep gorge. Our job is to rescue the little lamb, bring her down, and take her back to the fold of humanity. It is our sacred responsibility. Can we do this together?"

"My husband, your word is my command. Did you forget I read philosophy at the university?"

"No, my wife. You remind me every day."

"Okay, that's all right. I have studied the nature of knowledge. I understand reality. I understand existence."

"But my love, how does your study of philosophy help us?"

"As if you don't know my philosophy in life — I don't accept disappointment. I expect things to work. Leave this beautiful child with me. I will be her mother. I know how the Church members mock us that the pastor's wife has no child, no fruit of the womb. She will be our beautiful, secret child who has returned home."

"Very well, let us pray.

The Father of Creation,

The only living God,

The glorious God, the I AM that I AM, our Creator, our Maker, our Redeemer, the One who answers by fire.

Let your face shine on us now.

My wife and I have accepted

The gift of the child, Aishatu.

We have brought home the wandering child.

Show us how we may nurture her

In this country of wolves,

In this cesspool of corruption,

In this abode of the devil,

In this terrible land of Sodom and Gomorrah —

The land ripe for sudden destruction.

You who always answer us,

Answer us today too.

We ask all these in Jesus' Name.

Amen."

Beatrice opened her eyes and met Godswill's eyes, still closed. Her forehead furrowed. She was upset. She believed her husband's passionate hope for the redemption of Sofalia, but despite her Amen to his prayers, she still harboured doubts. The country's name said it all; it was the land of sufferers. The owl outside hooted repeatedly.

She saw his lips still moving — stealthily, silently, secretly praying. She rose to kiss him and cancel his secret petitions, whatever they were. Godswill opened his eyes. She lingered her gaze on his face, then gently whispered:

"So, are you extending prayer again after our prayers?"

Godswill looked back into her eyes, bemused.

"Not so, beloved. As we prayed, I heard a voice from above in my ears — the voice of the Almighty — saying: 'This girl is given to you as a sign of my love for Sofalia. She is a sign and symbol of a sick Sofalia, a raped Sofalia whose birth in hope was shattered in stormy adversity. Nourish her to redemption, to triumph.'

My Love, this child is Sofalia.

Her success or failure shall be the fate of Sofalia entrusted in our hands."

Godswill started speaking in tongues. His body seemed to be possessed by a powerful spirit. He shouted, jumped, and prayed with his eyes tightly shut. Beatrice had lost him to the spirit world again. It would take hours before her husband would become normal again. She watched the sweat on his forehead drip to his chin.

She usually left him alone to hear voices and see his visions when he became like this. But her husband was not the only one blessed with seeing visions. She also saw them. Each time she was blessed with a vision, one would appear like a cinema screen in her mind. On it, she would see a new life beckoning — a prominent and prosperous Church whose congregation would be among the richest and most powerful of the land.

She saw the rich and powerful from all corners of the earth bringing their offerings and tithes in billions of dollars so that their home, God's storehouse, became paradise on earth. She saw her husband praying and the presidents and kings of the world kneeling before him. This was her vision, and she held it in her heart by faith. There was nothing that would cause belief in God to fail.

14

THE SENATOR IN HIS PRIME

Senator Kanyi — "Mr. Cool" — was astonishing. This was the nickname the press gave him: nothing moved him. He was focused, unmoved, unflappable.

In Sofalia — a country living on the edge of the unexpected, where each day brought fresh disasters — such composure was considered a remarkable asset.

Yesterday's news alone was enough to unravel any lesser man: cattle herders had slaughtered more than a hundred farmers on the flatlands of the Central area. Emotions flared. Tribal anger boiled over. Religious leaders pitched their camps. The army was put on red alert — then told to stand down. Meanwhile, the Security Commander quietly withdrew two million dollars from the treasury for the "operation" and just as quietly transferred it to his offshore account.

The following day, at the unicameral National Assembly, senators broke into vicious quarrels. They hurled fists, hurled chairs. The Senate president's mace — symbol of their fragile authority — was seized by masked bandits, who fled firing shots into the air, speeding off on motorcycles. Rumour spread that they intended to hold an alternative "Senate" in the bush, with a live python as Sergeant-at-Arms.

It was here that "Mr. Cool" performed his miracle. According to the press, Senator Kanyi ran after the escaping bandits, grabbed a motorbike from his convoy, and overtook them near the Assembly. With his bare hands, he demanded the mace back, held it aloft, and rode back into the Senate chamber. Pure theatre.

He returned the mace to the humiliated Sergeant-at-Arms, who lay prostrate on the floor, face to the ground. The other senators stared in disbelief as Kanyi pulled the trembling Senate president — still cowering under the table — back to his feet.

Then, with effortless authority, Kanyi addressed his colleagues:

"Mr. Senate President, thank you for your precious time. Distinguished Senators, we have disgraced ourselves. We have humiliated our voters, defied the laws of this chamber, confirmed the propaganda of racists who claim the black man cannot rule himself. We have betrayed our oaths of office. In the name of all you hold sacred, undo what you did today. Unsay what you said. Apologize to each other, to our president, and to the people. This is a sad day for democracy."

As Kanyi returned to his seat between Senators Kelula Orfega and Akpaisong Effiong, the chamber erupted. One senator began to chant:

"Kanyi! Kanyi! Kanyi!"

The whole Assembly roared, echoing his name.

The Senate president smashed his gavel three times, shouting:

"Order! Order! One House, please, order!"

At last, the chants subsided. Kanyi raised his hands and, like a conductor of a grand orchestra, waved his colleagues back to silence.

That evening, the celebration began. Kanyi's mansion swelled with Sofalia's elite — politicians, contractors, consultants, embassy staff, journalists, businesspeople. Exotic cars jammed the street for miles, blocking neighbours' entrances without apology.

Foreign correspondents whispered about breaking news: Was this a coup d'état? A popular revolution? Or was it merely that a first-term senator, with a single dazzling gesture, had risen to national prominence and might soon seize the presidential ticket of the Chop-Me-Chop Party (CMC)?

But while the cream of Sofalia waited breathlessly in his mansion, Senator Kanyi himself was not even there. He was already in the skies, in his Challenger Commander jet, riding up front with the pilots.

He mused on the chaos of Sofalia. He was proud of his courage, his audacity, his instinct for exploiting crises. He blessed God that he had never wasted time in the country's educational system, which produced "idiots and morons" unfit to govern. His true power was language.

Kanyi thanked his brotherhood of Yahoo Boys, who had schooled him in the global lingua franca. English was his empire. He could slip into Oxford-Cambridge polish, or roll his R's in Ivy League cadence. To the English, he was nobility; to Americans, an Ivy League alumnus. He no longer wasted time speaking his native Lanneba tongue.

His poverty as a child did not give him opportunities for upward mobility. He had no toys to play with except those he constructed with his hands — little wire cars, ragged dolls, mud blocks. Play was invention, necessity turned into childhood.

His parents were devout Christians who grew up under a doctrine extolling the virtues of poverty, which was considered the admission card to Paradise. To be poor was holy; to be poor was safe. They did not attempt to exert themselves beyond subsistence living.

Even though his mother had skills in keeping livestock, his father forbade amassing more than five hens and a cockerel. To own more was to risk hellfire, for the Bible was clear that a camel would first pass through the needle's eye before the rich could think of heaven.

The parents did not encourage him to pursue his studies. There was no point. They believed every child was predestined to be what God wanted them to be, and effort was almost an insult to Providence.

But Kanyi wished to attend school, so at the age of seven he enrolled in Primary One. A week later, he was expelled from Kepe Methodist Primary School for stealing another child's lunch. His mother had fed him a meal of plain cornstarch in the morning, but when he saw the lunch of the boy, Cephas, the butcher's son, comprising bread and roasted beef, he could not resist. He gently pried the sandwich out of the box and devoured its contents while the other pupils were outside for the routine thirty minutes of physical exercise before the lunch break.

Theft, in any form, was a violation of a cardinal commandment and grounds for expulsion from the missionary school. His parents were shocked, bewildered. They wondered which of their lineages he had inherited this trait from — was it the mother's side, haunted by whispered talk of *spiritual husbands*, or the father's line, proud and ascetic?

That night, Kanyi decided to sleep outside his parents' hut. The heat inside was suffocating, and there was no breeze from the Atlantic. His parents, inside the hut, were again arguing — about why he had allowed himself to be expelled. His father told his mother that perhaps her mother's *spiritual husbands* were exacting revenge. First they had taken away their beautiful daughter, and now they had infected their son with the demon of theft.

His father was intent on salvaging the situation at the roots. He told his mother that a Pentecostal healer, Apostle Holy Fire, had recently come to town and was renowned for having no mercy with demons that entered children. His mother protested, reminding him of his duty as a Christian to pray to God directly for healing. But the father stood his ground and blamed her for failing to raise the boy properly.

Kanyi's heart, listening from outside, broke into a thousand pieces. He knew his father kept his word, especially when determined to win an argument. He thought he heard his father slap his mother and call her a useless, illiterate idiot who wanted to teach him how to raise a male child. He alluded again, callously, to her *spiritual husband*. Kanyi heard his mother's cries. It tore him apart.

He loved his mother so much. He decided, in a single whim of survival, that he would not be tortured by one Holy Fire, who was rumoured to kill children accused of witchcraft or possession. In his mind, he believed his father wanted him dead. He saw his father holding him down while the white-gowned Apostle Holy Fire drilled a hot iron rod through his heart. He imagined his life ending instantly in the church courtyard, the Apostle declaring to his grieving parents that he had killed the demon, not the child — and that their son's soul had ascended into heaven, purified.

He could not wait to hear more. He rose at once, and that very night he left Kepe town — his parents, his home, everything. He had no property, only a few second-hand clothes his mother had bought and the school uniform in which he slept. So he got up, faced the road they said led to Calanana, and walked. He was determined to be the captain of his own life. Whatever the future had in store was better than death at the hands of Apostle Holy Fire.

The street children of Calanana became his new community. They were the Atsan. Their mental food was hatred of the Ogas. They read from scraps of newspapers and books found in garbage cans. Kanyi loved it. The streets fed him and taught him all he needed. They drifted like tides, street to street, never knowing where they would spend the night, nor when the next meal would come. Yet the streets taught him to survive, to stay alive, even to beg strategically, saving little by little to build wealth. Yes, he became mono-maniacally obsessed with being ahead of the other urchins.

The girls did not last on the streets. They became guides for blind beggars, holding their sticks during the day. But at night, when the blind men felt their budding breasts, the girls became their sex slaves. Some bore children, only to be abandoned as liabilities. The blind beggars found new girl-guides and left the mothers on the streets to beg for their own survival.

Kanyi remembered vividly the day he raided the electronics store at Mpen Computer Village and stole a portable television set with rabbit-ear antennae. He and his gang lived in the abandoned No. 1 Kponti Market, which had been razed by fire. The government promised to rebuild it but never did. He found two half-burnt empty stalls and claimed them as gifts from heaven.

He assembled rags, straws, an abandoned mattress. He picked through discarded blankets and sheets, bunching them to create a makeshift bedroom — a lair, workshop, even headquarters. This was the humble beginning of his sprawling business empire. He found abandoned chairs, arranged a living room. His older friends helped him install the portable TV, his prized loot. The world beamed into his lair in the burned-out Kponti Market.

This was the miracle of his life — his Aha moment. For the first time, he could see how the rest of the world lived and fared. He and the others in Sofalia lived like animals: forgotten, abandoned, dehumanised, thingified. Yet here was a window to another reality.

He had existential dexterity — street smarts, survival instincts, razor-sharp resilience. He had been equipped with a natural radar that detected threats and opportunities. He rejected Sofalia's horrific reality, especially the condition of street children. It was intolerable. He determined to create his own alternate reality.

Now that he owned a TV, he hacked cable channels, defaulting them to CNN and sports. These became his lifelines to success. His life felt like luxury. He became a passionate fan of Chelsea Football Club. Each time his club lost, he would return to his lair furious, his face dangerous and brooding. He would dare any goat — literal or human — to bleat at his defeat.

Before going to the Senate, he avenged his club's losses with fisticuffs, kicks, even bites — these were street matches of loyalty. Whenever Chelsea won, he took it personally. Their victory was his victory. He boasted, celebrated without inhibition, taunting losers without end. He threw parties, and everybody helped themselves to food and drink.

CNN had its educational channel. To him, it was a channel dropped from heaven. He was now a big boy in the street-children's class. Bigger still — he was in a class of his own. He had an apartment, and he had a colour TV.

The day he heard and saw Larry King speak, something moved

simultaneously in his heart and mind. It was as if fate had finally given him a role model. He wanted to be Larry King — a fluent English speaker, a man who owned the room with his words. King was hilarious, profound, funny, severe, consummate. He wove stories into news and news into stories. He was always smartly dressed in his suspenders.

Kanyi decided: he would be Larry King. He would speak broadcast-quality English, like King, and study nothing else. He dressed nattily, too, wearing suspenders to hold his shirts in baggy trousers as the day's fashion dictated.

All the people who mattered — business tycoons, doctors, politicians — were indistinguishable in dress. What distinguished them was the English Language. Those who could speak did so. The better their English, the better their chances. It did not matter that he barely knew how to write beyond signing his name. When he opened his lips, phonology, cadence, the Queen's accent rolled out. That was partly why he seduced everyone — in politics, business, and the social elite.

He loved seducing people — mesmerising them the way light seduces moths. He was a shining beacon.

He was reminiscing on this when the stewardess, Edugie, wafted Chanel No. 5 around the cabin.

"Distinguished Senator," she said, "we will be descending in twenty minutes. Any snacks before touchdown?"

"No, thank you," he replied, steady.

He wondered why perfume carried such power over him. He watched her walk, her hips, her ease. Very briefly, their eyes locked. She lingered. He pulled away. He knew the allure of power and wealth: that intoxicant. She was his for the asking. But this was improper. Against his crocodile instincts. *A crocodile did not eat fish in its own water.*

Nevertheless, he permitted himself to admire female beauty whenever it manifested — in body, smile, touch, voice. He considered beauty like Sofalia's minerals: hidden beneath the surface, oozing out in moments of revelation. In women's faces, he saw God. They were gods, and to encounter a woman was to be in presence.

His mother was the pinnacle. She was his God. Thinking of her, Kanyi stiffened. She was his reality check. She found nothing admirable in the way he lived. To her, senators were jokers whose only job was sharing the nation's wealth. But his love for her was unmatched. Nothing on earth could replace her.

As for the hundreds of women angling for him, he picked and chose. He was not ready to live with a woman. Not ready to tie nuptial bonds or raise children — those little interfering bastards who broke ornaments, drained sleep, and schemed for inheritance. His immaculate home — *crystal walls, onyx tables, amethyst trays* — was too exquisite for them.

Though he respected his mother's insistence on continuity, he did not feel obliged. Children as patrimony? Dated. Passé.

The plane landed safely. Kanyi was whisked from the tarmac by his convoy.

"Sir, there is a huge gathering at our home," said his special assistant. The aide sat in front of the bulletproof limo.

"I know."

Kanyi pondered the man's words: *"our home."* Prebendal, he thought. Followers abdicating responsibility, attaching themselves to another's reality, ingratiating themselves as shareholders in his life. "Our home." How long could this last?

His convoy turned noisily into No. 1 Kanyi Street. The crowd was enormous, even bigger than before his trip.

As he exited the car, his orderly led him to a hidden corner of the mansion. The wall opened at his forefinger's touch. A lift descended. His orderly carried the bulky ostrich-skin briefcase stuffed with mint dollars.

Down on the lawn, a band played. Skimpily dressed girls danced to Swange music. The Algaita flutist mesmerised the crowd, cheeks ballooned, eyes bulging, lungs working like bellows. He played on, seemingly without breath — a legend unrecognised by the world. The dancers circled him, their backsides vibrating in electric spasms. It was mesmerising, art bordering on sensual ritual.

From the villa came two women, Adelene and her friend Mabel. They had flown in that morning from South Africa, where they had first met the senator in Johannesburg, during the finals of the Sofalia–South Africa football match.

The game was about to end in a goalless draw when Sofalia's captain headed the ball into his own net — an own goal that sealed their defeat. The brooding senator returned to the Four Seasons Hotel. In his penthouse chalet, dinner was served with Adelene and Mabel, two professional tour guides. He was in no mood for company. He gave each of them fifteen thousand dollars and gently ushered them out.

The next day, the Sofalian Ambassador to South Africa, His Excellency Guy Irtwange, tracked the women down. Ever the effusive host, he handed them first-class tickets to Calanana, each with ten-year Sofalian visas slipped into their passports. Adelene and Mabel knew what Kanyi represented: pleasure, protection, and escape from poverty. They would do whatever he wished.

It was their first time in Calanana. The senator's protocol officer drove them straight to his home, well away from the eyes of Sofalia's political class. Kanyi had no wish to share his South African *consolation prizes.*

But boredom set in. While waiting for the senator, they drifted to the swimming pool, drawn by the music from the garden where the Swange dancers performed. The rhythm swept them in. They joined the inner ring, ecstatic, their wet bikinis clinging to curves that drew louder cheers. The crowd leaned in, expectant.

The country itself was expectant, wide awake, hungry for spectacle. The dance sequence shifted. The lead singer launched into a praise song: first lauding the president, then slyly advising him to retire to his harem after his first term. The lyrics crowned him an "ancestor," a masquerade whose best was not enough. They called, instead, for Senator Kanyi. The girls voted with their hips, chanting him as their president.

At the poolside, CNN correspondent Isabella Huggins — thirty-one, Armenian-American — sipped Dom Pérignon, ate suya and shredded chicken, and filmed the commotion. When told the meaning of the lyrics, she snatched her notebook. Breaking News.

She realised she was watching the seed of a generational shift in Sofalian politics. The melodies, the chants, evoked in her a thrill like being caught inside an air bubble.

She muttered about Africa's endless paradox: a beautiful land, warm people, devoured by its rapacious elite. She spotted Adelene and Mabel, her age-mates, radiant in bikinis. She beckoned, iPhone in hand, hoping for an interview. They sensed the predator's scent of scandal, avoided her gaze, and retreated to the villa, where champagne and delicacies awaited.

Meanwhile, the senator's protocol team steered the evening smoothly. Ministers, senators, captains of industry filled the banquet hall. Food was served. The master of ceremonies — self-invited — drafted the programme: Christian and Muslim prayers, followed by introductions. Senators would be announced before ministers.

That order mattered. Recently, the Senate had scolded state protocol officers for ranking ministers higher. Ambassador Hilda Kperoga, a career diplomat and grandmother, had borne the humiliation. Senator Kanyi had lashed her publicly:

"You insult the Senate. Unlike countries bloated with bicameral loafers, Sofalia's legislature is unicameral. We are the Assembly. Apart from the president, we alone embody sovereignty. We can impeach a president. He cannot remove us. Ministers? Mere appointees. Unelected. Representing nothing. Do not compare us again. Go back and sin no more."

The ambassador sat in silence, blinking back tears. Male senators jeered. One offered her a tissue. She accepted, subdued.

Tonight, the MC knew better. Senators were served first, while ministers ate at a parallel buffet, pampered but ranked beneath. These were the men managing Sofalia's bleeding treasury, and they needed coaxing.

The evening's entertainment pivoted westward: Beethoven's

Moonlight Sonata, Bach's Suites for Solo Cello, Mozart's Eine Kleine Nachtmusik. Western ambassadors dined next, feasting on cuisine to their taste.

Dinner at Kanyi's home was always open. Every evening at seven, anyone could eat: ministers, senators, Atsan street boys, even fasting Muslims who broke bread and prayed at the mansion's mosque. Though Christian, Kanyi built both churches and mosques, sponsored pilgrimages to Israel, Greece, Jordan, Saudi Arabia. Politics demanded it. Faith was power, and he embraced them all. For Kanyi, religion was not belief but currency.

No expense was spared. Guests indulged in Sofalian and Western delicacies that rivalled the finest restaurants in Paris or New York. But despite the extravagance, a dull note lingered. The evening, laden with promise, ended without the dramatic flourish everyone expected. There was no speech, no declaration. The silence felt heavier than sound.

Kanyi entered the banquet hall, shook hands, called people by name, traded anecdotes, then excused himself with a courteous *"bon appétit."* Choice wines, spirits, and champagne followed. A live band replaced the string quartet, shifting the mood from dignified to festive.

The press had come for fireworks. Polls placed Kanyi well ahead of the incumbent president. Many believed he would announce his candidacy tonight. Yet he denied knowing what they meant, his evasions read as strategy — *political inoculation.* The more he demurred, the more they believed.

Commentators recalled his earlier shock victory against Senator Adura. They warned: to underrate Kanyi was to court ridicule. The master of ceremonies, emboldened, introduced him as "the incoming." Kanyi deflected with mock disapproval, deepening the riddle.

But instead of feeding the frenzy, he retreated. That night, he dined privately with his parents. They had waited beyond the seven o'clock hour, restless and hungry. The chef, Brian Cobb, served fruit juices and small chops, then fielded a sudden call.

"Brian, have you served my guests?" Kanyi asked.

"Yes, boss. They enjoyed dinner and went out to swim."

"But my parents don't swim."

"Oh — sorry, boss. I meant your other guests, the two ladies from South Africa."

"Serve my parents. They must not wait for me."

At last, the parents dined: pounded yam, goat meat, egusi and ogbono stews. Mama Kanyi teased:

"Papa Kanyi, you think you fit drink stout after all this swallowing?"

He ignored her, scooped meat, drank, belched.

"Mama Kanyi, let me enjoy while life lasts."

Her tone sharpened: "Enjoy? In the house of the son you almost lost — with your devil friend, that criminal God's Fire."

He bristled. "There you go again. Was it wrong to be concerned with my son's morality? God alone writes destinies. The day he disappeared from Kepe, you mourned like a hen robbed of her chick. But I told you — God's eyes were on him. He was in Egypt, hidden from the Herods of Kepeland. Years later, he returned to tell us he was off to America. Barely eighteen! I asked his forgiveness, and he asked ours. He is God's favourite. His hands cannot fail."

He paused, drank again, then added bitterly:

"You always heap blame on me, painting yourself the sainted mother and me the cruel father. It's the oldest trick. You seek the love of the son; I am left the villain."

She cut in, laughing: *"Baba Kanyi — heaven don butter our bread. Even a thousand lives, we won't go hungry."*

"So why complain over a bottle of stout? If God prepares a table, let me eat pounded yam in peace."

Conviviality returned. They ate in silence, each absorbed in culinary satisfaction.

As Mama Kanyi reached for a toothpick, Kanyi entered swiftly. He kissed his mother's hand, nodded at his father, still fishing out smoked tilapia from the soup.

"Forgive me for keeping you waiting. Today was hectic. I hope you have not heard the rumours — that I am running for president?"

They exchanged glances, palms turned upward. "No."

"Well then, I trust dinner was good?"

"You do well, my pikin," said his mother. "Thank you for the dinner."

His father cleared his throat for the after-dinner benediction:

"My son, your mother and I have lived in your home for almost a year now. We are cared for. We eat like kings — choice meats, European delicacies, and native soups. We are nearly too healthy."

"And drinking many bottles of stout for my husband," Mama Kanyi added with her usual candour.

Baba Kanyi resumed, his voice steady:

"But, my son, your too much love is killing us. Please, allow us to go back to the village. Your home is our home, yes — but your life here is a strange one. Your language is Western, your food is European, your friends are Ogas, and your politics we do not understand. Even though you are our son, your ways are no longer ours. Your wisdom, wit, generosity, and love of the people are from God. If you run for president, you have our blessing. But we do not understand politics. Please, allow us to go back home."

He turned to his wife. "Do you have anything to add?"

Mama Kanyi raised her hands, pleading:

"I no sabi politics. I won't lie. But my pikin Senator, allow us to go back to Kepe, our home. I beg you in the name of God. My fish, my snails, my goats don die finish."

The senator was stunned by her naïve vehemence. He felt betrayed — his dream of "upgrading" his parents had curdled into rejection. He sat, wounded, while his mother pressed on, even more furiously:

"This type of life wey you dey — person no dey do nothing! Wake up, eat, do nothing. Watch Knack Knack on television — immorality upon immorality. Do nothing. This your life, we no understand. Allow us manage our life for Kepe. Stay for your paradiso."

The word stung. *Paradiso.* Yes, he was in an earthly paradise, but his parents saw only exile. Their paradise was not his.

"Mum," Kanyi sighed, "this matter of returning to Kepe has

become our regular dessert each time we eat together. You once even said I had kidnapped you, that this place was a prison. I am sorry. You are right. I thought only of myself — that as a dollar billionaire, my parents' lives should also be luxurious. But I was not empathetic enough. Now I see it. Permit me just one more week.

"I have acquired two hundred hectares, and in six months, a mansion has risen there, in place of the hut I grew up in. Each of you will have a furnished suite, with walk-in closets, sitting rooms, even an Olympic swimming pool. Your home at Kepe will feed guests daily, just like here. Wolfgang Schuster, the German contractor, will hand over the keys next week."

"God bless you, my pikin," Mama Kanyi cried, her mood flipping to joy.

"God bless you, son," echoed Baba Kanyi, also moved.

"One more thing," Kanyi added gravely. "The house is secured with electronic gates and fencing. The Inspector-General has ordered twenty-four-hour armed guards. And beyond that, I have arranged private security only I know of."

Fear clouded his mother's joy: *"My pikin, fear don catch me. You say big house done complete — but I prefer my old hut. This new house go separate me and my husband."*

Baba Kanyi cut in firmly: "Nobody can separate us. Not when we were young, not now we are old. Just take us back to our old home."

Then Mama Kanyi dropped her bombshell:

"Our pikin, instead of new house, give us daughter-in-law and grandchildren. Na that one we want."

Her husband added quickly, more diplomatic:

"We cannot reject your new home, no. But also remember — family must continue."

Mama Kanyi leaned forward, eyes fixed on her son:

"What time you go marry, Kanyi? Or na true wetin dem talk — say Oyibo don change you into something else?"

Kanyi burst out laughing. "No way, Mama. No way. Not me."

"So why you never marry?" his father pressed.

"Dad, I have not put my mind to marriage. It is a distraction for now."

His mother, hoarse with exasperation, whispered:

"Because of why? You too old? Too rich? Or too busy?"

The father grew solemn:

"My son, they say there is no smoke without fire. Why then do they say what they are saying?"

Kanyi lowered his eyes. He adjusted his plate, pushed food around, and ate in silence. His mother stared fiercely, foreboding etched in her face. His father sat in taboo-breaking melancholy. The air was thick with unspoken fears.

15

GENTRIFICATION OF ATSAN

The whole country was pregnant with expectation, and everybody felt good about it. An American whose father was a Kenyan had been elected the first black president of the most powerful nation on Earth, the United States of America. His name was Barack Hussein Obama.

It was a great deal for every African politician. Sofalian politicians, too, keyed into the universal euphoria of the end of racism in the world. Minority tribes and disenfranchised peoples everywhere began to seek critical roles in their nations' politics. It was as if God Himself had raised the black American president to symbolise reconciliation — between black and white, between dreams and reality, between man and God.

The daunting challenges faced by any Luo tribesman in Kenya to aspire to the presidency, at the time of the American miracle, were staggering. Yet in one fell swoop, American exceptionalism had become the global dream — a world without dichotomies, where the African spirit, the Ubuntu spirit, would permeate the world.

Everyone had hope, and hope was everything. The human essence is built and nourished by hope. Hope, hope, hope became the rallying cry of humanity. A single speech was the butterfly's wing that unfurled hope until it seemed palpable; people felt they could see it, touch it, breathe it. In Sofalia, everyone wore Obama T-shirts to signify a new dawn of brotherhood and sisterhood.

Senator Kanyi rose in the Senate and made a Motion of Hope. He called for an Obama Week: a week when every form of work would stop, and men and women would party from dawn to dusk — and then from dusk to dawn — at government expense. The significance of this holiday, he declared, was to mark the end of the old, the death of an era, and the beginning of the new.

This speech lasted over an hour. In it, he praised America for liberal democracy — the best system of government. Sofalia, he reminded them, owed America its fledgling democracy. Like America, Sofalia was not only a democracy, but a republican Ogacracy. And not only a republic — it had a presidential system.

Kanyi said Obama was a role model for diversity, heterogeneity, and pluralism. Even though he was born and bred a Muslim, he was now a man of many faiths, honouring each in turn. Kanyi, who had once idolised Larry King, now quietly overthrew him. On the pedestal where King had stood, Kanyi raised Obama in his mind.

He devoured Obama's speeches on YouTube and felt validated. Obama was not lauded for legal briefs, not remembered for Supreme Court battles, but revered for a speech. And like Obama, Kanyi believed, he too — a senator — could become president of Sofalia through the power of speech.

After the motion for a one-week holiday was unanimously passed, Kanyi moved a second: to invite the U.S. President to Sofalia on an official visit. This was amended with a clause that the capital should receive a facelift before the visit. The Senate urged the president to nominate a beautification minister, whose sole duty would be to make Calanana a beautiful city.

Contracts for four-lane highways were expanded to eight. Streets were to be lit twenty-four hours a day. Flyovers would sprout at every intersection. If this meant borrowing more money from China, Sofalia should be willing — even if the loans demanded ports, airports, and police forces as collateral. The Sofalian press was aghast. The trade unions threatened a national strike. Ordinary citizens demonstrated against the selling of sovereignty for cosmetic upgrades. But it was done anyway.

The beautification minister was also tasked with clearing the streets of all "undesirable elements." The Atsan were to be carried away from uncompleted buildings to far-off detention centres, while their shanties would be razed.

At Kanyi's mansion, the parties persisted daily. Several cows were slaughtered — some for cooking, others for suya, and still others for frying. Kanyi's popularity did not decline, even though his political romance with the president cooled into tense civility. The two were bound together like mating canines — facing opposite directions, unable to part — entwined by shared ventures: money siphoned from Central Bank vaults, proceeds from illegal mining, oil block sales, and foreign kickbacks.

With the prospect of Obama's visit, hope soared again. But when *Daily Mail* editor Benedict Deli Gawan published his stinging piece, "Why All the Fuss?", the mood cracked. He called the five billion dollars earmarked for Obama's visit "a colossal and insensitive waste of taxpayers' money." He lambasted Sofalian politicians as "immoral and self-seeking spendthrifts" and "unconscionable kissers of Western arses." He further mocked Obama's black presidency as "a pure political masquerade of a black head on a white body."

Summoned to the Senate, the editor refused to retract a word. The next morning, as he drove to his modest one-storey newspaper office, he saw bulldozers tearing it down. On the machine's yellow flanks, the word "Beautification" was painted in bold black letters.

Dump trucks carted away computers, chairs, and water dispensers. An unmarked black GAC sedan sat nearby, two plainclothes officers watching. The editor knew better than to stop. He filmed the destruction on his iPhone, uploaded it to YouTube with the caption: "Sofalian fascist government bares its fangs... again."

Further along the Saalu Sabani Highway, he saw buses packed with squads of Mobile Police, rifles loaded, and tear gas hanging from belts. They were clearing the Atsan, "undesirable elements," and driving them towards an unknown destination. Calmly, he recorded and reposted on Instagram: "Class War in Sofalia." His caption read: "Finally, the war between the haves and have-nots has erupted in Calanana."

Crossing the bridgehead, he witnessed a final humiliation: police officers confiscating Queen Aisha's belongings, tossing them into a dumpster.

Having cleared all her belongings, Queen Aisha stood in the street with nothing. She hurled stones at the police officers and Beautification inspectors, naked, her body a spectacle of defiance.

The police lobbed tear gas. Spectators, who had parked to witness the macabre scene, erupted in protest. "Enough! Enough!! Enough!!!" they chanted. Their voices gathered into a single refrain:

"All we are saying is... this thing is enough."

Reinforcements were summoned. But before they arrived, a kind stranger — a yoga instructor returning clothes to a boutique because they did not fit — stepped forward. On impulse, she dressed Aisha in lace and damask party dresses. The woman worked slowly, deliberately, draping the fabric over Aisha's shoulders, fastening buttons, smoothing creases. Suddenly, Queen Aisha looked stunning, transformed from ridicule to regality.

Draped in borrowed splendour, Aisha cursed the police, railing against the violation of her "palace." The officers, reinforced now, clashed with taxi drivers who had stopped spontaneously to defend her. Gunfire crackled into the air; the crowd scattered. Aisha was beaten, clawing and biting, before four officers pinned her face-down. One sat heavily on her back as she was handcuffed and dragged away.

Soon after, the roundup began. Convoys of undesirables — the blind, the lame, the broken, and the merely poor — were herded like sacks of potatoes into trailers and makeshift buses fashioned from abandoned shipping containers. There were no windows. The bodies inside were pressed so tightly they could only lean against each other's sweat and smell.

The Atsan resisted with stones, bottles, sticks — any weapon desperation could yield. They shouted and cursed, searching for a leader. But when they saw Queen Aisha among them, clad now in silk and damask, her forehead bleeding, their spirits faltered. Even dressed as royalty, she could not save them. Even clothed, she was still one of them.

Operation Gentrification was carried out with chilling efficiency. Over seventy thousand beggars and Atsan were uprooted before dawn. Military tanks rumbled, helicopter gunboats circled, water cannons hissed. The state descended on its poor as though fumigating vermin.

Shacks were set ablaze; belongings destroyed. Fire engines sprayed water to "cleanse" the bodies of lice and bedbugs. Two blind men, fleeing from a jet of water, stumbled into the path of a fire engine and were crushed. Their fellow Atsan, who had failed to protect the truck from "damage," were beaten mercilessly. The truck's dent mattered more than the men's lives. Calanana city had taken sides with the rich and powerful against the poor and weak.

The corpses of the blind beggars were dragged like refuse to the edge of the clearing, then bulldozed into the garbage van.

16

THE ATSAN QUEEN

Queen Aisha mourned the loss of her castle, huddled inside a makeshift shack made of scraps of corrugated iron. These scraps were salvaged from the wreckage of several rows of shanty buildings that had offended the Ogas' sight as they returned from the Nick Agyo International Airport in Calanana. With President Obama's imminent arrival in Sofalia, the shanties had to be removed to ensure that the first black president of America wouldn't perceive his father's continent, Africa, as a place of debased humanity.

He could not view the Sofalians' existence as if the evolutionary process had been interrupted — as though they now represented the world's museum of humanity's ancestors in physical degradation and mental decline. The huts had to be removed. The new Mayor of Calanana, Chief Ekwensi Emike, encouraged by his Senate allies, was ruthless, pitiless, and intentionally cruel.

It did not matter how many natives were now homeless. An omelette must be made, eggs must be broken, and eggshells must be disposed of. The ordinary, voiceless, thingified Sofalia didn't matter in building a new modern state. They were worthless eggshells, the thingamajigs who merely existed — alive but without a life.

A rumour had circulated that Queen Aisha was dead; they said she had been raped and strangled by the beautification officers. The entire Atsan community was in deep mourning. They were implacable and inconsolable in their sorrow, and they swore silently of terrible consequence and retribution to avenge her death. They were so relieved that the rumour, though not baseless, turned out to be false. She was not dead. She was just battered and wounded as she lay in the corrugated shack. She was down but not out, molested but not murdered, and shamed but not silenced.

The dethroned Aisha lay in a feverish condition, silently grieving. The blood that had freely oozed where the police baton had impacted her temples had congealed and caked about her face. Flies gathered about her face.

She cried over her loss of all earthly belongings — including her beautiful broken iPhone 50 Pro Max.

She lay stretched out like a corpse, motionless and rigid, ready for viewing. And they came to pay their last respect. They were joyfully surprised that she was alive. They saw her sleeping on the bare earth floor, tired, hungry, and silently weeping. Her angry body shook like a caged stray dog.

Their commotion stirred her, and she woke with a jolt, startled, angry, and sad. As she saw so many faces peering at her prostrate, forlorn body, she remembered the brutal events of the previous day and the cruel, demanding, and exacting police of the beautification squad.

Her face dissolved into more tears, and then she started sobbing tremulously. Out of the crowd, a woman emerged with some cotton wads, a bandage, and a bottle of iodine, which she swabbed on Aisha's head wound. The wound had created a slight gap in her skin — a dark, crusted mouth at her temples.

Nurse Euphemia held her in her lap and began to cry along with her. There wasn't a face without tears as they watched this motherly, affectionate nursing.

At this stage, a strong voice roared out an address:

"Atsan, please, lend me your ears. Yesterday, we were free citizens of this country, exercising our rights to pursue happiness through carefree freedom and joy. Then they came and brutally captured us like rabid dogs or vermin and caged us here.

"Their soldiers stand on guard at the perimeter of this camp, where we are stripped of our human rights, self-esteem, and dignity, and two of our physically challenged comrades paid the supreme sacrifice last night.

"The State of Sofalia assassinated them in cold blood, then dragged them on the ground for miles before their bodies were violated and disgracefully disposed of in the refuse dump pit. Let us maintain a minute of silence for the souls of the departed."

There was total silence for a few minutes, and then the murmuring and chatter resumed. The speaker entered the shack to take his turn gazing at the tableau of Aisha's head cradled by the nurse Euphemia. The nurse looked at the speaker in silent awe and admiration. She asked him gently, "Who are you?"

"Nicholas Kenkan."

"I am Nurse Euphemia Longpod, formerly a psychiatry nurse with Calanana Medical Centre. I retired five years ago, and although I had hoped to live in peace, my gratuity and pension remained unpaid. I lost my home, where I had deposited a little mortgage money, and I hoped to complete payments with my gratuity. Now, all I have left is my life — nothing to live on, nowhere to lay my head. Then I became homeless, begging for food and sleeping wherever I could at night. Tell me, Nicholas, are you one of us?"

"Of course, we are together; I am one of us. Solidarity forever. I went to the university to study medicine. Tuition fees were suddenly increased, far too much for my parents' limited income. I had to drop out. When I returned to my parents' village, I could not face the shame. I moved to Calanana and found friendship on the streets among the Atsan. I am one of us."

The nurse turned to look at Aisha's still form and brushed off the flies licking the spittle drooling from her slightly opened mouth. She spoke loudly, asking nobody: "Does anybody here have Tylenol or

Codeine?" Without waiting for a reply, she explained: "She has a fever."

Cognition lit Nicholas Kenkan's face. He remembered the still form as that of the famous Queen Aisha of the Under-Bridge Castle on the Elhaj Saalu Sabani Highway. He recalled various anecdotes about her as a university graduate with a first-class degree in political science and philosophy. Still, crack cocaine had overcome her system, pushing her to the streets.

They said her skin was ebony black. But she paid a beautician to lighten it. The spa, where she had gone with black skin and came out blonde, was notorious for its miraculous skin transformations.

The lady who ran the resort boasted that she could create whole and quartered castes that the men craved, especially the Ogas on top. Every woman wanted her white skin to be admired by the Ogas. It cost a significant amount of money to change one's skin colour. But it cost far too much self-esteem to fulfil such an invidious racial death wish. Poverty and self-esteem are bad neighbours. They hardly exchanged greetings.

It was said that most white women in the homes of the Ogas were these selectively bleached individuals, whose buttocks remained dark and whose folds, joints, and other resistant parts still gleamed a rich charcoal black. It was also said that before her body was ravaged by crack cocaine, she had been captivated by the prominent Ogas of the land, who had discovered her at university as a compulsive and irresistible beauty, a symbol of Sofalian female allure.

Over four thousand people had been drawn to the miserable shack where Queen Aisha was condemned to rootless exile. They came because they were desperate and needed hope, partly because misery needs company to amplify and intensify it.

Many were unsure why they were drawn to the central clusters of shanty shacks in the vortex where the undesirables were discarded. They needed a leader, a voice of authority, someone with a vision to guide them out of the miserable captivity they endured. The Sofalian state had created its own leader of the oppressed.

Queen Aisha became conscious of the many eyes staring at her as she lay her head on Nurse Euphemia's lap. Someone produced a crumpled packet of Panadol and thrust it into Euphemia's hand. She eyed it suspiciously, narrowing her eyes silently as she searched for the expiry date. It was good on dates. She opened the packet, and another pair of hands handed her a pure water sachet, which she tore open with her teeth. Then she poured the contents into Aisha's mouth and lifted her chest. She dropped two Panadol tablets in her mouth, and Aisha dutifully swallowed.

Aisha was fully awake and calmly experienced the love and respect of the people around her. It had been since childhood she was last cradled in a motherly bosom like Euphemia's.

She coughed and demanded to sit up. She was still wearing the beautiful, flowery lace and damask dress that the kind Samaritan woman had generously and anonymously given her. She had wet the dress during the night, exhausted and in deep sleep. The urine now only formed a dark patch on the dress.

She rose and felt the bandage on her brow where she had been hurt by the thoroughly wicked and depraved beautification officers and police. The pain was numbing. Her brow had swollen to the size of an egg. It felt raw and painful, but the love she saw in the eyes that swarmed her was titillating. She drank it like nectar. She sucked it into her soul. It made her happy, but it also made her sad at the same time. Then she burst out laughing, her signature splenetic laughter, and everyone laughed with her.

She stood up and walked outside in the bright sunlight. It was still ten in the morning, and the crowd was buzzing, murmuring, and complaining in amazement and wonder at the intentional, vicious treatment that had been meted out to them, and how suddenly their lives had become a complicated mess.

The voice came from Nicholas Kenkan, whom the crowd waiting outside the shacks had silently endorsed with authority to speak, lead, and decide. Nicholas emerged with Aisha by his hand. Her eyes shone, and the spectators animated her face. She covered her eyes from the scorching sun and stumbled along with Nicholas to the middle of the crowd, where some cement blocks had been hastily arranged into a podium.

The crowd burst into celebratory chants as she stood on the podium, holding Nicholas's hands. Nicholas quieted them and declaimed:

"I salute you all. You can see that the Queen is not dead. They tried to assassinate her, but she fought them, fending off their batons left and right and knocking them to the ground. Had she not been overpowered by battalions of the state, brutalised, and forcefully raped, she would have defeated them all. But here she is."

The crowd roared in frenzy as they cheered their queen. Many of the women sobbed in joy.

Before Nicholas could finish, the adrenaline rush pushed Aisha forward, and with both arms stretched, she loudly shouted:

"Fellow Atsan of Sofalia, my beloved, I am furious that the wicked and corrupt government of Sofalia has committed apartheid-style atrocities against us, and they have dumped us here in this leper colony, lumping us all as undesirables. They have profiled us as criminals, dirty non-people, infected with deadly diseases, and vermin. They are doing this thing to look good in the eyes of one white man they invited to come and eat our pounded yams and goat meat — one Barack Obama — to eat our goat meat while our children starve.

"They borrow money from America to embezzle in their conspicuous consumption. This is why they have swept us from the streets where we have made our homes. We did not ask them to give us free medical treatment. We drank our traditional medicine and trusted God for healing. Our children cannot afford to pay for education; they stay with us and grow old, nurturing layers of ignorance. And we have silently borne these indignities, these insults from these people for so long — in silence, in tolerating self-abnegation, and with a deferential, sit-down look. Things have gone too far. It has become an existential threat to be poor, homeless, and hungry. They plan to eliminate us. They have brought us here to this concentration camp to kill us massively. Just like the Auschwitz holocaust. I ask you, what wrong have we done to be brought here for mass slaughter?"

The crowd burst out in clapping and shouting: "Nothing. We have done absolutely nothing!"

Then she continued, "We need to organise ourselves, we need to have a voice, and we need volunteers to address a petition to the Supreme Court."

The unbearable heat stole her voice. It became hoarse and faint. Someone gave her a sachet of pure water, which she drank a little of and sprinkled the rest on her head and face as a coolant. But it was too late. Despite the water, she fainted from the heat and was carried back to the shack. The audience responded with gasps and prayers.

Water was poured over her head and face. She regained consciousness and returned to the podium, but was held back by Euphemia, the nurse.

Outside her shack, thousands milled around. They clustered around her and looked up to her with hope. They saw in her an indescribable hope. Nothing was going to stop them from appropriating the hope she symbolised.

They surveyed their environment and were horrified to discover that it looked like an artificial lake a kilometre away. From this lake, a terrible stench arose: the Sofalian human waste dump. The sun's rays reflected on water mixed with human excreta and plastic bags, including black bin liners, plastic carrier bags, clear sandwich bags, and plastic bottles, making the *Lake of Death* a grossly surreal sight.

Plastic bags hung on trees, floated in the air, and settled among the bushes, drifting in the debris. Plastic sachets, containers, and envelopes were mixed in a gruesome, foul, swirling mess of filth. The sun shone over the horrific, treacherous lake, reflecting a tortured, battered, and wounded landscape against the sky.

This was the *Lake of Death*. They feared their surroundings. Nothing moved in this lake of hell; no vultures or even flies could be seen. Nothing was on the surface, and nothing lay beneath. Its contents were putridity, rottenness, and indescribable maggoty hellishness.

The sea of Atsan bodies held their noses and solemnly moved away from the sea of death, searching for water to drink. The land was barren, with few trees and little vegetation. The Sofalian outskirts had been deserted due to the constant felling of trees for firewood to provide food for its millions of inhabitants, who had planted no new trees.

The sparse vegetation had plastic bags hanging from the trees instead of fruit. Plastic bags floated in the air wherever a breeze blew. The heat was unbearable. The corrugated iron shacks intensified it to a boiling point. Rivulets of sweat ran down bodies. Sweat turned to steam.

It was past noon when the tired Atsan — mothers and children — clustered under the small-leaved Acacia trees dotting the undesirable reservation camp. By a miracle, three water tanks had been rolled into the reserves with the inscription: *Senator Kanyi's Grassroots Mobilisation Campaign.*

The Atsan rushed to take over the water tanks and pushed past the driver and water faucet operator, who were demanding voter cards from the Atsan before allowing them to drink.

There were no cups. Nobody owned utensils except their palms and fingers — no buckets, cups, or spoons. Nobody thought of these things. The government was in a hurry to expel its people, and this was perfected.

Nonetheless, the sight of water caused a great stir. There was a celebration. They would drink water from the devil, and since they were in hell anyway, who else would bring water to them? The Lord of hell. The devil himself. The crowd surged and surrounded the water. The attendants who had, moments ago, pushed the Atsan away were nowhere to be seen.

They fled for their lives after shouting, "Nobody will drink from this senator unless you have your voter cards." After shouting at the Atsan, the attendants expected the thirsty Atsan to meekly queue up with their voter cards and proceed one step at a time towards the tank water faucets, like humble communicants at the communion altar. But they saw an ocean of angry eyes screaming back at them. The angry eyes moved forward, and terror overtook the driver and assistants. All of them fled. The scramble for the water ran out of control.

Nicholas's voice boomed, "Order, order, my people, order." The crowd stood still. Parents whose children were rolling in the mud as the water flowed pulled their children out and held them close. Mud and water mixed with sweat, desperation, and hunger made them angry.

"Fellow Atsan," he continued, "you have wasted the little water God sent us by scrambling and fighting. We have lost more water than we use. Look at these water tanks sent to us by those who knew they had dispatched us to die. One man remembered we needed water. But look at these tanks. He is campaigning to be president and even gave conditions for drinking his water — not his water, but God's beautiful water.

"He wanted us to produce voters' cards before drinking water. How deplorable, how despicable. Now that God sent water, he shall also send down Manna from heaven..."

A loud voice interrupted him: *"No Manna here. We want rice and chicken from the heavenly kitchen, as well as pounded yam. Mama Maria must behold our fate and order his son to send down a suitable buffet of assorted food."*

And the people chorused: "Yeees and Amen."

A strapping youth had climbed one of the tankers and stood on top. He held his hand out as if holding an invisible microphone. He shouted:

"Fellow Atsan, we must organise or perish. My name is Princewill Awus. I have been in the detention cells of the Sofalia Secret Police. The most horrendous of their cells is far better than this wilful excretion, this criminal dehumanisation, and the horrible desecration of our humanity. We hadn't eaten for two days. Perhaps they intend to starve us to death.

"I beg you; we are all caught in this terrible state of human cruelty to its kind. We are all tied to a similar fate and face certain death unless we recognise that drastic and immediate action is needed. As a result, I propose that we choose our leaders now. We need volunteers and select people to lead us, to think for us, and help us reclaim our humanity and lives. We organise, or we agonise. This is an existential threat."

The crowd shouted in unison, "We want our Queen! We want Aisha!" An older man gesticulated wildly, making both commotion and an effort to climb the water tank where the young man was. He was pushed up the ladder to the top of the tank.

"Ladies and gentlemen, please listen to me," he shouted. "I also want Aisha. But you don't know her. I know her story. She is a tormented soul, the poor daughter of a fisherman who was rescued from the lagoon and brought up in the home of a highly respected man of God. This man of God, Godswill, was also my spiritual overseer. He entrusted her to my care."

The crowd booed at him: *"It's a lie, it's a lie,"* they chanted.

The older man shouted louder. "She later went to university, where I taught philosophy. However, at the hundred level, she began associating with a bad crowd. Her adoptive family, His Holiness Godswill and his wife, intervened. She would be taken along with many other girls to spend weekends with the senators and ministers in the city. She studied political science and philosophy and was elected president of the student government."

The crowd shouted, *"You are a liar, it's not the truth."*

"She was popularly nicknamed Angela Davis because of her powerful rhetoric. Unfortunately, she also learned the sad ways of the children of the Ogas. They introduced her to crack and shared her body among themselves, yet she managed to graduate at the top of her class five years ago. She served at the National Assembly during her one year of National Service. She contested in a beauty contest and was crowned Miss Sofalia."

The crowd was hysterical, *"Get down, you short devil. You should be hanged for sedition,"* they chorused.

The speaker grew more frustrated and shouted even louder, gesturing wildly. "She was an intern at Senator Kanyi's office, who had pinned her hopes of marriage on discovering they were both from Kepe."

Hearing this, part of the crowd chanted, *"The Senator is a rapist."* Others kept chanting and booing, insisting that all these claims were lies. But the speaker, undeterred, pressed on amid the noise.

"However, she was deeply addicted to crack cocaine. He noticed her decline and sent her to Abo Mental Hospital, from which she escaped after stabbing the night nurse and a guard. This is her story. She is a raving madwoman. She cannot be our leader. She is not even Atsan; she is frantic, angry, and dangerous."

The crowd chanted back with venom:

We want our Queen.

We want our Queen.

Want Queen Aisha.

They pelted the elderly Thomas Tikindi with pebbles, sticks, and mud collected from the tanker's pools of water. The crowd was agitated and angry as they marched off to fetch their Queen. The older man slipped from the tanker and fell to the ground. He continued gesturing at the indignant crowd, revelling in the righteousness of his intervention. He was quiet, intentional, and remained unruffled. The youth descended on him to finish him off for daring to speak maliciously about their Queen, but Nicholas intervened.

He jumped into their midst and put his hands around the old Thomas Tikindi, the retired but homeless professor who, after forty years of teaching at the university, retired with a pension that could not pay for electricity in his modest bungalow for a month nor his high blood pressure medication.

He was sure the government was impatient to see him dead altogether, so the pittance of a pension could be discontinued. His wife had died of ovarian cancer. Thomas decided to move to the Atsan community, where he became a street scavenger and beggar. His life had purpose again.

17

———

INSURGENCY FESTERS

Benedict swore to himself silently that the government of Sofalia would pay dearly for destroying the headquarters of his *Daily Mail*. He became a journalist by accident. He had wanted to be a lawyer. However, the law department demanded exorbitant fees, dress code regalia, and levies imposed by the department and the Sofalian Body of Benchers. He dropped out of law and studied journalism instead. Law demanded wealth; Benedict had only wit.

His family were rural farmers who paid school fees after selling farm produce. This sale depended on seasonal fluctuations — bad or good seasons. The parents could not afford to buy the improved seeds from European companies that had destroyed the natural corn seedlings.

The new, improved seeds killed all others around them but were unable to reproduce. Subsistence farming was halted this season. Farmers starved. The academic officer at the university was sympathetic and suggested that Benedict could still enter the university by choosing courses now reserved for students from low-income families: Religious Studies, Archaeology, History, Drama, Philosophy, and Journalism.

Journalism resolved the dilemma, and Benedict gave the course his full attention and zeal. He didn't just study Mass Comm; he swallowed it whole.

While he ran the story of his life like a videotape in his mind, he suddenly braked to avoid hitting a police barricade on the streets. He glanced to the side of the barricade and saw three police officers with rifles. They wore camouflage uniforms. He saw the young-looking police officer glance at him and, without saying a word, order him with a finger to move to the curb and park. The sun was piercing, the heat intense, the rifles and helmets gleaming at him.

Several vehicles were parked on the side of the road, and the police were conducting a thorough check of vehicle particulars, arresting those with expired licences and those without insurance. The questions came in torrents: Is the registration up to date? Did he have a valid driving licence? And where was he going?

He smiled. It was the end of the month, and the police were notorious for their tendency towards corruption, which they used to supplement their modest salaries, barely enough to see them through to the next month. He had nothing to worry about. The sergeant eyed him grimly and extended his hands. He bared his tobacco-stained teeth at him but remained silent. He simply glared: "Your particulars." The stench of stale tobacco, alcohol, and sweat hit Benedict.

Benedict pondered on this demand. It could mean anything. A quick pressing of a crisp five-sodollar note into the policeman's palm, as a bribe, was the illegal toll gate fee. He wouldn't do that. Helplessly, he looked back at the police sergeant, who stared back at him with murder in his bulging bullfrog eyes. He sighted the windshield stickers.

"Your driving licence and car insurance. I see your registration slip on the windshield," he demanded gruffly.

"Okay, I understand now," replied Benedict, rummaging in the glove compartment and retrieving the envelope containing all the car documents. They were all up to date. He handed the envelope to the sergeant with offended dignity, looking down at his shoes deliberately casual. The sergeant plucked them from Benedict's hands with insolence. He did not so much as glance at the documents when he blurted out:

"You big, educated people — you think you are so wise."

"Why, officer? What have I done?" Benedict demanded.

"Everything. Where is your fire extinguisher?"

He had anticipated the Sofalian police's predator-prey tactics. "Here, officer." He pulled the fire extinguisher from the floor under the passenger seat and handed it to the sergeant, who peered at it suspiciously and then flung it back into the car.

"I am taking you with me to the station."

"Why? For what offence?"

"My oga on top will tell you." Having stated the matter-of-fact situation, the officer invited himself into the passenger's seat and secured the safety belt across his well-rounded stomach, then ordered Benedict to drive to the police station.

Benedict's Toyota Corolla had been idling, hoping the sergeant's sickening joke would be over for him to travel out of town to visit his mother in Dokomaiko. His mother was the only person he believed would give him consolation for the calamity that had befallen him. He smelled a rat, and the rat was menacing his toes. He had to act fast.

"Officer, I am not going to the station with you." He switched off the ignition, removed the car key, and went out, leaving his car at the police checkpoint in the hands of the bewildered sergeant. The sergeant called out to him in vain, then shrilly blew his whistle, but to no avail. Benedict kept walking.

In his mind, the scenario was all too plain. The system — the oppressive system of neo-imperialists — had hijacked the government and the Sofalian treasury. And they needed to lock him up. As a journalist, he should have been with the Ogas. His persistence in speaking truth to power was not only intolerable insouciance but positively dangerous to the government, and he was now officially undesirable. This was why his newspaper's headquarters was destroyed, and they were trying to arrest him.

He waved down a motorcyclist. The rider had carried three

people on his Honda motorcycle, but he stopped nonetheless: the more, the merrier. He piled Benedict on top of the other three passengers while he sat on the petrol tank with his legs spread out. This was acrobatics. The driver asked him his destination, and he told him. That was almost twenty kilometres. This acrobatic stunt mode was taxing.

When they were halfway to Dokomaiko, the rider told them to look to their left. Benedict looked left at the soldiers sealing off a long perimeter wire fence around the road. The soldiers were fortifying the area menacingly.

"Look at those soldiers. They are from the 'Beautification Ministry'. This is where they keep all the undesirables from coming out and going to town." Benedict told the rider to stop.

"Please stop. This is where I drop!" he ordered. The motorcycle stopped abruptly, pitching the passengers toward the roadside ditch. The angry biker demanded an inflated fare; he refused to move until Benedict paid.

Benedict Deli Gawan crossed himself with an exaggerated sign of the cross and stepped toward the gauntlet of soldiers who kept the undesirables from returning to Calanana. He walked to the newly constructed gate and met a ring of stern-faced soldiers, rifles at the ready. Their lunch lay scattered nearby — crates of beer, bottled water, half-open takeaways — abandoned like spoils. Benedict raised his hands in a gesture of peace.

A marksman ordered him forward for inspection. One step, then another soldier barked, "Who are you?"

Anger and fear braided up inside him. They were dangerous companions. He thought of lying, of bargaining, then remembered: these guards were not judges; they acted on orders. Truth was the only modest weapon left.

"The name is *Benedict Deli Gawan*."

"What do you want?" the marksman called from his watch-post.

"I want to enter that fence. My brothers and sisters are inside. When they came for them, I was away. I came to join them." Benedict forced a harmless, foolish smile. The soldiers sniggered at his audacity. He did not look like an Atsan. They nicknamed him "a visitor." He had chosen solidarity with the Atsan out of rage. It was more meaningful to be with these powerless and abandoned people than to visit his mother. It is duty first before family.

They radioed their superior. Captain Chris Udeng arrived in a mini-Jeep, an impassive silhouette, his "Batman" perched on the hood with a machine gun. The captain scanned Benedict and, with a thin politeness, asked, "I hope you have not brought trouble?"

Benedict kept his hands raised. "No, sir. I am unarmed." The captain drove off in a cloud of dust. The sergeant at the gate opened the barrier and waved him through.

"This is the gate of no return," the man said as Benedict crossed. "You will not come back through here."

"I know." Benedict answered quietly.

"You will not need your wristwatch, jacket, or phone."

He handed them over, charmingly theatrical. He had concealed his iPhone and Wi-Fi properly on his body. They took the analogue phone, his jacket, shoes, and wristwatch — symbols of the life he had maintained until now. As they gathered his belongings, he thought: he now resembled the person he once looked down on — the Atsan.

The irony arrived whole: the medium is the message. Benedict remembered McLuhan and smiled inwardly. His concealed iPhone would still carry proof; the global village would watch. The *Daily Mail* building had been razed that morning — he had vowed revenge — and now the world might finally see Sofalia's face. He felt energy gather inside him, righteous and dangerous: the pen — no, the camera, the upload — might yet be mightier than the AK-47.

Memory pulled him backward: the campus newspaper, *The Sabre Tooth*, the exposés, the death threats, the *Daily Mail* versus Sofalian State, court victory. He had earned international commendation — the PEN America Award for Courage — but here, stripped of credentials, he was officially "undesirable." That label, he decided, would be the headline.

Outside Queen Aisha's shack, the Atsan had already rechristened the place *The Palace of Queen Aisha*. Their anger at Thomas Tikindi's slander had crystallised into resolve. Nicholas Kenkan — ex-student, accidental leader — held the crowd together. They needed a rudder; they needed hope. As student Union president he had led the million man march to demonstrate against the high cost of living at the presidential villa. He was highly organised and respected for fearless and timely decisions.

Nicholas had read everything on leadership — Machiavelli, Sun Tzu, Mandela, and Obafemi Awolowo — an eclectic catalogue that made him both mockable and oddly magnetic. He lectured the Atsan about organisation: without leaders, he told them, *"We are Dodos."* They laughed and then listened.

Nicholas Kenkan told them no leader is perfect; followers must accept flaws for the greater good. Queen Aisha might have tried crack, he admitted, yet she had a first-class degree and had been thrown away by the useless oligarchs running Sofalia's kakistocracy, who never saw her as a person with wounds, not as a "disabled woman" in a land of widespread brokenness.

Kenkan said Aisha suffered bouts of depression treatable by both herbs and modern medicine. *"We are all naked like Aisha,"* he declared — clothes do not make the human. This was his theory of clothes: after the Industrial Revolution, the fashion explosion produced what he called Structural Disfigurement — adornments that hide character rather than protect it. During the million man march to the capital, he threw away his clothes and marched nude to the capital.

He praised Queen Aisha for embodying that theory by refusing to let clothes define her in the past. But now that she'd been crowned Queen de facto, her subjects insisted she be given plumage.

Nicholas announced his Plumage Theory — peacocks as case studies — and said that without plumage an eagle, peacock, and chicken are equally edible. Plumage, he argued theatrically, was the enthronement of precariat nobility.

Euphemia Longpod installed herself as palace chief medical consultant. The women surrendered their best garments so the Queen could be decked in finery: a makeshift wardrobe appeared, shoes, coats, and dresses arrayed like trophies. Aisha, who had once eschewed clothing, now enjoyed being Queen — it had taken lifetimes to arrive here, and the sudden recognition intoxicated her.

By acclamation, Nicholas became Prime Minister. As they organised the Queen's cabinet, the Atsan dragged in another prisoner — a man caught trying to pass as one of them — and, amid cries, they bound and marched the defiant Professor Thomas Tikindi and the *Daily Mail* editor, Benedict Deli Gawan, before the Queen.

Aisha saw Dr. Tikindi and screamed, "My Professor — who tied you like this?" Her confusion broke the crowd's practised fury; she accused Nicholas and Euphemia, puzzled that they had failed to answer her simple question.

Nicholas replied, "This man said terrible things about you at the university, Your Majesty."

"Release him. He was my philosophy teacher," Aisha said. "Yes, I was a bad girl. People believe what they prefer to hear. We hear what comforts us. Free him; make him my adviser."

They obeyed at once.

Benedict was shoved forward. "He was caught spying, trying to pass as one of us," someone announced. "We recommend he be hanged tonight; his solar-powered iPhone will be palace property."

The Queen looked directly at Benedict, wagging her right forefinger at him. With a voice slow, firm, and measured, she asked, *"Are you one of us, or one of them?"*

Benedict stared, stunned by the turn of events. In thirty-six hours the naked madwoman under the bridge had become a crowned sovereign; he had gone from editor to prisoner before that transformed figure. He swallowed and spoke carefully:

"Your Majesty, I am not a spy." He raised his hands palms up. "I came in peace. The government destroyed my newsroom today. They want me silenced. I seek asylum."

"I am Benedict Deli Gawan. I hold a B.Sc. in Mass Communication with Honours." His eyes filled with tears and anger. "Please don't kill me. I will serve you as Press Secretary. I can get our story to the world."

Nicholas watched him, admiration and calculation mixing. He

unclasped Benedict's wristlocks and freed him. Turning to the Queen, he declared, "This man speaks truth. Forgive him. He is a progressive public intellectual. If he chose to join us, it proves poverty is not stupidity."

"It is often said that in every nation, only two per cent think. Three per cent believe they think but don't think at all. The ninety-five per cent would rather die than think. Sofalia leaders belong to ninety-five per cent of the unthinking population, and we, the thinkers, are ironically undesirable. Here in this undesirable reserve, we are the thinkers. And if we are the thinkers, then we must prove the theory that poverty is not a lack of brainpower. Poverty is not stupidity. Ideas have power."

The Queen beckoned Benedict forward. "From now on," she told him, "You will be the Chief Press Secretary to the Queen. You will live here with me in the Palace." She adjusted herself. Her eye caught the iPhone in Benedict's hand. "Give me that phone," she ordered.

She held it to her ear, touched it repeatedly with her fingers, and held it to her ear again. "Hello, hello, Senator Kanyi Mulaake?" There was silence from the other side. Queen Aisha was frustrated. The crowd gasped in awe that their Queen was calling Oga directly.

Benedict, anxious to help, said, "Your Majesty, I have Senator Kanyi's direct line."

"Then, could you call him to speak with me?"

"Yes, please, Your Majesty."

Saying this, he proceeded to call the number. With the first dial, Kanyi came online.

"Who is this?" he asked.

Aisha grabbed the iPhone from Benedict's hand. "This is Queen Aisha."

"Where are you calling from, my love?"

"Senator Kanyi, I am Queen Aisha."

"Queen, who? Which Aisha?" he asked, not entirely understanding the situation.

"Has my becoming a queen changed my voice so much?"

"Sorry, I don't remember your voice. Please, tell me which Aisha?"

"Very well. You don't remember that Pastor Godswill's daughter was sent to the Mad People's Home after you betrayed me with false promises and abandoned me for your prostitutes in your demonic empire?"

"What! Is this a joke?" he asked incredulously, adding, "Who gave you my number, mad woman?"

"Kanyi, you and I are from Kepe, and you know that Kepe is a leveller where the citizens have each other's backs. We are all poor, all our neighbours' keepers, but here in Calanana, it is dog-eat-dog. You are the Oga on top, and I am the Atsan Queen below. You defend your perch. I assert my perch. By now, your shameless water supply tank drivers should have told you that we are not quaking, shaking, or intimidated.

"We are not to be held hostage because you stole money belonging to the people, and then you offer us our water for a piece of a damn useless paper called a voter registration card to vote in your sham elections. Senator Kanyi, I am a living philosopher and would like to persuade you and your colleagues to reconsider your approach. I demand that you remove us at once and return us to our place on the streets. We are not giving anybody trouble.

"We, the Atsan people, have committed no crime. We are all dignified poor people. Poverty is undesirable, but how can being poor make us undesirable people? All we want is to leave this settlement, this undesirable colony, this apartheid enclave, and return to where you found us, or we found you. Poverty is not a crime." She turned and looked at the crowd, which nodded in unison. *"We are poor but not undesirable. We are poor but not stupid."*

For good measure, the Queen told the senator: "Senator Kanyi, we shall meet in Kepe soon. And, Senator Kanyi, remember that destiny has fallen on you and me to help Sofalia escape the poverty trap. I have the answers, but you have no clue. We must help Sofalia escape the neo-imperialist trap.

"You and I are trapped. I am trapped in a foreign body, and you are trapped in a foreign mind. We are the trapped Sofalians and Kepeians. This is why it will be an honour for you to marry me, and then we can both work out our salvation to save Sofalia. Goodbye, Kanyi. We will meet in Kepe or on the streets of Calanana," she stressed.

She returned the phone to Benedict and let out her pathetic, shrill laughter, glancing left and right at the eager Atsan gatherings.

Dr. Thomas Tikindi jumped up and down, repeatedly exclaiming, "Pure genius, pure genius! The Queen of Sofalia, and next, Queen of Africa. Sofalia will witness liberation."

18

____

TICKET TO PARADISE

The Paradise Reformed Assembly, also known as the Paradise Church or simply the Paradise Building, was an iconic landmark. It celebrated the triumph of human faith, resilience, and innovation.

It stood on the highest point above sea level in Calanana. At night, the searchlights from the steeple could be seen hundreds of nautical miles away across the Atlantic Ocean.

Many ship captains navigating the West African Coast would exclaim with joy upon sighting the light on the steeple.

"There, we behold Paradise," they would say, before mentioning Calanana or even Sofalia. The sailors called it Paradise because of the rest it assured from storms and dreary hours at sea.

It was designated the National Shrine and became an essential tourist destination. Many tourists came from all over the world to marvel at the righteousness of this impoverished African country, whose hearts and wallets were with God.

His Holiness, the Founder of Paradise, Godswill, preached a fire and brimstone sermon the following Sunday, in which he demanded that the people of Calanana not take things into their own hands to cause any breakdown of law and order.

He reminded his congregation that the God they worshipped could defend His Church. Caesar overreached and wanted to rob God of the offerings and tithes. He ominously alluded to swift retribution that would soon come, affecting the land over the great evil being planned against their faith. He alluded to politicians who were robbing God by not paying tithes from the vast wealth they amassed through politics.

The building itself was designed in the shape of a Cross. It sat on a massive landmass on the choicest real estate in West Africa, if not Africa. Inside the Church building, there was a profound sense of holiness. The sight, sounds, and silences all reflected the overweening glory and presence of the Almighty. The pews were arranged in rows, signifying the arms and legs of Jesus that bore the nails.

The centre of the Church building was its chest, symbolising where Jesus's heart was. This chest served as a place for miracles and wonders, regarded by many as stage performances. Here, manifestations of God's powers were displayed for everyone to see. This space separated the congregation from the clergy, who sat at the altar.

The golden altar was the crown jewel of the building. The choir sat on the left side of the altar, all dressed in immaculate white. They wore white gowns with extended, seamless wings attached from the shoulders to the hands. Their heads were covered with gold and white runner hoods. They were angelic and theatrical to say the least.

The angel-like wings imbued the choir with a swooning grace, especially when it sang songs like, "We raise our hands to the Great I am who was, who is and is to come," and when angelic hallelujahs and hosannas were sung. The spiritual mood sucked the worshippers into rapture. Tourists cynically shook their heads and whispered to each other: "Nothing but theatre."

The altar was two metres high, and the railings separating it from the paradisiacal space for signs and wonders were pure gold. Above the altar was the hemispherical dome forming the ceiling. If those at the altar looked upwards to the dome, they would see paintings by

Michelangelo and Baroque artists, with astonishing realism, as if heaven were opened above and angelic beings could be seen ascending and descending.

The four piers of the Church, representing the four corners of the globe, were communication and lighting points. If, at first glance, one had hastily concluded that Paradise was a theatrical masterpiece, one could be forgiven. But if one's iconoclastic and disrespectful conclusions persisted at the time of worship, one would be a sadly confirmed atheist.

This was when the supersized video screens that covered the entire altar wall in thrust formation came alive on three sides facing the audience. "The Holy Holy Holy" song, or any other chillingly apocalyptic songs of worship sung by the choir, with bass reverberations, would begin the worship.

The congregation would swiftly take their seats, only to rise again and join in the hymns of worship and praise. The white lights, the ethereal tones, the Alto and Soprano voices, and the Angelic presence all contributed to the otherworldly atmosphere and feelings. The images of Christ crucified and His ascension to heaven on the large screens came alive with the sound and sights of the choir in a profoundly spiritual reverence. The captivating combination of sight and sound engaged the senses, leaving the soul fully alert. This was the essence of worship. Beneath this immersive spectacle lay millions of dollars hidden away in deposits, blue chip shares, and exclusive estates.

The Church could accommodate a hundred thousand worshippers, who came in cars, SUVs, motorcycles, and even on foot. Over five thousand people were responsible for orderliness, and a full-time security force was accountable for it. The church's car park had twelve floors and could hold forty thousand cars.

The padded pews were arranged in sixteen rows, extending through the four corners of the Church, down the sides and nave, and out to the periphery of the overflow. The overflow watched the services from raised television screens.

Those inside the national shrine, Paradise, sat on pews made from ornate wood species. Great care was taken to carve the pews as masterpieces of art. The Church artists, like Bezalel and Oholiab, were ordained by the General Overseer, given the heavenly commission, and filled with the Spirit of God. The dazzling combination of gold, silver, and bronze liberally splashed on the altar railings and the edges of the pews inspired awe.

Each pew was a donation from the over one hundred thousand members of the congregation, whose names were boldly etched on gold-plated plaques mounted at the back of the pews. This spread out the pews' golden appearance and the rich texture of the golden congregation of Paradise.

The day the Church was commissioned, the heavens liberally opened, and a shower of dollars came from all corners of the earth from those who came to behold or participate in visualising where redeemed humanity was headed: Paradise. They opened their palms and pockets and locked their treasures away from where neither moths nor rust would assail them in this heavenly treasure home. These same worshippers declined to offer alms to the deaf and blind beggars who stayed outside the perimeter of the church building.

The dollars were gathered in large sacks, piled high like a mountain toward the dome. It was indeed a matter of remarkable tact and decorum that the First Faith Bank Plc of Sofalia had brought dozens of bullion vans and hundreds of military escorts to the Church to transport over one billion dollars in rain to the bank vaults. God, Yahweh, had filled the Church's coffers to the brim.

The highest donors were given a mini golden master key to open their heavenly mansion in paradise when their time came. These were the ones who sat in the front pew of the Church and whose feet were planted on the firm terrestrial space of wonders and miracles. Those at the back pews saw them as saints.

One vacant seat belonged to the Distinguished Senator Kanyi Mulaake, representing the Core-Southern States of Isive, Iwiken, Brownstone, Serekana, and Creek State. He hailed from Kepe town in Creek State, which had territorial jurisdiction off the Atlantic Coast over seven islands: Olu, Wole, Denor, Amalin, Illah, Salamu, and

Nasida. These islands were flung into the Atlantic, yet they produced natural gas for which Sofalia had claimed world fame and, sadly, infamy. The senator was both benefactor and beneficiary of paradise.

On the day the Church of Paradise opened to the public, the heavens blessed the general overseer, Godswill, beyond his expectations. He saw the sky above open, and a dollar rain deluged him. Dollar bills and bundles came from all sides. Godswill held the rim of the large jars into which money and gold bars rained, driving the ushers and deacons in a frenzy, scrambling to catch all.

He had moved away from Calanana and the Mega Church, His Voice Must Be Obeyed Church of God, where he had served as senior pastor for twenty-seven years — even after the death of the general overseer. He had moved away from the urbanised mega-Churches whose congregations were only for the rich, who paid handsome tithes. He resolved to minister to the lost sheep of Sofalia in the mud-walled rural slums.

He stoutly insisted that their lives were as meaningful as those of the urban politicians who came to wear their church membership like talismans to harvest a robust Church voting population. He was shocked at the unsavoury task of giving communions to these depraved political souls who conveniently only crawled to the Church altar, especially during election times.

His life had undergone a remarkable transformation over the past decade. A miracle took place on the corner of the beach at Kepe, a small outskirts town on the banks of the Atlantic Ocean. Godswill awoke with a vision from God, in which a sign was given to him of the mighty assignment God had prepared for him.

The sign of a young lady who had died and gone to heaven. God Himself told her it was not yet her time. And though a thousand drowned by her left hand and ten thousand drowned by her right hand, she did not drown.

She returned from heaven to the earth, and her mission was to be born again in Godswill's household as their daughter. When the whole village turned its back on her, Godswill took her in, and as soon as he took her in, things began to change for his small church.

His fame spread around the world. People claimed to have been healed by him. The free advertisement was that he even raised several people from the dead, including the same girl.

His wife, Beatrice, patiently taught Aishatu at home. Within one year, she completed her papers, took the matriculation examination, and passed with very high marks. She was then admitted to the University of Sofalia and graduated with a First-Class (Honours) degree in Philosophy and Political Science four years later.

Beatrice exerted immense pressure on her husband, claiming they had outgrown the local surroundings and urging Godswill to relocate the Church to Calanana, where the major donors and tithes were. She had envisioned a vast Church with a generous congregation, with growth only limited by their imagination. She was the First Lady Of the Church.

Upon their return to the capital, they began assembling at the small Blessing Time Hotel on Titor Avenue, off Igbabur Street. His congregation was small until a rumour began circulating that Godswill was not just an ordinary pastor but a prophet. The new Elisha returned to Earth and was set apart from other men of God to do exploits and bring healing to the afflicted, life to the dead, and fruits of the womb to the despised, lonely, and barren.

He had been an exceptionally worded man of God and began holding outside crusades at the Calanana Stadium. The size of the Church continued to grow in proportion to the spread of poverty and intense suffering in the land. Corruption became endemic, and everyone, including the Churches, was affected and infected.

The General Overseer's name was a household name. His pictures with his beautiful wife smiled down from billboards throughout the capital cities and all the Sofalian towns. Nobody observed any particular concern about the billboards having no images of Jesus. He was more popular than the politicians who, envious of the G.O.'s popularity — as his Church members fondly called him — tried to introduce a bill to compel Churches to pay taxes over their stupendous wealth to the government.

This measure could not have been more unpopular. On the first day of reading the bill, thousands of Church members marched through Independence Square and occupied the National Assembly. On the second day, hundreds of thousands marched through the provinces and joined the others in Calanana, demanding that the president resign and withdraw the unpopular legislation.

They were incensed that their faith was under attack. They took over Calanana. They occupied all intersections, and traffic came to a standstill. The university students joined in. The Christians and Muslims joined the demonstrations against the terrible government, which was not just attacking the Churches but all faiths. Prayer mats and rosaries lay side by side at the Independence square.

The chairman of the traditional idol worshippers slaughtered one thousand rams at the Independence fountain, and the blood of the rams flowed through the streets. The smell, heat, cries of animals, and the shouts of the demonstrators filled Calanana with dread. He announced that he saw a vision of terrible bloodshed that was imminent and how the leaders would be slaughtered like rams.

The presidential palace gates were now barred by protesters, who bared themselves naked and were soaked in the free beer the breweries provided. The demonstrators told CNN that they bared themselves because faith was the only thing every human being possessed, and if the state robbed them of their faith, then they were left with no dignity, no human rights, and left nude.

The president was secretly evacuated into the bomb-proof building, and his security adviser advised him to leave the matters to Senator Kanyi Mulaake to appease the demonstrators. Very reluctantly, he called the senator.

"Hello, Kanyi, are you there?"

"Yes, Your Excellency. Thank God you called. I heard they have taken over the palace."

"No, not yet, but things are bad. The National Guard is not taking orders. They all claim their faith has been attacked. I have been evacuated to Mars."

Kanyi smiled at himself. What a wimp the president was. He had abandoned the ship and was now whimpering from an underground bunker they had nicknamed Mars. There was an awkward pause, and Kanyi could hear the president's breath labouring, unsure what to say next. Then he said:

"But Kanyi, you are a member of the Church?"

"Your Excellency is not suggesting..."

"No, my senator. I only suggest you talk to this G.O. Godswill to get the people off the streets so we can do what we were elected to do."

"But, Your Excellency, all the senators have been confined within the Assembly building. We cannot leave this place. There is nothing we can do. How I wish I could also go to the streets and watch the different naked women on the streets."

"Senator, this is no time to joke. Besides, you have watched more than your fair share of naked women in one lifetime. I beg you, please talk to your Church people to go back home. I beg you."

Kanyi laughed cynically. Fate was beckoning. The general elections were just seven months away, and this was a chance of a lifetime.

"Mr. President, your word is my command. But, Mr. President, I would rather you address the nation. Get the television crew to record your compassionate address. I believe the people will obey you."

"Senator, I have also been following the polls. This is your moment to stand up for the nation and rescue us. Our Ogacracy has become a mobocracy, and mobs have no pity; they are unthinking and speak only one language — violence."

"Your Excellency, the demonstrators are relatively peaceful. They are having a wild party. This is cathartic and purgative. They will soon wear themselves out and go home."

"Senator, I am kneeling here on Mars, begging you. I have been in politics for too long not to perceive a regime-changing revolutionary movement. I beg you. The calm is deceptive. When people are shorn of dignity, they are pushed to the wall. They must march forward in rebellion and violence, attacking to destroy. Do something."

"Your Excellency, please don't kneel for me. It is an abomination. I will go out and see what I can do."

"Very well. Please, address the nation, pour in the tranquilliser, and save our democracy."

"Your Excellency, your word is my command and filled with wisdom. I will speak to our citizens and report back to you."

A few minutes later, a figure carrying a megaphone emerged from the National Assembly. He was completely naked, standing on the overcrowded steps of the Capitol, microphone in hand, ready to speak. Yet, he said nothing. The crowd, in hushed silence, held its collective breath and surged forward to hear him. The megaphone crackled, and Senator Kanyi roared:

"Fellow citizens of Sofalia. I am one of you." They looked at each other and back at the naked speaker, and they surged toward him, shouting, "It is Senator Kanyi; It is our Kanyi."

Kanyi started walking toward the Cenotaph, where a raised platform featured a vintage podium. The crowd followed him, chanting his name repeatedly. He truly belonged to them. He stood naked but unashamed.

They picked him up and carried him on their shoulders to the cenotaph. They placed him standing on the peak with the sculpture of the unknown soldier. The sea of naked people surrounded him. Kanyi felt a rush of adrenaline. He knew that crowds intoxicated him. They electrified him. He faced them with his nakedness and began his address:

"Fellow citizens of Sofalia, I am one of you. When you are hurt, I am hurt. When you are happy and make merry, I rejoice and dance with you..." There was total silence. "Government actions have deeply hurt us in the last few days. We were hurt because all governments on earth must make their people happy. This is the cardinal responsibility of governing. This government doesn't exist for itself. It exists for us, the ordinary people."

A sharp crackle rang out, followed by rolling, thunderous applause. Kanyi smiled, knowing he had them exactly where he wanted them. He repeated, "Yes, the government must ensure that we, the people, the ordinary folks, are happy." The applause continued to grow.

"But fellow citizens, we have left our homes, families, and responsibilities unattended. Here we are on the streets of Calanana, acting like mad people. Yes, here we are. Look at you and me. Where are our clothes? Why have we decided to throw decency to the wind and flaunt our bodies at one another like barbaric perverts just because the government has attacked our beliefs? And we have every right to be angry at the government.

"But we have no right to be angry with each other. Turn to face one another. We are shameful, yet I repeat, we have every right to be outraged at the government and frustrated with ourselves for electing this government to power. However, our freedom to be upset should not infringe on our neighbours' right to happiness."

The crowd looked downcast and confused. Murmurs rippled through the gathered thousands; sidelong glances were exchanged in silence. Kanyi continued:

"Fellow citizens, this is a domestic misunderstanding. It is a domestic quarrel. This misunderstanding occurs occasionally when the teeth, tongue, and the brother and sister in the mouth have a misunderstanding. There is pain when the teeth mistake the tongue for food and bite the tongue. This attack on our faith was a terrible misunderstanding. The teeth of Sofalia have mistaken the tongue of Sofalia for food. We have been savagely bitten." The crowd murmured in muted agreement.

"This is why we are crying on the streets. But the teeth and tongue can never separate and go their separate ways. They must put the pain behind them. They must put the blame game behind them. And they must again work together to save the body. Forgiveness is key.

"We must forgive the government for this unintended mistake, and the government should immediately release the students arrested yesterday for protesting with us. Then, God Almighty taught us that we had sinned against him. Walking about naked like Adam and Eve after their cardinal sin of pride was also our sin. Fellow citizens, the government is sorry. And there will be no church taxation now. Cover yourselves and return to your duties. May God bless Sofalia."

The audience was subdued, and the mob began to drift away and disperse gradually, like a tide retreating, in eerie silence. The nightmare had ended suddenly. The sirens of power started to wail again on the streets of Calanana.

Later in the night, a crowd gathered on Kanyi Mulaake Street. They filled his house. A Christian band and a Muslim group were singing inside Kanyi's mansion. The rich soundscape entertained people with gospel music and Islamic Koranic recitations. Drums, hymns, and chants blended under one roof.

They expected the announcement to be made. But there was none. The president returned from "Mars" dressed like a pregnant woman waddling in oversized belly-padded fatigues. He drove in a private car and arrived at Kanyi's home. Nobody recognised the wealthy pregnant woman who was taken upstairs to Kanyi's Library by Secret Service agents.

Kanyi looked at his president, and President Kila took his hand.

"Senator, please excuse my strange costume. I just came to thank you for saving our democracy earlier today. Tomorrow, a grateful nation will honour you with the honorific title of Grand Commander of the River Lafa, GCOL, our highest honour for any citizen. And I also confess that if you are interested in running for the office of president in the next election, I have no objections. The nation's unity is more important to me than our ambition. You are the man of the moment."

Kanyi smiled at the president. He said: "His Excellency, you are a beautiful bride." They burst out laughing. The president countered: "A bride the nation had already wedded to chaos."

19
____

TRANSFIGURATION

The thirty-fifth Convocation of the University of Sofalia was underway. Out of the forty thousand enrolled students, twelve thousand graduated. June the fourteenth was permanently etched on the university calendar as convocation day.

Aishatu graduated at the top of her class and was chosen as the valedictorian of the convocation. Out of the twelve thousand graduates, only twenty-five achieved first-class honours across all six colleges: Law, Natural Sciences, Medicine, Humanities, Computer Technology, and Agriculture. She was the sole first-class graduate in the Humanities and the Department of Philosophy. The graduands, guests, and visiting senior government officials applauded in awe and gave her a standing ovation.

The vice president of Sofalia, the university president, and key officials from the Sofalian government were in attendance. They gave speeches, but by far, the highlight was the valedictory speech by Aishatu.

The day before the gathering, her foster parents, His Holiness, the G.O. of the Church of Paradise, and his spouse, Her Holiness Lady Beatrice, had held an exceptional thanksgiving service for her, where her parents, with twenty-five pastors, laid hands on Aishatu's head as she knelt at the Church altar. His Holiness prayed:

"The mighty God, my father, my guide, the Elohim, the Adonai, Yahweh Nissi, the El Shaddai, Jehovah Rapha, Jehovah Jireh, Jehovah Shalom, The Highest El Roi, Abba Father, One That Answers by Fire..."

He declared that this was the child entrusted to their care after the miracle of Kepe seashore, and that today, they were fulfilling their oath as her foster Godparents. He prophesied that she would always be the head and never the tail, never lack, never be sick, her table always full, her enemies confounded, and her wisdom surpassing even Solomon's. Aishatu was overwhelmed by the weight of these prophecies and wondered in her heart if the blessings might wear off and she might fall from grace to grass.

The spouse and the pastors chorused a resounding "Amen!" after each pronouncement, creating a rolling wave of sanctified affirmation.

After the Church service, Aishatu was presented with a white Mercedes 500 convertible. Her Holiness Lady Beatrice Godswill took her to her luxurious bedroom in Godswill's palatial residence. The world's leading palace furniture house, the Lynda Clifforde of Milan, had made it elegant. The royal purple, white, and blue curtains matched the settees and divans. The bedroom was lavish, with a tasteful bathroom and spa configuration.

Beatrice and her husband lived in separate rooms, each needing space to converse with God in tongues and silence. This was essential to ensure that either partner's presence would not disrupt the smooth flow.

There was a sitting room next to the bedroom, but Beatrice took Aishatu into her bedroom, and they sat together on her plush, oversized king-size bed, which was made of rich oak and royal mahogany wood. They sat on the handcrafted luxury mattress covered with lace, velvet bedsheets, and ostrich feather pillows. The duvets were black and white, with matching piles of pillows and a large valance at the rear of the bed.

Beatrice embraced Aishatu. "My sweetheart," she kissed her gently on the cheek.

"Yes, Mummy."

"You have made me proud with your legendary educational achievements. You allowed me to home-coach you successfully, and within one year, you passed your O levels and the University Matriculation Examination. Then, in a record-breaking three years, you bagged the Bachelor of Arts in Philosophy, First Class, from the University of Sofalia Calanana."

"My mummy, I am prouder of you. You and His Holiness have breathed life into me that I did not dream of having."

"No, sweetheart, you are a beautiful soul." She paused and looked into Aishatu's eyes. "I want to present you with our small graduating gift."

She thrust the keys of the all-white, black rooftop Mercedes-Benz 500 convertible sedan into her daughter's hands. "Here, my daughter, take this car." She brought out a jewel case. "And for your graduation dress, have these emeralds for your outfit tomorrow!"

Aishatu's eyes lit up at the emeralds in the impressively decorated case. "But mummy, these things are too expensive; I am just an ordinary girl."

"Nonsense. Nothing is too precious for you, my love. You are the apple of my eye. You are not ordinary. This is why you must promise me one thing."

"What thing, Mummy?" Aishatu shyly asked.

"Yes. You are not ordinary. That is why you must promise that you will never touch hard drugs again."

Aishatu's face crumpled with features of abject misery. "Mummy, it was the devil that pushed me to become a victim of crack cocaine. I promise I will never sully my lips again with that vile stuff."

"Sweetheart, that was well said, but it is by God's grace and grace alone."

Both mother and daughter held hands and looked into each other's eyes. Aishatu's eyes were imploring, afraid of the future and vulnerable, while Beatrice's eyes were steady, challenging, and hopeful.

The next day, during the University of Sofalia's Convocation ceremonies, Aishatu stood on the podium among the graduating students. She paced back and forth eight times, collecting the top prizes in Logic, Aesthetics, Ethics, Political Philosophy, Epistemology, and Metaphysics. She received the Dean of Arts award for the faculty's overall best graduating student. Afterwards, she was awarded the Chancellor's prize for the best graduating student in the entire University. Each time she accepted an award, murmurs, whistles, and songs accompanied her as she returned to her seat.

Aishatu stared at the ocean of students in academic gowns, the faculty members, and finally, the state box, where the vice president, senators, and ministers sat among the university members of the Council, the Pro-Chancellor, and the Vice-Chancellor. A tremor of fear and anxiety crossed her body and sweat formed on the tip of her nose.

When the time came for her valedictory speech, she spoke clearly into the microphone in perfect English diction, with emotional tenacity and cadences that earned her a standing ovation. It was challenging to connect the image of the immaculate, flawless diction of the graduating Aishatu with the earlier broken, abandoned pile of humanity on the beach.

"Good afternoon, Vice-President, Distinguished Senators, Honourable Ministers, our beloved Vice-Chancellor, his beautiful wife, the deans, the directors, and the faculty. My special greetings go to the parents and sponsors of the graduating students. Without you, there would be no graduating class. On behalf of the graduating students, I say thank you."

There was mild applause.

She paused for the applause to die before continuing:

"Permit me, ladies and gentlemen, to especially mention my parents, His Holiness, the G.O. of the Church of Paradise, and my beautiful mother, Her Holiness Beatrice Godswill, the First Lady of the Church of Paradise.

"I stand here as an unlikely candidate for any degree, let alone receiving many prizes." The audience clapped long for her humility and self-effacement. "I am equally an unlikely graduating student to receive the most coveted award for being the best graduating student in this incredible citadel." Aishatu looked up, searching for a glimpse of her parents in the audience. She paused and, with a tremor in her voice, said, "My parents!" She called out to them. Her voice trembled. "You found me when hope was lost, when I was broken, helpless, and left for dead. My wonderful parents and models of true Christian love, I love and thank you." The audience was silent and leaned forward, and she continued:

"We live in a world today where uncommon challenges assail us, and often, we are overwhelmed by change. There is a constant reminder to us by nature that our destiny is not really in our hands but in the hands of the Almighty God, our Creator. Science and technology have allowed us to live longer and more leisurely due to technological advancements.

"The younger generation has the world at our fingertips like no other generation before us. The world faces a global civilisation crisis and a generational call to responsibility. We can rally our peer group worldwide toward a New World Order of justice for all. My fellow graduating students today resolutely refuse to accept the slogan of being leaders of tomorrow. The youth of today are leaders today.

"We speak this with respect to our elders, parents, and the politicians present here. We are the leaders of today, embodying the new slogan of responsibility and commitment to serving Sofalia. As the graduating class, we recognise our generational duty and obligation to support those in need, the underprivileged, and the socially marginalised. Our pledge is to ease the suffering of the majority who endure backbreaking labour. Yet, our country's elite exploit the resources, while we, the people, hold the horns of the cow being milked by them for their benefit. Our sweat sustains their banquets.

"The graduating class embodies the new spirit of representation, which is the idea that I am because you are, and vice versa. *Aya tutu* teaches togetherness, showing that we are all bound in an inseparable mutuality. When one of us is diminished, we all stand diminished. When one of us is celebrated, we all share in that celebration. We call on all Sofalians, especially those like us who have benefited from the formal education system and earned degrees, to give back to the nation with love.

"Let us give back this love by reaching out to the untouchables and unlovable among us — those who have a presence but lack a voice to express it, the vulnerable among us: the beggars, the sick, the homeless, the children, the elderly, and the women. We see many on our Calanana streets every day. They are us."

She stared blankly at the audience, suppressing a smile and trying to control her emotions. The audience stood up and applauded.

She continued, raising her voice:

"Let love abound as we build a new society of communal responsibility for a shared destiny built on justice, equality, and freedom. May God bless the University of Sofalia and all of you. Thank you."

Everyone was on their feet, and the applause was deafening. The vice president beckoned to the pro-chancellor, who whispered to the vice-chancellor. Then, the Master of Ceremonies beckoned Aishatu, who was in the protective embrace of her foster parents, their Holinesses, to follow her. She was ushered into the bulletproof state box, where the vice president sat for a presidential handshake.

The vice president shook hands with her and passed her over to the senators and ministers, who gave her their business cards and extended job offers. Whether the offers were to harvest political capital and enhance their standing in the media, no one could tell at that moment.

Then she stood directly in front of Senator Kanyi, the rich, handsome, and most eligible bachelor in Sofalia. She felt vulnerable as the senator undressed her with his eyes. She extended a handshake, but instead of a handshake, Kanyi stood up to embrace her, pressing his palm against her waistline and gently rubbing it delicately and suggestively.

He thereafter addressed her thus:

"My sister from another mother, I am proud of you. We Kepe people are excellent in our character and DNA. Do you know me?"

"Yes, sir, you are Senator Kanyi, an important pew member of my father's Church congregation. And you are from Kepe. You are my senator."

"Were you present during the commissioning of the Church of Paradise?" he asked.

"Yes, sir. You paid ten million dollars in tithes." She looked at him and intentionally taunted, "I suppose the oil business and the Senate business pay well." She had the authority to know the business details of her parents' church.

Senator Kanyi looked bemused and alarmed. Could she have known in her uncanny spiritual way his illegal diamond mining businesses, his kidnapping portfolios, and the fact that he was bankrolling insurgent activities in several neighbouring nations like Nigeria, Chad, and Burkina Faso?

Kanyi recalled several rumours that she was the legitimate owner of the Church and that she was a sea creature, the Queen Mami Wata, from the sea, who allowed herself to be washed ashore at Kepe to live among humans. The moment the pastor, Godswill, had taken her into his household, his fortune and that of his Church changed. The senator became even more eager to include her in his life to create more wealth.

"I am happy I met you today. I have an opening in my office for an intern, and you seem to be a good fit for the position. Perhaps you can help me the way you assist your father and mother. And with your brilliant mind, who knows where you will end up?"

He turned on his sensual charm and tried to look into her eyes. She averted his gaze and said:

"Who knows, indeed. Maybe I would be a senator someday if your patriarchal, misogynistic society would allow me."

"But you are the Queen. That is why you could guess exactly how much I donated anonymously that day."

"Everybody saw your staff pile your sacks of dollar tithes at the altar. It was not an unusual donation but a curious one. Mum is directly responsible for the tithes, and I help her. The First Faith Bank tallied it to your name. My father gave you your golden key — your heavenly mansion, completed now." Kanyi forced a laugh.

"Oh, my beloved sister, you are right. He gave me the key to my heavenly paradise but also prayed that I should not be rushed to experience the splendour of my heavenly mansion until I am married and have children."

Aishatu found him greatly attractive and humorous. Yet, she was not too eager to be counted among the statistics of Kanyi's female conquests. Her heart skipped even as her mind warned her.

She laughed with him and said, "I see; I now know why you are still unmarried. Fear of death and going to heaven now?"

"No, not at all. I am not married yet because I have not found anyone so beautiful, intelligent, and from Kepe. Now that I found you..."

Aishatu was pulled away by her mother, Her Holiness Beatrice Godswill, who was determined not to let Aishatu fall easy prey to Kanyi. If he wanted her, then he should do the right thing. Aishatu was dazed by the day's activities and her encounter with Kanyi.

Yes, she would ask her parents' permission to start working as an intern in Kanyi's office immediately. As she absent-mindedly walked to her parents' limousine, she smiled. Today was the best day of her life. Life was good. The sun was shining brightly. God was alive and on the throne in heaven. She had no idea how quickly shadows could gather after such brightness.

There was a paradise here on earth if human beings cared to find the truth that could set them free. God was not dead. She had graduated into a life of luxury. In her naivety, she thought that she would never have any needs in her life.

She was her parents' only child, and at her father's demise, her mother would become the General Overseer of the Church. If her mother died, then by God, she might one day be the General Overseer, the spiritual leader of the World of Paradise. She imagined herself leading a massive spiritual revival crusade in the United States, in New York, addressing a million worshippers, all ready with their offerings and tithes.

She must persuade her parents to let her intern in Senator Kanyi's legislative office, thereby gaining work experience, and perhaps even consider marriage if Mr Right were as handsome and wealthy as Senator Kanyi. While contemplating marriage, a flicker of doubt crossed her mind; sometimes she wondered if Mr Right could also be Mr Wrong.

Her knees were weak even thinking about him as both parents led her back to their corner, outside the convocation square, and into their vehicles. The Convocation had ended. Life had begun — and paradise demanded its price.

20

THE COMATOSE MENTALITY

Six months after her triumph, Aishatu lay unconscious, delivered by ambulance to Calanana Specialist Hospital.

Her Holiness Lady Beatrice Godswill, Aishatu's mother, noticed her absence from Sunday Church service for the third consecutive time. Her white Mercedes-Benz was not in her allotted space in the Paradise car park.

Aishatu had excused her previous absence from Church attendance due to her involvement in state affairs at Senator Kanyi's office, where she was an intern.

The first time, she accompanied the senator to Madrid, Spain, to attend an inter-parliamentary meeting as his protocol officer; they stayed at the Hotel Santo Mauro.

The senator was not at the Conference. He went shopping with Aishatu along Serrano Street and Galena Canayas. After a day of extravagant shopping, they dined together for two hours. The bill came to three thousand nine hundred euros for both of them.

The senator had a stack of credit cards labelled platinum and gold. He gave the steward one of them, but the steward rushed back to their table. He announced, "Sir, there is a mistake."

"Is there a problem with the card?" Kanyi asked.

"No, sir. You mistakenly tipped one thousand euros for the meal, sir," the waiter explained, seeking the senator and Aishatu's approval of his righteous action. The senator laughed with his eyes.

"No, waiter. That is my tip. You deserve more. I am here on honeymoon with my bride, and your meal made us very happy." Aishatu's eyes opened widely at the Senator. She rolled her eyes at the waiter and both connected, dismissing the senator's lie with a knowing smile.

The confused waiter produced the receipt and returned it with the Banco de España Platinum card. Aishatu collected the card and receipt while the senator stood away, making his usual secret calls. She glanced at the receipt for Euro 4,900, and her face froze — as if at the sudden sight of a cobra poised to strike.

"My sweet Aishatu, all is well," the senator soothed her.

"No, senator, look at this receipt for one meal: Euro 4,900." She turned to face the senator, her face etched with pain at her dawning complicity. "All cannot be well. This bill for a mere dinner is a crime, sir. We have just robbed our citizens. One meal is equivalent to paying the minimum wage for fifteen Sofalian graduates for one year."

"No, don't bother about these trifles; life happens. Please enjoy. This is our first trip abroad together. It will be a constant feature of our life." She forced a laugh.

"The waiter believed you when you said we were on a honeymoon. That was an expensive joke. You have yet to propose marriage and are discussing the honeymoon with a server here?"

"My sweet Queen, we shall see to that. We shall do the right thing."

They returned to the Santo Mauro and became intimate, and Kanyi promised her that she would be First Lady if he won the election as president. She was worried that the senator discussed serious matters too casually. She closed her eyes and said a silent prayer to God, asking for protection from disillusionment.

Her car was missing from the car park for the second time.

Aishatu had called her mother, Beatrice Godswill, the First Lady of Paradise, from Hotel Nassour Hof, Wiesbaden.

The phone purred for a few seconds before Beatrice answered.

"Hello, Princess Aishatu. Which part of the moon are you calling from?"

"Mummy, we are in Wiesbaden; we just flew in a few hours ago."

"Is this another official conference?" Aishatu swallowed hard.

"No, Mummy, and yes," she answered ambiguously. "The senator came for a medical check-up. All expenses paid by his office, of course."

"Yes, I know; let him know we are praying for him. But let him do the right thing. Don't let him seduce you with his sweet tongue and money. We also pray for him to succeed in the number one position."

"Thank you, Mummy."

"Of course, when our prayers work and he becomes president, you will be the First Lady of Sofalia."

"Wonderful, Mummy. May God hear your prayers."

That evening, the senator was absent from the Hotel. He had gone out to dinner with the Managing Director of IKK Germany GmbH. They discussed road contracts and other private matters, but Aishatu was not interested. He left her in the hotel. But no sooner had he left the hotel than the phone rang for him. It was a connected call.

"Hello," answered Aishatu.

"May I speak with the senator?" a female voice demanded.

"And may I know who is speaking, please?"

"Is this Senator Kanyi's room at the Hotel Nassour Hof? May I speak with the senator?"

Aishatu detected a Sofalian lady's accent. She became suspicious and impatient.

"May I know who is calling, please, and where are you calling from?"

"And who are you to know my name or location? I want to speak to the senator and not any other person."

"What is the problem, Ma'am?"

"It is none of your business; you don't need to know my name."

Aishatu dropped the hotel receiver in shock at the caller's unwarranted rudeness. In a fleeting moment, she felt both jealous and afraid. Who was this woman, and why did she feel so entitled?

She wondered why women hovered around the senators like flies and then justified her own actions by claiming she was not merely hanging about the senator but working; however, more than that, she was not just working — she was understudying the senator to imitate the lifestyle and demeanour of the Sofalian elite. She reflected on her Kepe roots and her new position and surroundings. God was indeed on the throne.

This was because, although she was born poor in Kepe, fate had smiled upon her, and now she had made a class catapult.

She also quieted the demon in her mind, condemning it for the adulterous relations she had cultivated with the senator. She knew or believed that she was unlike many of the women the senator had used and dumped. Her case was different. After all, they were all from Kepe, and she naïvely believed that this mattered to Kanyi.

And she didn't need his money. She had hers directly from Paradise.

The phone rang again, and she reluctantly picked it up, just in case it was the senator or some emergency in Sofalia that required them to get in touch.

"Hello," she said before the voice angrily said, "Just let the senator know I am Lady Akember Gungun. Let him also know that my husband took the bullets for him. He is all but dead, a mere vegetable here in Herst Schmidt Kliniken Hospital in Wiesbaden. Let him know he must come to the hospital in person and apologise to Gungun and me. Let Kanyi know that my husband is not dead. He is a snake whose tail has been cut. His head is intact, and his fangs have a lethal reach." She paused, but the pause conveyed inexplicable anger and a menacing note.

"The Senator isn't here. He went out to dinner with friends. I'll let him know that Lady Akember Gungun called."

"No, tell him everything I said. Tell him he has made me a widow in my prime. My husband is dead from the neck to the toes. Only his head is alive. The senator should do the right thing and apologise instead of seeing his henchmen, contractors, and lithium buyers." Her fingers trembled on the receiver, her mind refusing to absorb the words.

"Yes, Lady, I will tell him."

The caller insisted. "Also, it's important to let him know that my husband could significantly hinder his presidential ambitions. Kanyi owes my husband twenty million dollars in agent fees for illegal mining and other ventures. He must settle this payment within thirty days." The caller abruptly hung up, leaving Aishatu's hand numb as she struggled to return the receiver to the cradle. She was in disbelief that she was now so deeply entangled in corruption.

Later, when Kanyi returned to the Nassauer Hof, he appeared tired and upset; the dinner had not gone well. The Managing Director of IKK Germany GmbH complained that the contracts were shrinking, and Sofalia seemed to have followed the new trend of African leaders by joining the Chinese bandwagon.

Chinese loans and manpower were undermining IKK's long-standing business relationship with Sofalia. They demanded Kanyi's promise, signed by both parties, that only IKK Germany GmbH would serve as the main contractor when Kanyi assumed presidency.

"Why, senator, you do seem glum and pensive. Did your dinner go well?" she asked as she tried to rub his neck.

"Oh, yes, the dinner went well. Hoffman was lively, as usual, with his jokes. But these Germans are ruthless though."

"Ruthless jokes?"

"Nope. Jokes aside, mean and ruthless."

"Really? Like what?"

"Like they want me to mortgage Sofalia before they would support my presidential campaign."

"How?"

"They want my guarantee that when I become president, the government will give all the significant contracts to IKK Germany GmbH alone. They even added that if I agreed, all Western countries would endorse my presidential election, support us with billions of dollars, and not interfere with my government after I win. Things will be as they have been for Sofalia and the West since independence. Do I have a choice? No."

"But Senator, how has seamless exploitation been between the West and Africa? You are experiencing neo-imperialism, the last stage of capitalism. The leadership is impoverishing Africa so that the West will continue to live in unbelievable luxury! How can you of all people be led like a sheep to slaughter without a bleat of resistance? Where is the strategy of freedom from this new slavery for Africa?"

"My Queen, let us not bother about it. I have no choice. No African leader has any choice. We are trapped."

He reverted to a false sense of gaiety. He withheld far more than he was willing to share with a politically insignificant young woman, armed with theoretical indignation, who didn't realise that one could not engage in politics using Hail Marys or govern with Hallelujah choruses!

"No, you are not trapped. Our leaders do not listen to the cries of poverty that surround them. The distant Western melodies of greed and the illusion of power and fame tempt them. But you have a choice to make. You have a destiny to choose for Africa."

"Aishatu, Sofalia is lucky. When I am president and you are the First Lady, we will have two brilliant presidents. Two for the price of one. What a bargain!"

"Senator, please don't flatter me with sweet words. The decision is yours. And there is another matter."

"What is it?" Kanyi asked with unusual curiosity. His heart began to beat faster, and his eyes were cast down.

"Somebody, a woman with a Sofalian accent, telephoned to speak with you."

"Did she leave a name?" Kanyi asked nervously.

"Certainly. She said she was Lady Akember Gungun, that you owed her husband, Gungun, over twenty million pounds, and if you did not pay within one month, her husband would scuttle your presidential ambition."

Kanyi was quiet, then sighed deeply, nodding a cynical melancholy.

"I knew it, the ungrateful thing I dug out from the dung pit and made my trusted business ally. Gungun chose to confront the military and almost died in the encounter. I brought him here to the best hospital in the world so he could live again, and now that he has gained consciousness, I get this?" He was bluffing and talking tough, but Aishatu detected anxiety and nervousness in his tone. It was dawning on her that all that glitters is not gold, and Kanyi was a base metal, a duplicitous person.

"After lying in a coma for ten months and having become conscious again, he is showing his gratitude by threatening me! And the idiot prostitute of his, who calls herself Lady What? How did they get my hotel room? My German host must have carefully managed all this to manipulate me to sign that agreement."

Aishatu disappeared into the bathroom for a while. What she had just heard was unsettling, so she let her mind wander. Although she knew he had never proposed, he continuously referred to her as the First Lady of Sofalia when he became president. For some mysterious reason, he never turned off the lights at night, even when they lay together in bed.

She remembered one night when he was crying and calling out, "Aishatu, Queen of the Sea, please don't kill me." She wondered why he referred to her as Queen of the Sea when she was merely the Princess of the Church of Paradise. Did he see her as some sea monster transformed into a woman? And was that why he insisted on keeping the lights on, even during moments of intimacy?

When she returned to the bedroom, he was already there and seemed brighter and more in control. "You took your time in there," he said.

"No, Senator. I plan to go to the Wilhelmstrasse Shopping Mall tomorrow to pick up some gifts for a few girls at the National Assembly. While I was in the bathroom, I thought about my mental shopping list. We all dress well for you to maintain patriarchal dominance in the Senate chambers, you know," she added with a hint of wry humour.

"My Queen, let's go to bed. It's been a tiring day. I've already told the pilot to prepare the crew. I planned for us to return to Sofalia in the morning and be in our chambers to avoid missing the president's supplementary budget speech the next day. He needs more funds to combat the insurgency. Luckily, the presentation has been postponed, so we have plenty of time."

"Can we please put off the lights so I can get a good night's sleep?" Aishatu implored.

"No, my Queen. I keep the lights to behold your goddess-like beauty."

"You are talking nonsense, Senator; I am no more beautiful than those of your other girls."

She wondered if the senator was all right, calling her goddess and queen. People said he had not been to school, but he was a fine gentleman, infernally handsome, and spoke with the refinement of Obama, his secret role model in oratory.

The senator fell on the bed and, in no time, fell asleep. She snuggled closer to him. He was startled and opened his eyes slowly to behold her, his gaze filled with inexplicable fear. "Too tired to make love, my Queen. Please, forgive me," he mumbled. He turned his back on her and fell asleep.

Aishatu couldn't sleep. A migraine hit her. She tossed and turned in bed. Finally, she got up, walked to the living room, and tried to watch a movie. It was filled with too much sex and foul language. She scrolled through the paid entertainment channels. For a moment, she paused on the adult entertainment channel.

She turned off the TV and felt hungry. She hadn't eaten for twelve hours straight. She had been busy all day and sensed a deeper hunger and loneliness in her soul. While the food she ordered eased her physical hunger, her spiritual hunger became more intense. Once again, she had missed the church service, which might be why the migraine had returned, prompting her to reminisce.

At the university, her boyfriend had introduced her to crack cocaine. It was the latest trend. Young people no longer smoked due to the fear of dying young. Instead, they vaped and took crack. One day, she took an unusual dose and was raped by several male students. They left her for dead in her hostel accommodation.

She had woken up after over twenty-four hours to find her body sore. They had punched bruises into her sensitive body. She crawled to the bathroom and squatted before a mirror to inspect the wreck left of her carefully protected body. Cuts, scrapes, and blood caked her privacy. She cried till her eyes were swollen, and no tears came out again. She blamed herself for choosing a low life of humiliation and degradation over the lofty class God had placed her in. She saw herself as the pig that, after it is bathed clean, goes back to the mud.

She could not report to the authorities. Moreover, she dared not. She was afraid she could lose her life. She knew the boys — members of a notorious campus secret cult — wanted to teach her a lesson for being a nerd. She loved studying and was always ahead of her professors. Her peers both admired and resented her. Yet, she was reluctant to report them. They would deny it. Then, the doctors would use the lacerations from her intimate wounds as evidence to convict the boys. Still, conviction in a patriarchal judicial system was uncertain. She would be a double victim, facing unwanted negative publicity.

This humiliation was her watershed moment. She crawled back to her mother, Lady Beatrice, who arranged a discreet medical examination and was relieved that Aishatu had not contracted HIV from the gang rape. However, the medical report showed a significant amount of cocaine in her blood. Beatrice kept it away from her husband.

It was a woman's secret with her daughter, and she again discreetly arranged for her to enter a drug rehabilitation facility to clean her up. When Aishatu returned to school, she became diligent in academics. She was determined to excel in all philosophy courses and achieve a first-class grade. And first-class she made. Her room had piles of notes and flasks of coffee and kolanuts to keep her awake. She studied for eighteen hours each day. She did nothing else.

She returned to the bedroom, turned off the lights, and lay on the bed. She tried to hug the senator, who was startled and woke up.

"The lights are off," the senator cried out. "Why did you turn off the lights? No, don't touch me," he almost screamed as if he were in that dream again, and had seen a snake about to strike him. He clutched the bedsheets, recoiling.

She got up grumpily, turned on the lights, and returned to bed. But she slept in a small place, at the very edge of the bed. She was angry that he had said, "Don't touch me," as if she had been a dreadful monster or a danger to him.

She began to doubt all these mannerisms. She asked herself if it was not symptomatic of empty campaign promises that would be broken and remain unfulfilled. She imagined the promises rebuffed and repudiated, leaving the unfortunate victims in a state of discontent. She wondered if she, too, needed to sign a pre-election and pre-nuptial agreement, compelling him to marry her on the day after the presidential election, if he won, or even before.

The third time Aishatu's white Mercedes-Benz 500 convertible was absent from the designated parking lot at the Church of Paradise was dramatic. While the Holy Ghost Anointing Service was on, Lady Beatrice received a written message from the chief security officer of Paradise: "First daughter at the Sofalian Specialist Hospital. Seriously ill."

Beatrice felt numb. She didn't want to panic her husband or the congregation. A vital service was taking place, her husband was ministering, and the Holy Spirit descended upon hundreds of people. Some lay flat in the pews, while others knelt at the altar, contrite, imploring, and yearning for the Holy Ghost Fire to purify them.

She wondered what might have transpired between Kanyi and Aishatu that necessitated hospitalisation. It could be stress, an appendectomy, or an accident — anything, she thought. No sooner had the last Amen been uttered than Lady Beatrice rushed out of

Paradise to the emergency ward of the Sofalia Specialist Hospital, Calanana.

But she was late. Even without informing the family, Aishatu was already on her way, authorised by the Office of the Distinguished Senator, to the dreaded Sofalia Mental Hospital Abo, a facility fifty kilometres outside Calanana — an impregnable fortress with barren high perimeter walls and barbed wire.

The consulting specialist, Dr. Ndu, neither a Christian nor a Muslim, did not feel intimidated by the imperial presence of Her Majesty, the First Lady of the Church of Paradise.

He refused to discuss Aishatu, her condition, or her medical records. The office of Senator Kanyi had brought her to the hospital, and the doctor asserted he could not share details about her condition with Lady Beatrice because he was unaware of her identity. Appalled by the doctor's disrespectful attitude, Lady Beatrice confronted him.

"I am appalled by your decision to send my daughter to the Mental Hospital. This conduct is a clear case of malpractice!"

Dr. Ndu relented. "I understand your concern, Madam, but I assure you, our actions were necessary. The lab found twenty milligrams of Diazepam and fifteen milligrams of Temazepam in her system, well above the toxic threshold. They also found a large number of opioids. And with a self-inflicted laceration on her wrist, we had to take precautions."

"Precautions?" retorted Lady Beatrice, angry and refusing to accept the medical evidence. "You are accusing my daughter of being suicidal? Can you imagine the stress that young women undergo while working for these individuals at the National Assembly? My daughter is not suicidal. She is just stressed, that's all."

Feeling undermined and disconcerted by the malpractice accusations and determined to have the last word, Dr. Ndu replied: "With all due respect, Madam, stress doesn't explain the combination of pills she took. We need to evaluate her mental state to prevent future attempts. It's standard procedure."

Lady Beatrice was now in a fit of rage. She was determined to interrogate the doctor and immediately put him in his place. "What standard procedure? You are just covering yourself. Do you imagine the stigma the poor girl is in? You hurriedly and with malicious intent, sent her to the asylum, certifying her a mad woman?"

Lady Beatrice's intensity took the doctor aback. He became suspicious that, like mother, like daughter, Lady Beatrice might also require some care, as her escalating temper and anger exhibited all the signs of a mood disorder. He gazed into her eyes and tried to pat her shoulder in a reassuring gesture. She stepped back and turned to leave.

Ndu said, "I understand your distress, but I must prioritise your daughter's safety. The mental hospital will re-evaluate her condition after the mental health assessment. I assure you that we're doing what's best for her."

Lady Beatrice drove to No. 1 Kanyi Street, and because of her status, she quickly gained access to the mansion's inner sanctum. She met the senator at his villa's swimming pool, where he was in his swimwear, playing with two young women from Las Palmas who appeared to be underage.

Lady Beatrice stormed in, "You deceitful, manipulative monster! You promised to marry my daughter, and then you humiliated her like this. She is lying critically ill at the Sofalia Mental Hospital, and doctors allege she was trying to take her life. And here you are, cavorting shamelessly with these underage girls. Why do you humiliate the Paradise family like this?"

Senator Kanyi (smiling): "Lady Beatrice, calm down. There is nothing to worry about. I was entertaining myself a little. Your daughter had no reason to go overboard to try to harm herself. It is not the first time a girl has been denied marriage."

Lady Beatrice was outraged: "You are entertaining yourself with two girls half your age? After you promised Aishatu marriage?"

Senator Kanyi (shrugging): "Aishatu knew she imagined things. She knew the score. She was just a distraction until some better things came along. And by the way, a man in my position is entitled to good things even if they come underage. This is not your Church, and you have no authority to judge anybody."

Lady Beatrice was furious, and the two girls, sensing danger, left the pool and headed to the guest chalet, away from the venom of a mother whose daughter had been spurned by big money and presidential hope.

"You used my daughter, broke her heart, and now she's fighting for her life! You are responsible for her attempted suicide."

But the Senator was unfazed. "That's not my problem. She should have known better than to trust or attempt to own men like me. All women are playthings."

Lady Beatrice, genuinely shocked at his slur against all women, looked at him as if he were some vermin. She faced him as if ready to attack, flicking her wrist with gold bangles. "You are disgusting. You'll pay for what you've done to my daughter."

The senator (laughing): "I doubt. I am Senator Kanyi, Lady Beatrice, generally considered above the law here."

"I know about that, too," she replied. "But you are not above the laws of God Almighty, the One who answers with fire."

"Madam, you can't threaten me. Let me inform you that I'm not too fond of your golden key to heaven. My God is now a crocodile, Ambe Loko, of the River Loko. It has already swallowed your golden key and lies in the river bed with its sharp teeth moving against the fast-flowing currents.

"Everyone knows that Aishatu is a sea creature brought to empower and enrich you and your husband, as well as to protect against local con artists from Kepe. Please leave my home at once. They say you sold your womb to the devil to get a demon child who made first class without studying. Don't threaten me."

Lady Beatrice looked heavenward and wished a fire chariot would descend and carry her away from this abode of hell. She spoke in tongues, spewing dangerous prayer patterns and curses on the senator and his home. Then: "We shall see. You have not just sinned against the body and blood; you have cursed the Almighty Himself."

Her orderly led her out while Kanyi returned to the pool to enjoy his romp.

Lady Beatrice did not go to the Sofalia Mental Hospital Abo. She was shocked by what the senator had said: repeating the rumours that Aishatu was an incarnated Mami Wata from the bottom of the sea, and how the Paradise church was a cult wholly dependent on the magical powers of this adopted sea monster. She needed to return to her husband, who had greater faith in God and could handle the situation. She could hardly walk back to her car, and when she finally entered, she went into a prayer sequence while her hands trembled on the wheel.

21

THE RESURRECTION OF GUNGUN

Akember Gungun walked beside the hospital scooter where her husband, the feared bandit of Sofalia's Midlands, Gungun, sat. A blanket was draped over his form from chest to feet. He was a living testament to the marvels — and the eccentricities — of Western medicine: more than thirty operations later, he survived. He could still see, smell, taste, swallow, think, and whisper; his voice came through the respirator as a rasp that revealed both iron will and fragile flesh. But from the neck down, he was a stone: paralysed, a man trapped inside a body. Robots had given him hands — articulated, pale, humming with servomotors — and those hands moved at his thought. The miracle was clinical and unsettling.

After Gungun's incapacitation, SLAP's command had split and reformed: Barkin Banka claimed visible command, but it was Akember who stitched the threads in the dark. The banditry and kidnapping endured despite the public drama of Gungun's "death" and the macabre images shown on the channels. Her money — the millions SLAP had hoarded — bought access, lawyers, false papers, parties, and the occasional chapel sermon when necessary. Akember moved between Binda Cave and Calanana with the fluidity of someone who belonged to two worlds: the jungle and the marble.

She had learned to speak polished English in private jets and on verandas where senators and oligarchs smiled like auctioneers. A Yale diploma — stolen, purchased, or imagined — slid well into parlours that preferred pedigree. Kanyi seduced her habitually: not only with charm but with leverage, promising elevation, access, and a future throne. She accepted what she needed — warmth, influence, and access to the machines that might return her husband to life — until the night she realised she had been an ornament in a larger rack of bargains.

On that night, she took Kanyi's Beretta Pico while he slept and pressed it into his open mouth. The memory of this act — ludicrous, intimate, toxic — haunted the senator's face. Akember felt the pistol's cold against his gums and a rage that tasted like the metal of the gun. She awakened him with that brutal intimacy and demanded answers. He fumbled with excuses; she shot into the mattress to underline her point. Kanyi's eyes widened. His life and his political ambition were all at the whim of this dangerous woman. He blamed himself as a self-inflicted victim of his moral turpitude. His face sunk and his hands trembled.

"Take me to Wiesbaden," she said. The demand was not merely about travel: it was restitution, reclamation, and a test. She knew how to move state instruments with a pistol and a show of diplomatic swagger; Kanyi's status cleared borders and smoothed visas. On the tarmac in a pale dawn, she walked with him as both hostage and possessor. She hid the gun in his gown folds; insiders were rarely searched. The senator's private jet lifted them over the Atlantic and his private complacency.

Herst Schmidt Kliniken was discreet about its miracles. The Rupa Wing — funded by ex-presidents, oligarchs, and curious philanthropists — reeked of antiseptic and power. The ward names sounded like honourifics that whitewashed culpabilities: the Rupa Presidential Hospice, the Schuster Wing, the Leben Neu Gestalten research suite. Gungun lay in a gilded enclosure under fluorescent mercy. His body had been turned into a laboratory and a reliquary; visitors were allowed only at specified times and were required to sign confidentiality agreements. There were "No Phones" and "No Photography" signs on the walls of the wards.

Akember entered with the choreography of a woman who had rehearsed rage. She stood at the bedside and touched the man she had owned, who now seemed at once fragile and vast. He smiled — muscle in his cheek pulled by an old habit — and the robotic fingers twitched, a ghostly applause. His voice rasped, surprising her with a calm she had not expected.

"My love," he said, "a new vantage opens when you are high and still. I see things differently."

Akember's face crumpled. Anger, exhaustion, and devotion braided her words into a single thread. "They took him, Senator. You took him. You used us as... as commodities. You sit with your suits while my man lies as a talking head. I want recompense." She spat the last word like a bad coin, the memory of her bandit army flashing across her mind, giving her bravado.

Gungun's eyes — small, searing — fixed on Kanyi when the senator was brought in, escorted by two stone-faced IKK partners who had been waiting in the quiet corridor, their hands tucked against a ledger of contracts. Kanyi's face was a map of equations: fear, calculation, the thin sheen of the man who had once thought himself invulnerable. He had arrived with apologies on his lips and deals in his briefcase. The power of proximity to men like Gungun, even diminished, still translated into leverage in Sofalia's markets.

Akember stepped forward. She kept the pistol hidden but held the moral weight of a woman betrayed. "You brought him here as a trophy," she accused Kanyi. "You brought him to die under someone else's knife and then kept me. Where is my man's due?"

Gungun watched them argue like a high priest judging supplicants. He moved his lips with deliberate difficulty. "Akember," he croaked, "revenge is a narrow gate. I have lain in the valley. I saw the thing that made me whole and the thing that unmade me. Power is a mirror. It shows you the worst of yourself." He paused, the breath in his chest whistled, and he lifted a robotic hand that trembled like a newborn limb. "I do not desire your blood. I desire... to be known. To be listened to."

Akember's jaw tightened. "Your speeches turned men into markets while you emptied coffers for IKK bills," she said. "Words won't buy back a spine." The accusation landed like an invoice and a curse. Still, in the small private theatre of the hospice, the political math shifted: Gungun's moral pronouncement would either neutralise a vendetta or reframe it into a campaign. Gungun continued, "I look forward to a time to make a full confession and seek the forgiveness of those whose lives we destroyed."

In the corridor, Barkin Banka waited — not the grotesque butcher of rumour, but a man whose face, when seen close, betrayed the scaffolding of ruthless competence. He had kept SLAP's networks functioning and had consolidated power in the absence of his boss. He came in only for the briefest of bows and a soldier's nod; his eyes moved like a hawk tallying players. "Gungun," he said in a tone that threaded loyalty and calculation, "your voice can return us honour or ruin. The boys are restless. Some want a purge; others want the old ways."

Kanyi, trembling with a politician's fear, tried reasoning. "Gungun, I served you. I brought you help. You know I saved you." He said it as a bargain, then as a prayer. The room smelled of antiseptic and impatience. Akember stepped back to the window and stared at the cliff of winter light falling into the hospital courtyard. Her silhouette was a map of irresolution.

From the bed, Gungun said, with a thin, dangerous humour, "Save me? Or use me? The world taught me to take, Kanyi. Now it asks me to speak." He turned his head toward Akember. "If you seek justice, choose a path that does not leave the dead as coin. Choose to build a legacy that can't be bought with blood."

That night — in the hospice's hush, with punctuated monitor bleeps and the distant clank of carts — a new scheme was stitched. Gungun would not sign their death warrants. Instead he asked for a list: names of those who had profited from the conflict; receipts of deals; dossiers. He would speak. He wanted his enemies to be exposed in the light, rather than hunted in the shadows.

Akember reacted first, like a storm coalescing: she refused. To her, without the old reckoning, the scales would never tilt. Barkin Banka weighed her words and the room like a judge. Kanyi, counting votes and donors in his mind, offered money — again — as if currency could anaesthetise history.

Gungun watched them bargain and smiled, a small, terrible smile. He was alive in a way that alarmed them all: diminished in flesh but magnified in consequence. His resurrection had not merely returned a man; it had returned a story the elites wanted buried. He would be a witness; that was enough to unbalance the plates.

Outside, in the Wiesbaden dusk, diplomatic cars glided past, oblivious. Inside, in a room where the dead were revived and the living bartered for power, Sofalia's next convulsions were being negotiated — not with guns fired into mattresses, but with lists, testimonies, and the fragile wish that a parable could alter a nation. A radio beeped from Akember's handbag. It was her orderly in Binda checking on her. She tapped a message back: *"Kettle not boiling."*

Akember only cried the more, her shoulders shuddering with a tremor that felt like a breaking rope. She began to hyperventilate, the words tumbling out in jagged bursts: "I don't know if I can — or want — to. My hurt is too deep."

"That's okay," Gungun replied in that thin, raspy voice that had the calm of a man who'd already crossed a private river. "Please, don't be so worked up. Because you see me like this, you're all angry. Our German friends will make you feel at home. A hotel nearby lets you rest; you can visit during the day. I have found a strange peace. I hope you will find it, too."

Akember refused the hotel. She refused to be consoled into calmness that felt like erasure. Even as nurses came to sponge Gungun's lips and adjust the machines, she remained in a furious vigil.

She saw in his hollowed body the end of the life she'd married; she saw in the machines the last proof that money and medicine could not undo the ledger of debt and shame. She vowed, without saying it aloud yet, that she would not forgive the world that had taught her obedience and then sold her husband's flesh as spoil.

Akember had never liked being told to fall in line. Orders chafed her like cheap fabric. She had chosen another path: fixer, cleaner, and final arbiter of problems whose answers were bullets and ledgers. Violence had its own accounting, and she had learned to read the books.

She watched Gungun's head — dangerous, fragile — and decided she would not be a mere consort in the background. If he had softened, she would sharpen her edge. Barkin Banka would be removed; the throne of SLAP would have a new Oga. She clenched her fist around a hospital tissue to punctuate the vow.

When at last the exhaustion of rage took her, she curled on the ward's sofa and slept like a sentry. The machines hummed their indifferent lullaby.

"Poor thing," Gungun thought — an interior whisper the reader feels rather than hears. Gazing at the sleeping woman, he began to speak to himself in those inaudible motions of lips and jaw that the prisoned monitors could not translate.

She is right to call me dead, he thought. *Yes — in some ways I am dead, both physically and morally. I am dead to what I was; the ghosts of my victims, the faces of the families I destroyed, press against the inside of my skull.*

"I, Gungun, am haunted by the ghosts of lives I have taken, by the innocence I stole, and by the futures I crushed," he mouthed. *"I am ashamed of nights spent drunk on the rush of the gun, revelling in power for the sake of power. For what? A façade. A distraction from the hollow that was inside me — the empty pit at the valley's bottom. Should I dare to cry to God for redemption?"*

Then she came — angry, tender, unforgiving — as an accuser who knew the ledger of his life better than he did. *"I trained her,"* he admitted to himself. *"I made her sell death as a service. She loved me with the ferocity of the weaponised. She traded in the satisfaction of endings."*

He watched the fire of hate in her eyes and recognised it as the same fire that had once animated him: that appetite that left wastelands in its wake. *"Why can't she see what I see? Who can pry open her eyelids to show her the ruins we have made?"*

She calls me weak. Physically I am feeble; spiritually I might be hollow. But that does not mean I am nothing. I am Gungun. I was made for something beyond the scoreboard of killings. My time is short; perhaps there is redemption on this lonely path. Perhaps I must walk it alone.

"How can I be saved, when she — the one in whom I planted seeds of hate — now harvests an apocalypse?" he wondered. He was trapped inside a body that would not obey him; regret was the only muscle that still responded. Still, he hoped she might find her way out of darkness before it was too late.

22

FIRE IN PARADISE

The conference hall in Paradise was enormous, modelled after the United Nations' General Assembly Hall. The delegates for Paradise's annual conventions represented all nations where the Paradise Church had established congregations and beyond. They were known as Overseas Overseers. Each delegate pledged allegiance to His Blessed Holiness Godswill and reported their daily activities to the headquarters in Calanana — in person, via Zoom, or through teleconferencing.

Godswill and Her Blessed Holiness, Beatrice, were tireless stewards: efficient managers of people and materials. Every dollar given to the work of God in all nations was accounted for. The best financiers diligently calculated all the offerings and tithes, and no nation dared demand taxes from Paradise.

Every Sunday, the global harvest of dollars for God in Paradise reached nearly two billion dollars. These figures were rising, especially from the most significant economies: the US, China, the UK, the EU, Russia, Japan. The looming fear of a third world war prompted many billionaires to donate to Paradise as a form of eternal insurance.

The Church had hired Assets Plus, Wall Street's best hedge fund manager, to multiply God's money. There was already talk of trading in Paradise stocks. The hope was that Gerald Owens, the head of Assets Plus, would not become another Banker of God like Paul Marcinkus.

Paradise responded to billionaire benefactors with elaborate rituals of grace. Each was granted forgiveness for present and future sins, along with a three-dimensional brochure of their mansion in heaven, complete with a *golden key*. These brochures showed radiant palaces built of gold and diamond, adorned with emeralds and sapphires, illuminated by sun, moon, and stars — all controlled by the mind of the keyholder.

The hall itself was frigid with overzealous air-conditioning. Delegates wore thermal underwear to guard against pneumonia. They endured the cold willingly, for in Paradise the desire for warmth was framed as a longing for hellfire.

Delegates from Canada, Russia, and the Nordic countries congratulated Sofalia, marvelling that a poor, underdeveloped state was exporting holiness and grace to the rest of the sinful world. No one could explain the mystery of God's mercy — why Sofalia of all nations had become the gateway to heaven on earth.

The Annual Conference of overseers was underway, unaware that Paradise itself was ablaze. The unthinkable had not only been imagined but had manifested: Paradise was tainted.

The stain began the day Aishatu, Paradise's first daughter, was admitted to Sofalia Mental Hospital. When Her Blessed Holiness Beatrice Godswill confronted Dr. Ndu, the consultant at Calanana Specialist Hospital, and later Senator Kanyi about her daughter's condition, she did not yet know Satan had ignited the fire in Paradise.

Beatrice refrained from entering Sofalia Mental Hospital at Abo. Though maternal instinct urged her to rescue her daughter, she hesitated. Every vigilant Christian knew the power of the devil: unclean spirits dwelt in the mentally afflicted. The Bible said little of Satan, but much of demons, legions, and madness.

Beatrice feared the legion now residing in her beautiful daughter,

Aishatu — her faith shaken by both Kanyi Mulaake, Satan's agent, and the destructive lure of crack cocaine.

So Beatrice turned instead to her husband's altar, deep within the mansion grounds of Paradise Church. A glowing red light above the door bore the inscription: *Silence, you are in God's holy presence.* Inside, she knew, Godswill lay prostrate with his Bible, refuelling on divine strength. Knocking would be futile; the chamber was soundproof.

Yet delay was dangerous. There was only one way to pull him away — to confront the invasion of Paradise by Satan and secure Aishatu's release.

She pulled the fire alarm.

Fire engines roared onto the grounds. Penitents, mid-prayer, flooded into the Prayer Stadium. The chief fire officer advanced with a hose toward the supposed blaze. At last, the altar door swung open. Godswill emerged as the officer broke into the mansion, hose at the ready. Beatrice's nails dug into her husband's hand as she whispered: "Our daughter is burning."

They found her still in her Sunday finery; when Godswill and the fire chief saw her, both demanded, "Where is the fire?"

Beatrice first addressed the fire officer. "Please go back. There was a mistake. There was no fire. I activated the alarm by mistake."

The officer stood puzzled; an alarm was not the kind of thing that simply sounded by accident. He moved to investigate. Beatrice raised a hand to his face. "Quickly — tell everyone to return to their places. The fire has been contained." The fire chief acknowledged her authority and returned to the station to reset the alarm system remotely.

"Very well, Your Holiness." He saluted, turned, and drove back toward the Prayer Stadium to calm the panicked crowd.

Beatrice pulled Godswill to the privacy of their mansion. He was flushed with prayer sweat; worry furrowed his brow. His prayer-worn hands turned upwards in a plea. "Why did you pull the fire alarm?" he asked, voice fraying with anxiety.

"Just follow me," she replied.

"No — I must return to the altar. I was in the middle of... I —" He tried to explain; his spiritual discipline felt interrupted. Beatrice held his hand tighter. "No, my husband. *Paradise is on fire.*"

"But where, Beatrice? Where did you disappear to after the service? The chief deacon could not get your signature on the bank teller before the offerings went — I had to see to it myself." He sounded half amused, half nervous.

She led him into the living room; portraits of the first family watched them as they sank into the royal-purple velvet settee. The walls glimmered with group photos: overseas branches, smiling overseers, golden plaques. "What on earth — and what in heaven — is happening?" His Holiness asked, curiosity sharpened by the absurdity of her behaviour.

Beatrice began to speak.

"While I was in the Holy Ghost Service this morning, the chief security told me the First Daughter was at the Emergency Room of the Specialist Hospital."

"Oh — so that is why you hurried off." His heartbeat quickened. "Is she —?"

"I don't know. By the time I arrived, the doctor had certified her as a madwoman and committed her to the mental institution. He did it without calling us." Beatrice's voice was the edge of a blade now; her adrenaline tightened. She felt the ground drop out beneath her.

Godswill stared. "They've committed our daughter? Just like that? Or has she gone back to — crack?"

"I don't think so," Beatrice snapped. "I spoke to the doctor. He was dismissive. His voice was clinical, his eyes unreadable. But I know who is behind this — Senator Kanyi. He means to ruin her, and I will not allow it."

Godswill excused himself and padded to the perfumed bathroom. He unburdened himself with the private ritual of relief, washed, padded his hands in the warm towel, and returned. He tried for calm: "Beatrice, sit. Let's eat something."

"Go ahead," she said. "I am not hungry." She watched him take a bite — pepper-spiced salmon, cauliflower rice, roasted veg — food that spoke of the church's wealth and the comforts it brought. She watched his face and thought of Kanyi's taunt: the *golden key* lost in the crocodile, the rumour that Aishatu was a sea creature.

"So you went to Kanyi's mansion?" Godswill asked. "What did he say?"

"He insulted us," Beatrice said. "He was romping in his pool with girls who looked barely of age, while our daughter was branded mad."

Godswill made a short, incredulous laugh. "Kanyi is like that. He says whatever comes —"

"He is Satan himself," Beatrice cut in. "He promised marriage, humiliated her, and now he locks her away. She overdosed on a cocktail of pills and cut her wrist —"

"Attempted suicide?" Godswill's face went pale.

"I can't say he intended it — blackmail, maybe. Our daughter needs nothing from him."

"Let me call him and straighten this out," Godswill said at last. "We should correct him — he's of our flock."

"No," Beatrice said, shaking her head. "We will fast and pray tonight. Kanyi has thrown down a challenge — his powers and principalities versus our Jehovah who answers by fire."

"It is late. Let us fast and pray; tomorrow we'll storm the hospital with three hundred priests — each with a flask of anointing oil and holy water — and exorcise Calanana."

23

THE GREAT ESCAPE

An uncommon drama unfolded at night at the mental hospital. Aishatu woke with a start at four in the morning. Her feet and arms were tied to the bed, her right upper arm receiving a blood transfusion. Three pints had already dripped into her veins. She gasped, "Where am I?! What is going on?" she asked no one in particular.

The bright ceiling bulb burned into her eyes like a miniature sun, causing her head to throb. She closed her eyes, attempting to piece together the fragments of her memory. Senator Kanyi. The vicious quarrel. The two black-skinned women in his bed. His jeering voice: *"Sea creature... crack cocaine junkie..."* His words had shattered her heart into a thousand pieces.

And still, like her addiction to crack, Aishatu was addicted to Kanyi. The more he insulted her and her adoptive parents, the more she loved him. When he told her to go to hell — or back into the ocean where she belonged — she decided to take her life quietly. Life had no purpose. Yet now she was here. The horror of the realisation hit her: she was in a mental hospital.

Kanyi's desire for lighter skin had led her down a dangerous path. She scoured markets for hydroquinone, mercury soaps, lemon juice, cassava paste, even paying a beautician twenty-five thousand dollars to immerse her in a whitening solution for eight hours per session, four weeks straight. It worked. She became the pale "white" woman he wanted. Yet, after all this, Kanyi still preferred imported black pygmies from Congo. She caught him red-handed. He hurt her deeply. She now regrets the loss of her beautiful, dark skin and the doctors' warnings about cancer from bleaching.

She had gambled everything — education, health, wealth — for the love of a man unworthy of her. Waking up in a mental hospital felt worse than death. Yet she had failed even at suicide. But she would not fail at escape.

She glanced around at fourteen rows of young female patients lying or sitting on narrow creaky beds with thin, worn-out mattresses and faded sheets. The walls, painted blue and white, peeled like old skin. The floor near the baseboards was yellowish with dirt. The woman nearest her had sunken eyes, a bulging tummy, and large ears, which she poked with her fingers, laughing. Across the room, beyond another row of beds, was the nurses' station.

She had heard whispers about the dreaded Abo Mental Hospital, where ordinary people were broken down with drugs and abuse. Patients manacled like dangerous animals. She believed she would be better off dead than remaining there. Her case was likely to be "reviewed" in the morning — meaning tranquillisers, sedatives, and injections to push her over the edge. She decided not to wait.

Letting out a blood-curdling yell, she shook the ward. Nurses and attendants rushed to her side.

"What is the problem, madam?" asked the stout, buxom matron.

"I need to pee."

The heavyset woman called for a bedpan. One was fetched and placed beneath her. Even as she relieved herself, the matron studied her identity card bearing the National Assembly emblem.

"So, you work at the National Assembly, my daughter. Your records say you tried to harm yourself. What happened?"

Aishatu felt a wave of embarrassment as she realised she was entirely naked after the bedpan was removed.

"Where are my clothes, madam?"

"They were filthy — faeces and urine. You'll get a decent hospital gown when the doctors arrive to review you tomorrow."

She imagined the "review": tranquillisers, injections, madness manufactured to order. She thought of her parents, whom she hadn't called in weeks. Her mother would fight like hell to get her out. But the shame she had brought! Bleaching her skin. Attempted suicide. Incarceration.

She sighed. Death was preferable to shame. Still, she looked the portly matron in the eye and pleaded politely:

"Madam, please help me. I work at the National Assembly and must return to work Monday morning. They will sack me if they find out I was here."

"My daughter, you're unwell. This place will look after you. The National Assembly is a glorified mental facility, lacking specialised care," the matron said.

"Yes, ma'am," Aishatu replied, already calculating her escape.

The matron's own daughter had taken her life the previous year with a friend by overdosing on sleeping pills. That memory made her soften. She noticed a strange resemblance between Aishatu and her dead girl.

"Please, madam, I'd like to sit up."

The matron ordered the attendants to remove the ropes binding Aishatu. Aishatu sat up, stood shakily.

"It is almost morning," she said wistfully. "How I wish to see the sun rising over the mountains in Calanana."

"You can take a walk around the ward," the matron said. "But I warn you: the guards outside will kill you if you attempt to escape."

"Thank you, madam. First, let me stretch my legs."

As Aishatu approached the open door, she saw the armed guard at the gate, deeply asleep, snoring in his chair. Beside him on the floor lay an automatic weapon. Her heart hammered. A golden chance. She dashed for the gun.

24

THE CONCLAVE

The Annual General Convention of the Paradise Church resembled nothing less than the United Nations General Assembly. All UN member countries were represented, with their leaders seated in designated chairs in the vast congress hall. Before each delegate's desk stood two flags: the national flag and the flag of Paradise. Beyond the pristine Church grounds, one hundred and forty flags rippled in the wind.

At the very centre of the parade stood the enormous banner of Paradise itself: plain white, with images of His Holiness Godswill and Her Holiness Beatrice Godswill in the middle. Their flag was ten times larger than any national symbol. The lack of a cross, saint, or image of Jesus was unsettling; the area radiated a cult-like, shrine-style atmosphere.

By six o'clock, delegates were filing into the congress hall. Security was strict, involving iris scans, fingerprints, and blood-type checks. Phones and devices were confiscated before entry. Delegates were then guided into the robing hall, where they bathed in sacred showers and dressed in royal-purple, white, and gold cassocks, embroidered with intricate motifs.

From there, they proceeded to the Hall of Emptiness, where each knelt to "empty themselves of worldliness" before being escorted to their seats.

At precisely seven in the morning, the steeple bell rang seven times. A thick white cloud, conjured by theatrical lighting, engulfed the hall as sacred polyphonic music rose with intricate harmonies. The effect was hypnotic, reverent, otherworldly.

Through the cumulus descended the magnified figures of Godswill and Beatrice, arm in arm. The solemn notes of *Miserere Mei Deus* pierced the hall. Delegates, transfixed, watched as their Holinesses seated themselves upon the thrones.

The chief scribe rose. The day's proceedings began with the Lord's Prayer, intoned in austere, monophonic a cappella.

"For thine is the kingdom forever and ever in Paradise. Amen."

A silence followed — thick, suffocating, intimidating.

Holy Shepherd Godswill's golden staff was carried to him. Rising, he descended to the podium at eye level with the congregation. The lights blazed like noonday. He stood before a forest of microphones, cleared his throat, and began:

"Fellow labourers in Paradise, the Lord's vineyard. Today marks the tenth anniversary and the seventh Annual Convention. I welcome you all as representatives of the brethren in the Paradise Church of the Lord of all Nations.

"The world is in turmoil, but this is our unique opportunity to rescue and reign. Revelation 5:10 tells us: 'He has made us gods, kings, and priests: and we shall reign on the earth.'

"Last year, we opened Paradise Bank, whose shares are listed on the New York Stock Exchange. Its value is guaranteed in solid gold. Our universities rank among the top ten in the world; five of our professors have won Nobel Prizes. I have myself been nominated for this year's Nobel Peace Prize, for our modest efforts in rolling back the nuclear programmes of Iran and North Korea, and resolving crises in Darfur, Nigeria, Chad, and Somalia.

"Yet we face new dangers. The information revolution has made the world a village, but cyber-attacks, hacking, and social media disruptions are tools of Satan — the serpent of the underworld. We must remain vigilant.

"Remember: John 10:34 gives us this authority: 'Ye are gods.' *We are gods.*"

The proclamation lingered, filling the hall. Some delegates bowed their heads in awe; others exchanged furtive glances.

Godswill continued with business.

"The University of Miracles in Jerusalem has grown but faces difficulties. Its current Overseer Chancellor, Prof. Donatus Tippering Goddard, has struggled with mental health and transparency. I therefore move for his removal."

The vote was unanimous: "Aye."

"I now nominate Professor Ching Un Chang, Overseer of the South Korea Precincts, as his replacement. Those in favour?"

Another resounding "Aye."

The proceedings ran with immaculate order. Delegates remained completely isolated from the outside world for twenty-four hours. Devices had been surrendered. Meals arrived at the push of a button; dishes vanished as if spirited away.

Celestial lights, mists, and projections of past triumphs circled the revolving walls. Delegates enjoyed impeccable washrooms, fine wines, and abundant feasts. Waste disappeared without a trace.

During the recess, older members visited the celestial spas, where virgins of Paradise massaged aching joints. Others lay prostrate in the adjoining chapel, whispering the mantra:

"The God of Godswill, Abraham, Jacob, and Isaac — help me to be a good shepherd. The God of Godswill, Abraham, Jacob, and Isaac — allow me to be a good shepherd."

The twenty-four hours were dedicated to worshipping God, praying for the nations, and reviewing the progress of the church's expanding charity outreach. Free food was supplied to the world's starving populations in conflict zones and to those in need in developed economies. The convention also considered applications from the government of Sofalia for loans — two billion dollars to improve Calanana's infrastructure and another two billion dollars to fight insurgent Islamist extremists. The convention rejected these requests and upheld its long-standing policy of neutrality in secular governance and politics.

This blissful state of innocence, perhaps self-imposed ignorance, made the following morning horrific for Paradise. Headlines screamed across national and international outlets: "Paradise on Fire!" "Mega-Church Called a Scam!" "Paradise — Home of Satanic Rituals?" "Abuses, Deceits of Paradise Church!" "Mami Wata, Queen of Paradise!"

A horrifying scene unfolded at the entrance to the Sofalian National Assembly while the convention was in session. Security officers arrested a naked, white woman armed with a gun. She had surrendered despite being armed. She claimed to be a staff member for Senator Kanyi; he disowned her when contacted. He warned the press and security not to associate him with the woman, calling her a Mermaid who had taken human form and claiming she was the spirit behind Paradise's success. Kanyi's press secretary held a press conference where he dissociated his boss from the Mermaid scandal. He completely denied even knowing her, let alone being her employer.

When Kanyi disowned her, the woman's eyes shifted toward the security post's armoury; she clenched her teeth, shook her head, rolled her fists, and demanded Paradise be called — she insisted on speaking to the parents she would not stop naming. Attempts to dress her were rebuffed. A policewoman offered her a wrapper to cover herself. She shoved her away.

The National Assembly police had little choice but to take her to police headquarters and charge her with breach of the National Assembly, indecent exposure, and slander of a serving senator.

Her presence at police HQ caused an immediate media frenzy. Within an hour, naked pictures of Aishatu spread across TikTok, Facebook, Instagram, Twitter, WhatsApp, Snapchat, and Telegram. Social feeds exploded with sensational captions: "Hidden Truth of Paradise Exposed!" "Satanic Queen of Paradise, Finally Unmasked!" "Day Sofalia Stood Still!" "National Assembly Visited by Mami Wata!"

It was a media circus. The most popular social media influencer, DaBrowning, with two million viewers, was mainly responsible for the news scoop and spread the story online globally.

The world was stunned. The Christian Association of Churches in Sofalia (CACSO), with a membership of forty-five million, convened an emergency meeting and publicly disassociated from the Church of Paradise, accusing it of dubious activities and demonic rites. They warned Christian communities to be vigilant against a Satan who had come disguised as an Angel of Light.

Photos of Aishatu were photoshopped with wings and a mermaid tail and circulated widely. Delegates quietly fled Sofalia — not through Nick Agyo International Airport but via bush tracks and smuggler routes to Ghana; others slipped out from Kotoka International Airport. Nobody wanted to be seen. Bishop Herman Kings of the United States Parish sought refuge in the United States Embassy where he was taken to the airport at night and whisked through immigration and customs under diplomatic cover.

A more devastating tsunami was engulfing Paradise from within. Godswill and Beatrice were caught in the storm; their Holinesses faced the shocking reality of their daughter's dishonour. Godswill stared, stunned, at the naked, outstretched images of his daughter circulating on screens. How could God permit such a thing to fall on His Church? The Church must be protected at all costs, he resolved. Beatrice read the social reports, bit her lips, and cried aloud as if touched by a live wire.

Beatrice told him what she had learned: Aishatu had escaped from the mental hospital that night, stealing a rifle from a sleeping guard, firing into the air as she fled, grabbing a motorbike, and speeding to the National Assembly, where she was arrested at five in the morning. The guard on duty was inconsolable; he cried that his career was over and tried to run after the sputtering motorcycle.

"Where is she now?" Godswill asked with grave concern.

"She has been with the police since her arraignment yesterday, while we were at the spiritual retreat," Beatrice answered. "My poor girl! Godswill, you must hold a world press conference and clarify this mess. I am going to the police HQ to get the Inspector-General to release her immediately."

Godswill, watching CNN, said angrily, "Beatrice, look at CNN — our stock has crashed; we could be ruined by tomorrow. Let me seek God's face instead of rushing to a press conference. There is more to this than meets the eye. It is Armageddon."

"Any minute delayed is putting the life of our daughter in danger. Let me go and bring her back," Beatrice pleaded.

Godswill flinched as if slapped. "Which home?" he demanded.

"You asked which home?" Beatrice fumed.

"Yes," Godswill repeated. "And I command you not to go anywhere. This is an attack by Satan himself. There is more than meets the eye — the furious media campaign against Paradise." He held the golden staff of office with trembling hands and planted it on the ground.

"But she is our child; I must bring her to our home."

"No, Beatrice, you will not bring her here."

"My husband, I am disappointed. She has become the world's most vilified object. Her naked body is circulating like a demon. Where is the compassion you convinced me to teach? How can we be selective with God's love and deny our own daughter? This girl has been through a lot. Remember, it was after her rape in college that she fought back and made first class. Let us not abandon her when she needs us the most, my husband. She is our daughter."

"Regarding her real identity, my wife Beatrice, I have started to have doubts. Could it be that the Mami Wata killed the real Aishatu, possessed her body, and was then cast ashore? Beatrice, could the devil have deceived us, and suddenly, the real Mami Wata manifestation is emerging and shattering our understanding?"

Beatrice snapped: "Godswill, I refuse to listen to your cowardly, image-conscious hypocrisy. I reject what just spewed from your lips. It is not Godly. My husband, money, fame, and power have changed you. Can't you see? The secular political god of Sofalia, Senator Kanyi, wants to break our family. If you will not straighten this out, I will do it myself."

"You will not do such a thing. You could ruin Paradise forever. I do not intend to return to Kepe, a failed man of God. I forbid it. You speak of money and fame? Look at yourself in the mirror and tell yourself that. This whole Paradise enterprise has been your idea from the beginning. I wanted to be a simple rural shepherd, working in the Lord's vineyard, tending to plants and nurturing new tendrils. I was sceptical about moving to the city and becoming entangled in wealth."

He pointed a trembling finger at her: "The lives of the rural poor, thinly clad and oppressed, are just as precious to the Lord as those of the rich and powerful, who have used the Church as talismans for elections and personal gain. I cringe at our immense wealth, tainted with blood money from robbers, kidnappers, and demagogues. Their tithes are the foundation of Paradise's empire. But you, my wife, like Adam's Eve, prepared a feast of fame and power."

He concluded coldly: "No. Let Aishatu be. The wage of sin is death. If she refuses to repent, she should face the law. I will pray for her. But I forbid you — for our marriage, and most importantly for Paradise — not to go near her or involve our identity with hers. Leave her alone. May God have mercy on her soul."

Beatrice, shocked beyond words, visibly restrained herself. She looked at her husband with a mixture of pity and anger. Seething with restrained fury, she opened her palms and, trembling, said: "My husband, apart from God Almighty, I know you better than any living soul. I know you better than you know yourself. I pity you for deciding against your conscience.

"Let's not deceive ourselves. God entrusted her to us, and I made a promise to God to care for and protect her. The first day she received communion in this church and knelt at the altar, I knew I could never turn my back on her. Whether we bring our daughter back or leave her among the wild beasts and principalities of Sofalia is a moral test of our conscience and creed. How we handle this will shape our future in Paradise."

Godswill rose, clasping the Bible in both hands. "No. As head of this Church, I forbid you. I denounce the Mami Wata spirit that has lived in our home and sought to corrupt the Church. There shall be no mercy.

"Any member who takes her in will be excommunicated. Anyone who offers her charity will be suspended, burial rights revoked. She is the State's responsibility. I wash my hands of her. If Sofalia has a mental health policy, let it handle her. Leave the Church of Paradise out."

Lady Beatrice sealed her lips against his rage. Exhausted, she nevertheless forced the last word: "So be it, my Lord, your Holiness. I wash my hands of this matter. Let the sins of Paradise fall upon you. I will not reach out to my daughter, as His Holiness desires. May God have mercy on your soul."

25

CHOP-ME-CHOP PARTY

Senator Kanyi awoke between two young women. Matilda and Jitini, undergraduates at the University of Sofalia, had been stranded in the city. Their lecturers were on strike, and with transport fares to their distant home provinces skyrocketing, they had accepted Kanyi's invitation to stay.

The government had been raising petrol prices relentlessly. It was an election year. Behind the scenes, meetings with the IMF and World Bank had secured loans — not for "elections," at least not officially, but for "Critical Infrastructure." Everyone knew what that meant. The loans came with conditions: devalue the currency, remove subsidies, and slash the civil service by a third.

The fallout was immediate. Middle-class families vanished. Civil servants and university teachers parked or sold their cars. Bandits terrorised villages, driving peasants into cities as beggars. Beneath the farms lay the true prize — gold, lithium, and oil.

Matilda and Jitini, meanwhile, thrived in the shadow of collapse. Bright, calculating, from opposite ends of Sofalia, they became friends — and partners. Their mothers and fathers, worn down by poverty, had little authority left. The girls pursued survival as an art:

cultivating older men in the Oga class, collecting gifts, maintaining beauty, and plotting escape from Sofalia.

Their arrangement with Kanyi was simple. He provided dollars and a palace lifestyle; they provided companionship and obedience. Condoms were not negotiable — at least not with him. Kanyi mocked their protests, declaring: "Great generals die on the war front." In his world of sexual athletes, the battlefield was a bed, and threesomes were his chosen formation.

Matilda and Jitini knew better than to compete. They shared, rotated, whispered jokes about who would one day be "First Lady." Kanyi reinforced the fantasy, insisting he would marry when it suited him, and that any of his consorts might wear the crown.

The girls lived off-campus in well-furnished one-bedroom flats. They entertained lecturers with food, drink, and intimacy to safeguard their grades. "Investment," they called it, not scandal. In Sofalia's moral economy, scandal belonged to the Ogas; the girls remained largely invisible.

That morning, after the senator rose for his ritual spa routine — an hour of bathing, massage, and grooming — the smart bed crooned a lullaby:

"All earthly creatures, great and small, begin your chores, or lay your sleepy heads back on ostrich-feather pillows."

Matilda whispered: "First Lady Jitini, remember me when you enter your kingdom with Kanyi."

Jitini laughed, answering their shared script: "And First Lady Matilda, remember me in Kanyi's kingdom."

It was a private joke, but today the stakes were real. For while the university remained shut, Sofalia's political circus was wide open. Kanyi was heading to the national stadium for the Chop-Me-Chop Party's convention — to nominate its presidential candidate.

And everyone already knew who the man of the hour would be.

"First Lady Matilda, how could God permit these kinds of riches to such people in this country?"

"First Lady Jitini, these riches are not from God. They are from the devil himself. The devil grants them a span of years to reign, but when the pact ends, he takes their souls just like that."

She told the story of an oil magnate from her town in the south — Sir Sylvester Akutuku Daang Doo II, a governor who abused wives, grabbed traditional lands, and grew monstrously rich. When his pact with the devil expired, he withered, toe to chest. He made a final donation to build a chapel in his name, then died. His funeral at Yommie Kodjou Stadium was lavish — Milanese pallbearers, Bach's Prelude and Fugue, tributes from the powerful.

But then, a villager seized the microphone:

"Your Excellencies, our village gave birth to a treacherous monster. He stole our wives, raped our daughters, jailed innocents. His only gift to us is his death."

Silence. The villagers walked out. The ceremony ended in shame.

The bathroom door opened. Matilda and Jitini fell silent. Kanyi emerged in flowing baban-riga robes of red, black, and white — the ceremonial colours of power. Today, he would be nominated as the Chop-Me-Chop Party's presidential flag-bearer.

"Girls," he said, without looking at them, "a car will take you to the university. History will be made today. My assistant Idris will give you ten thousand pounds each. Do not miss class. And tune in to Sofalia National Television for my speech."

Outside, party loyalists thronged his residence. Ministers, officials, and delegates scrambled for space. Traffic wardens were deployed around No. 1 Kanyi Street. Hotels overflowed; supporters camped wherever they could.

At the poolside, dancers gyrated to pounding drums. At the centre was a dwarf performer, Pigmy Toto, famed for her lewd thrusts and shrieks of mock ecstasy. Rumour had it she was also summoned to Kanyi's bedroom as a charm for electoral fortune.

The senator's convoy stretched over a kilometre, sirens wailing, Algaita horns blaring. At Tigers Square, the half-million-seat stadium roared. The emcee announced with relish: "The eagle has landed!"

Kanyi descended from his Escalade convertible, mounted a white charger draped in gold and silver trimmings, and rode a circuit of the stadium. Delegates erupted, surging to meet him with dances, songs, and bundles of cash.

The reality was messier. Toilets overflowed; the stadium stank of open defecation. The PA system failed, and nobody could follow the programme. Food vendors and hawkers mingled with delegates, each delegate clutching their price: a quarter of a million dollars.

Foreigners had flown in on private jets the night before, bearing suitcases of cash. They had chosen their man. Kanyi — charismatic, ruthless, and sartorially resplendent — was their willing proxy, the neocolonial agent who would keep Africa's resources flowing outward as they had for four hundred years.

The president of Sofalia had completed his second term and, like other regional despots, attempted a third. Togo, Guinea, Senegal — he pointed to them as precedent. But Sofalia's National Assembly moved to impeach him. His own party accused him of violating their manifesto's spirit: step aside, let another feed.

His ego bruised, the president blamed the vice president for leading the rebellion. In retaliation, he vowed to thwart the vice president's ambitions too. The ruling party, fearing a split, persuaded the vice president to shelve his bid "for party unity."

That left Senator Abume Abami, a wealthy ex-governor, in the ring against Kanyi. He had oil, gas, and telecom money and could match Kanyi dollar for dollar. But overnight, the Supreme Court quietly convicted him on twenty-nine charges of corruption and "conduct inimical to democracy."

By dawn, Abami resigned. The party's National Secretary announced that the senator had withdrawn "for personal reasons."

The convention was now a coronation. At forty-two, the son of a commoner, Senator Kanyi Mulaake would be crowned the CMC party's presidential candidate.

He dismounted his white stallion before the State Box, cameras flashing, the press ambushing. The masters of ceremony ushered him to the spin room for the press conference.

"Senator Kanyi," asked Chris Anapoor of CBN, "how do you feel now that your opponent has resigned?"

Kanyi smiled a menacing smile. "I feel sorry for him. A wealthy man, convicted by our highest court. A tragedy."

"But Senator," Anapoor pressed, "is it not suspicious that every opponent you face resigns at the last moment? Don't you feel responsible? Ashamed?"

Kanyi glared. "And you, madam, are you not ashamed to bombard me with insolent questions on a day when democracy is at its prime? Who feels shame in the face of favour? Next question."

He nodded to a friendly hand — SBC, the government's mouthpiece.

"Sir, President Obama has cancelled his Sofalia visit, citing corruption and human rights concerns. Your reaction?"

"Obama has snubbed Africa's crown jewel," Kanyi sneered. "But he is a white man in black skin, an apostle of white supremacy, pretending to be black. A flawed man with a flawed perception. When I become president, Sofalia will not need Obama's visit to prove adulthood. We will show the world we are no one's poodle."

Hands shot up. He gestured at random, then chose a young woman.

"Mr. Senator," said Edugie Enobakhare of *The New Herald*, "do you plan to marry before the elections?"

Kanyi smirked. "It is possible. You will know in due course."

Before the feeding frenzy could resume, his press secretary declared the session closed. Kanyi strode boldly to the State Box, where the president had arrived. The national anthem was sung.

The Convention

The rest was carnival: dances, songs, chants. The opposition parties existed only to provide entertainment. The election had already been won and lost.

The CMC party's victory was not built on a manifesto. It was secured because every commissioner of the Sofalian Independent Electoral Commission (SIEC) was a card-carrying CMC member. Offshore accounts had already fattened them for life. All twelve commissioners were present at the convention, sitting smugly as "impartial observers."

Meanwhile, at Kanyi's Mansion, Jitini and Matilda were glued to the television, watching the live coverage of the convention, and practising the First Lady walk together, with high hopes, as Kanyi was crowned the presidential flag-bearer of the ruling Chop-Me-Chop party.

26

QUEEN'S DILEMMA

On the fateful day, thousands of Atsan gathered outside Queen Aisha's Palace. The Atsan had been creative and resourceful. They dug holes for water and foraged the surroundings for edible plants, mushrooms, insects, rodents, and non-venomous snakes. They even managed to waylay truckloads of provisions and rob them of essentials, including bread. This bread was freely shared among the Atsan and with Princewill Awu's, who became Robin Hood for the Atsan.

He led a group of youths to the Sofalian rice depot, which was situated in a remote area out of sight of the Sofalian police. They overcame the few security staff, who eagerly helped load several thousand bags of rice into the commandeered trucks and transported them to Atsan City — but as soon as the Atsan departed from the rice depot, the hungry citizens of Sofalia stormed the facility.

The government security personnel on duty were among those who took matters into their own hands, but for a good reason. They brought out bags of rice and freely distributed them to the masses. All over Sofalia, the dog whistle for mass action had been blown, and food depots were pillaged for the common good of the people.

At six in the evening on the twenty-seventh of June 2014, as the sun was setting and colouring the sky yellow and red, the crowd outside Queen Aisha's palace gathered quietly. Nurse Euphemia had ordered a supply of suitable medication to treat Queen Aisha's psychiatric condition. Her condition was notably stable.

Nurse Euphemia marvelled at how easily she could keep people with mental illness off the streets. She was confident that after about seven months of treatment on the same drug regimen, Queen Aisha would be entirely cured. And yes, she was beautiful. Dressmakers from the Atsan community crafted her stunning, flowing royal robes.

At precisely 6:05, a procession emerged from Queen Aisha's palace. Nicholas Kenkan led the procession, carrying a wooden pestle as a mace. Thomas Tikindi and Benedict Deli Gawan followed closely behind. Next came the Queen's men and women, who solemnly walked in two lines behind Her Majesty, who was carried on a makeshift cane chair. Four young men lifted Queen Aisha on their shoulders in the chair. The crowd chanted love calls and sang of the Terra Cotta palace provided by the Atsan masons, builders, and bricklayers. Their marching was precise and rhythmic.

They had built a six-foot-high podium with six steps. They positioned the Queen high above everybody else. The rest of the procession also sat on the podium, facing the audience on three sides. Musicians and their instruments filled the arena. Famous high-life star Jim Kum Pax X sang his hit song, "Sofalia Suffering and Smiling." This song was an instant hit on Spotify, garnering over five million listeners in its first week of release. The royalties from the songs were unlikely to reach the Atsan.

The congregation outside Queen Aisha's palace welcomed her to this hit song. As the music subsided, the master of ceremonies quieted the crowd. Everybody stood to catch glimpses of the Queen, who rose to address her subjects. Queen Aisha was elegantly dressed for the special day. She stood tall and spoke into a microphone brought in that morning by the scavenging squad, which had literally established a vast network across the nation. They had scavenged the top-rated public address systems, and now, the Queen was ready to address her public.

"The good people of Atsan, today is a great day, and I bring you salutation, love, and peace. Before I go to the subject of our convention today, I wish to apologise for the circumstances of our imprisonment in our country. We have all been made thieves and kidnappers. We have been forced to make life-or-death decisions. So, I absolve our scavenging squad for foraging in Sofalia's cities to sustain and support our lives here.

"We have borrowed, and frankly, even stolen food and many other items to make life here more tolerable. We have stolen critical drugs necessary to help those here with diabetes and high blood pressure, as well as other medicines for our community. If we stole, it was the state of Sofalia that made us steal. I, therefore, absolve all of you, our gallant youth, of the responsibility and declare you without blemish." The crowd erupted, cheering, yelling, singing, and dancing.

Thousands cheered and urged the Queen on. She continued: "At the end of today's deliberations, we shall cast a vote. But let me now call on Prime Minister Mr. Nicholas Kenkan to give a short report on the state of our community today."

Mr. Kenkan took the microphone and bowed before Queen Aisha: "Your Majesty, the Queen, long may you reign over us, the Atsan of Sofalia, for whom we stand in commitment to serve. Today, over seventy thousand Atsan are in this community under your Queendom. We are loyal servants and subjects to the Queen, whose wisdom has united us.

"It is now clear that Sofalia's government truly intended to kill all of us and hide the truth from the world. Three days ago, the president of Sofalia received a message from the president of the United States of America. In the message, the US president expressed his inability to visit Sofalia due to human rights abuses and regretted any inconvenience this might cause the Sofalian government.

"The president cited the endemic corruption and ongoing persecution within Sofalia — Christians and Muslims by animists. The United States, a pretentious country, considered the persecution of Christians and Muslims unacceptable.

"Our Minister for Religious Freedom responded to the US

president, claiming that Christianity and Islam were foreign religions tolerated in Sofalia. Our people, called 'animists,' had abandoned their indigenous beliefs in favour of these Middle Eastern faiths. The minister framed religious conflict as a form of foreign interference.

"Our Minister argued that Christianity and Islam have turned Sofalia into their battleground. Their religious texts endorse both peace and conflict simultaneously. Their followers choose arguments from these verses to justify violence. Their principles of peace have been abandoned.

"Mr. Kenkan noted that English, the conquerors' language, was the language of administration, scholarship, and commerce in Sofalia, which was also a concern to the Atsan. But the palace was considering further action, and they had to wait for Her Majesty's speech, carefully crafted by Benedict Deli Gawan, the Press Secretary and Chief Strategist.

"Anything that could be used to strike at the Sofalian government and remove it from power was fair game. Benedict had sent several petitions to the United Nations and the International Court of Justice in The Hague, but had been unsuccessful. They had yet to receive a response. They had made the human rights abuses in their country a focal issue on social media and major international outlets, yet CNN, Reuters, BBC, *The New York Times*, Associated Press, Fox News, Russia Today, *The Washington Post*, China People's Daily, and other global opinion makers refused to acknowledge their plight or even their existence.

"The Atsan under Queen Aisha had to take their fate into their own hands; no other help was forthcoming. Big business had seized control of the world's governments, and the new rule of the media was: 'If it profits, then it's news. If it doesn't threaten the lifestyles of those who control world opinion, it should be ignored.'

"For survival, the Atsan had to unite under Queen Aisha's leadership. This woman provided them with collective security. They felt hope just by looking at her face, and when she spoke, all their sinews came alive, and they yearned to act. Today, the Queen needed to inspire the Atsan to act. They chanted her name and waved banners featuring her photo."

The Queen patted Prime Minister Kenkan on the back, warming his heart with a radiant smile. Then she spoke. Her words exactly as written:

"Thank you, Prime Minister. Thank you, fellow citizens of Sofalia, fellow Atsan, suffering citizens, my comrades, and the keepers of Sofalia's conscience. It is with great distress that I address you today.

"Our intelligence indicated that three days ago, the President of Sofalia received a letter from the President of the United States stating that the request for a state visit by the US President to Sofalia had been rejected. The US government clearly stated that, as long as there is widespread corruption, religious persecution, and narco-trafficking abuses in Sofalia, the US President will not honour Sofalia with a state visit.

"The US's attitude and stance have always been to prioritise US interests above all. This is why we were not surprised that the abuse of power and the terrible human rights violations of the current Sofalia kakistocracy were not mentioned in the US president's refusal letter.

"The US prioritises its interests. However, the Sofalian government looks after foreign interests, and the Sofalian government and its henchmen may profit from this. Frankly, it does not matter to us whether the US president visits Sofalia or not. All we want and need from the US is to recognise our sufferings and engage with our oppressors to stop the wanton human rights abuses, erasures, and victimisation.

"Last night, the Sofalia government, all three branches, convened, lamenting like children that their beloved mother, the mighty United States, had refused them a state visit. They complained about the loss of honour on earth; the president of the US had betrayed them. They quickly devised new plans to win over the United States government. They proposed imposing a corruption tax on all our citizens, a form of self-punishment for endemic corruption, payable to the United States government. This will be another tax burden on the ordinary people who do not engage in corrupt acts. It will amount to a double punishment.

"They proposed doubling the interest Sofalia pays on the loans it took from the World Bank for infrastructure. Of course, as we know, the three arms have quietly siphoned the money provided by the bank for infrastructure into private pockets in offshore accounts. Nobody mentioned us, the Atsan. Nobody referred to any plan to improve the human rights record of the Sofalian government that has now enslaved the people. No one mentioned the apartheid-style detention without trial of more than seventy thousand Atsan by the Sofalian government.

"It was a deeply disheartening shock to hear that the National Assembly had swiftly passed an Act to permanently prevent our people, the Atsan citizens, from setting foot in Calanana. The National Assembly passed an Act to make it a capital offence not only to beg but also to be present within the Calanana City Centre, appearing as a beggar, loafer, or impoverished.

"The Beautification Ministry was empowered to establish an armed squad to shoot on sight any semblance of human poverty within the city centre. The President of Sofalia issued an executive order authorising the mass deportation from the Maidadi and Abosko districts of Calanana of anybody whose net income was less than a million dollars. Senator Kanyi, now the presidential candidate of the Chop-Me-Chop Party, boasted on the nine o'clock news that if elected, he would make Calanana the cleanest city on earth." The crowd jeered, shouting, *"Shame, shame."*

"This is where we stand today. I have emphasised extensively that a rescue plan for Sofalia is long overdue. The talk of a coup d'état by the Sofalian army is baseless. These soldiers have no moral right to oppose the looters and abusers of the Sofalian people. They were accomplices in all the atrocities committed against the populace. They lack moral authority; they are tainted, and they have become evil and contemptible. It is time to take our destiny into our own hands.

"Accordingly, I suggest that the Atsan march to Calanana City and overthrow the current regime. We should seize the State House and remove the illegal dictatorship, the corrupt and malicious kakistocracy. Instead, we should install our own Queen Aisha as the Queen of Sofalia, end the sham republic, and return to our sacred roots as a monarchy. We shall hold a referendum on this proposal. The alternative is to disappear.

"They will wake up tomorrow and see us no more. We will go to the mountains, forests, and rivers. We will set up a colossal guerrilla operation that will look inward. We no longer look to the Western or Eastern powers to liberate us. We will deliver ourselves from our oppressors. We will kidnap the Ogas, their family members, and their oil workers. Their money will provide us with the finances to topple them.

"I now yield the floor to our representatives to debate and demonstrate our stance on whether to hastily invade Calanana, capture the city, and seize power immediately, or to delay and gather more resources for a revolution to reclaim our country and establish a monarchy."

Having finished her speech, the Queen was escorted back to her seat amid a rapturous ovation by her beloved Atsan. A water flask was opened, and Nurse Euphemia produced a handkerchief, gently wiping her brow like a child. The Queen smiled contentedly as Prof. Tikindi took her place on the podium. Here is what he said:

"My fellow suffering citizens, the time to fight for our rights as human beings and as Sofalian citizens is now.

"The history of our country's relationship with the outside world indicates that the world might not be particularly interested in us. The West only seeks to keep Africa and Sofalia mired in chronic poverty. The illusion of Western civilisation and modernity relies entirely on maintaining us in ignorance and deprivation. Our political leaders are compromised, as highlighted in Francis Bini's new best-seller *Black Skin, White Tastes*, written as a sequel to Frantz Fanon's *Black Skin, White Masks*.

"Our leaders are infants, pleading and cowering before their foreign masters for validation. We are too blind to see foreigners milking our cows, extracting the cream, and leaving us with just the drips from old cows that provide little nourishment. Yes, we are holding the cows' horns, but those beneath our cows are getting away with the milk.

"My fellow Atsan citizens, we must no longer be ostracised, vilified, or stigmatised simply because we are poor. We refuse to accept discrimination based on the size of our pockets. At the start of her address, the Queen promised to enable us to make our own choices freely. We may decide to rush and seize control of the government tonight.

"We might disperse into the forests and hills of Sofalia to gather resources and engage in guerrilla warfare against the corrupt government. Alternatively, we could retreat to Calanana with our tails between our legs, forgiving past injustices and agreeing to be slaves forever to the Ogas. The choice is yours.

"Refusing to choose is already a choice to remain as the other — the rejected, the scum, and waste of Calanana, discarded in the refuse dump. It is the choice of a living death, neither dead nor alive. It means being nothing. It means being nameless and non-existent. It means losing human dignity and rights and being reduced to a zero. The choice is ours to make now. We should adopt the first option: let us rush into the city tonight when they are least prepared." The audience yelled, shouting: *"Yes, let's rush tonight and take the city. Yes, yes, tonight, yes!"*

"Professor Tikindi, that was a great speech," said Nicholas Kenkan.

27

BONDS OF CREATIVITY

The human condition has always shaped human creativity. When the Sofalian government imagined that herding the poor into a camp would lead to starvation and death, they underestimated resilience. Within months, what was meant to be a graveyard became a city. Waterholes were dug for drinking and washing, streets were carved out of the dust, and families marked out their plots. Out of disorder, the Atsan built a community.

Queen Aisha became their symbol of authority, and with her blessing, a police force was formed. Though officially barred from Calanana — and pointedly dismissed when the U.S. president declined to visit Sofalia — the Atsan refused to vanish.

Bricklayers and artisans raised a terracotta palace. Queen Aisha's own residence was enlarged, and Nurse Euphemia, long beloved by the people, was promoted to Director of Health Services for the city. The motorway bore a blunt sign: *Atsan City — Home of Low-Income Residents.* The inhabitants took no offence. There was nothing shameful in poverty.

Teachers, engineers, journalists, mechanics, and scientists — the poor were never talentless. Within their queen, they found dignity.

Within themselves, they found the right to steer their own lives. Schools opened for the young, staffed by their own.

Princewill Awus oversaw law and order. He strapped a sawed-off shotgun to his chest. At first, survival blurred into desperation. Gangs of Atsan, led by him, robbed commuters at night. But once food barns filled and stability returned, Queen Aisha urged them to abandon crime. A new phase of farming began. Land outside the enclave was distributed, and families were encouraged to cultivate it.

Yet, farming was a torment for the urban poor. They were educated, restless, and skilled for city life — not endless days of weeding, fertilising, and waiting nine long months for a harvest. The work felt like an exile into the past, a forced march into the lives of long-forgotten ancestors. Many yearned for the energy of Calanana.

In despair, some Atsan wrote the Sofalian president, begging for mercy — even offering to return as slaves to the Ogas. The Inspector General's reply was merciless: the Atsan were carriers of disease — HIV, malaria, dengue, hepatitis, typhoid. They were contagion. Sofalia could not risk their return, not when a North Korean presidential visit and possible defence pact hung in the balance. The city gates were sealed with fresh military garrisons.

Benedict Deli Gawan, a veteran journalist, refused to let silence settle. He urged the Atsan to appeal to the United Nations High Commissioner for Refugees. His letter catalogued their suffering: forced removal, hunger, lack of clean water and shelter. The UNHCR replied, asking whether they had suffered physical harm. Forms were distributed. Seventy thousand came back — each recounting some form of abuse.

The Commissioner offered advice: applicants citing persecution for sexual orientation would be prioritised. Benedict relayed this, only to be met with outrage. The Atsan were poor, polygamous, and proud of it. Same-sex identity was foreign to them, even unthinkable. Their population was growing rapidly, fuelled by polygamy — and in a democracy of numbers, they would one day outvote the monogamous elites.

The UNHCR rejected their applications. Polygamy, while legal in

Sofalia, was deemed "sexual greed" by Western standards and discriminatory against women. The High Commissioner herself, a same-sex partner, expressed regret but stood firm.

That night, disillusionment spread. Many declared they would rather march back to Calanana and face bullets than surrender polygamy for Western monogamy — or worse, same-sex monogamy.

But Benedict urged patience. "Do not give up so easily," he said. "The West is founded on reason and logic." Appointing himself solicitor, he drafted an appeal to the High Commissioner, herself once a refugee from East Timor:

"Your Excellency, the Human Rights Commissioner for West Africa:

"I have the honour of most respectfully representing the asylum-seekers of Sofalia, a people upon whom their government has wrought untold hardship — subjecting them to discrimination, stigma, and horrendous denial of human rights, in violation of the Declaration of Human Rights of 1948.

"I specifically wish to petition your esteemed office to reconsider your recent refusal of refugee status on the grounds of polygamy. In Africa, polygamy is recognised as a human right, allowing men and women to live in inclusive communities where the extended family protects offspring and sustains a collective economy.

"In Sofalia, even the Christian minority has embraced polygamy, if only to keep pace with the demographic growth of Muslims, who would otherwise dominate elections.

"Margaret Mead once called monogamy the most difficult of all marital arrangements — and also the rarest. While we respect Western nations for their monogamy, your own scientists have demonstrated that polygamy is natural, while monogamy is not. Why, then, do you punish my people when Western marriages collapse under the unnatural burden of monogamy?

"Permit me to suggest that the global community might benefit from polygamous families, who uphold the very institution of marriage now faltering in the West. Tolstoy's *Anna Karenina*, Hawthorne's *The Scarlet Letter*, even Lawrence's *Lady Chatterley's*

Lover reveal the misery of failed monogamy. My clients, by contrast, could enrich your nations.

"Moreover, over ninety per cent of our applicants hold university degrees and are fluent in English. Your Excellency, I therefore request you reconsider the rejection of seventy thousand applicants and grant them status without delay."

Benedict signed on behalf of the Atsan, but events moved quickly elsewhere.

Princewill Awus's stature grew. He was popular among the Atsan for maintaining order, while Sofalia's armed forces seemed content with containment. Their mandate was simple: keep the Atsan from entering Calanana. In that, they succeeded. What happened inside the enclave — or beyond it — was ignored.

Anecdotes spread about the "mad woman" of Calanana now running a government of thousands of exiles. To the ruling elite, it was laughable, a parody of authority.

Meanwhile, Calanana itself glittered. The new mayor, Mbom Adams, eager for a long political career, cleared the streets of the poor and unwanted. Pavements blossomed with mango trees, bougainvillea, masquerade trees, and dahlias. Investors from Lebanon and China financed gleaming hotels, their courtyards spilling with flowers. Grocery stores multiplied, their shelves filled with imported goods.

Not a single impoverished loafer marred the polished city squares.

The shops carried Chinese names. Owners, many once fishermen, had traded nets for suits after disputes in the South China Sea made fishing untenable. Their broken English amused customers, who saw them as proof of Sofalia's "new reality."

From time to time, Awus swooped into Calanana like an eagle, targeting white tourists, often oil company employees. They were easy to locate at the Hilton Omega and All Seasons hotels. Awus was a paradox: impeccably dressed, wealthy, feared — and revered by his people as a Robin Hood.

Ransoms were demanded, enforced with torture when needed. Money flowed. With it, he procured contraband arms through sympathetic customs officers, shipping containers filled with weapons from Russia, China, France, and the United States. He called himself neither a criminal nor an entrepreneur, but a freedom fighter — an agent of distributive justice.

Awus was dangerous, but his charisma was undeniable. In student days, he had commanded stages as Kongi in *Kongi's Harvest*, Dedan Kimathi in *The Trial of Dedan Kimathi*, and Commandant Kwaghmande in *Mulkin Matasa*. His talent for revolutionary roles foreshadowed the orator he would become.

On campus, he rallied student parliaments to organise national demonstrations against poverty. On television, he denounced leaders as "ignorant idiots who knew next to nothing about governance." When anchor Yinqa Adudu pressed him to apologise, he refused:

"These misfits, who have rigged themselves into power, are businessmen and traders. They treat citizens not as people but as customers."

The phrase stuck. Electricity, water, petrol — everything priced beyond reach — became proof of a government that saw the people as clients to exploit, not lives to serve.

Awus concluded that Sofalia's leaders valued flowers and buildings above citizens. So he bribed police and customs alike, stockpiling arms within the Atsan enclave. What Sofalia had intended as containment, Awus remade into resistance — a parody of apartheid, yes, but also a cradle of revolt.

28

KANYI RUNNING

Kanyi had built a palace for his parents at Kepe that outshone the traditional king's. The commoners of Kepe gathered there every evening for free food, unlike the palace of the paramount ruler. Kanyi's palace smelled of the aromas of food, smoke from cooking free meals, with the constant sounds of drumming, singing, and feasting. The royals were angry, but they had to suppress their anger, for resentment could have jeopardised their standing with the commoners and even with Kanyi, the king of the underworld money empire, the foremost political figure, and the prospective president of Sofalia.

He employed numerous servants to attend to his parents' needs. They lived as if they were staying in a five-star luxury holiday resort. His mother's chicken and goat business was carried out to her satisfaction. She freely distributed money and food to the Atsan of the region, and they affectionately called her Mama President, a name she was not accustomed to, as she was more widely known as the Mother Theresa of Kepe, due to her natural good nature.

Her husband, Kanyi's father, spent his days watching films and drooling over lascivious pictures of beautiful film stars. He had no friends anymore since his sudden elevation to a different class had inevitably ruptured his relationship with his old peers. Money, property, and the attitude of the rich had damaged friendships between the rich and the non-rich. Kanyi's father learned to play golf and had a retired national golf coach accompany him daily on the course.

Kanyi's mother was too occupied with her charity work to notice that her husband had altered his wardrobe, often dressing in shorts and T-shirts around younger women who visited his palace, as he called it. They had constructed an Olympic-sized golf course, but only the coach, police officers, and the Secret Service personnel who protected him ever used it.

Baba Kanyi's focus on playing golf involved some risks. Baba insisted on having Itoro Abak, a beautiful and well-endowed former judoka now working as a wellness coach, as his caddy. Baba often lingered in the spa with Itoro to receive massages: Swiss and Shiatsu with hot stones placed on his back while Itoro's fingers gently kneaded his lower back beneath the thick white towel.

Mama grew suspicious when her husband insisted on playing golf even in the rain. One day, she decided to go and see what was happening. But upon arrival, she saw more than she expected. On the massage table in the gym, with the door slightly ajar, Baba was groaning beneath the weight of Itoro, who sat on his steaming back with oil dripping onto the table. Baba softly urged her to press harder.

Mama Kanyi cried:

"Chei! Baba Kanyi! My God don catch you today!"

Itoro slid off Baba's back, dropping her towel to the floor. Her gorgeous body gleamed at Mama, who stood facing her with the massage table between them.

"Chei! Chei!!" was all she could say while her eyes killed both culprits at once. Itoro retrieved her towel, and Baba stared at his wife, muttering under his breath:

"Mama Kanyi, I did nothing. We did nothing."

"You Ashawo, harlot. Let my eye never see you in Kepe again. Pack an go your place. You no shame come sit on your granpa back? Wetin you come

see in him? You think na him money? No be him money. Na my son money!"

Itoro, shocked and embarrassed, ran out of the gym, leaving the older man alone. The villagers whispered that Mama Kanyi was a witch and that it was her witchcraft brought from her village that made her son so rich. They whispered that if Itoro had slept with Baba, their sex organs would be glued together, separable only by surgeons.

Baba Kanyi carried himself with offended dignity for a whole week, charging his wife to stop being petty, mean, and provincial. He did not once admit that Itoro had aroused him each time he saw her, nor that he was wooing her slowly with the promise of a Daihatsu Mini car.

Mama warned him sternly, threatening to report him to their Pastor and bar him from taking Holy Communion. She also insisted she would not be "provincial" again from that moment, and that they would play golf together. She would wear shorts, accompany him to the golf course, and get an athletic young man to massage her in the rain. Needless to say, the golf course fell into disuse, and weeds overtook the Olympic-sized course.

But Mama Kanyi was worried that her son, the most eligible bachelor of Sofalia, had not shown an interest in marriage. She groaned to her husband:

"Baba Kanyi, e be like your son no wan marry. Something dey wrong."

"Mama Kanyi, tomorrow we will spend the weekend with him and give him a piece of our mind."

"Baba Kanyi, and this campaign war do me. I no likam at all. People say Kanyi na white man wife!"

"Abomination! Not our son. They badmouth him because they see him pass them all. Na envy."

"Baba Kanyi, tell your son to marry. The people of Sofalia wan first lady. We must insist this time."

They ate quietly, promising to confront Kanyi the next day and demanding his plan for a wife. The neighbourhood owls and bats liked gathering at Kanyi's countryside home at night. This was an ominous sign, but the house's security was robust. Forty-eight police officers were stationed there, rotating their positions except when Mama and Baba were bathing in the bathrooms or requested privacy.

The environment was so stifling that, one day, Mama asked Theresa, her police orderly, to step back from her.

"Theresa, you talk say na which region they born you?"

"Central Region."

"Ma, na which tribe?"

"Larpan."

"You say?"

"I say Larpan."

"Na de place that General Afikun come?"

"Exactly. Na General Afikun dey same village with us. But they kilam."

"Why dem kilam?"

"They say he wan do coup."

"A person wey do coup no palaver; one wey wan do coup they kilam. God dey!"

"Na so soldier wahala."

"No election, just bang bang bang, fellow Sofalians!"

"Blah blah blah, coup."

Mama liked Theresa. She had been married earlier, but her husband wanted to oppress her because *"e no get boy pikin."* So Theresa left him and carried away her two girl pikin, who dey university now. Mama liked Theresa.

Life with Mama was paradise. Theresa did not have to perform tedious police duty to serve the wife of Oga and then serve Oga. She had spent nineteen years in the police force and was still a corporal. Now, in Mama's house, she had time to read. She liked Mama, who was generous to her. She was able to save her salary for her children's school fees. She even planned to stay after the elections when the senator became the president of Sofalia. But things didn't seem alright, things were swirling around.

Mama asked Theresa if, in the white man's country, men married men and women married women. Theresa had also heard rumours that Kanyi was attracted to both men and women, but she did not want to explore that aspect. It was too personal and intimate, and Kanyi denied the allegation. After parading a host of beautiful, eligible Sofalian girls, he gave press conferences saying he had not met Miss Right, and no Miss Right had met him.

Mama asked Theresa, *"My pikin, you think this problem spoils Kanyi's chance to be president?"*

"No, mama, no. Ee no spoil his chance to be senator. Ee no spoil chance for president."

"God dey, my pikin."

"God dey, mama."

As the election campaign progressed, there were no reports of violence. Three candidates emerged: Senator Kanyi of the Chop-Me-Chop Party (CMC), Chief Abudu Akodu of the Involved People's Convention (IPC), and Prof. (Mrs.) Mildred Amuci of the Sofalian Mass Congress (SMC). But things degenerated. The parties became polarised along regional lines and deep-pocketed cleavages.

Kanyi Mulaake hailed from the South, although his mother was from the Eastern region. He was among the wealthiest Ogas. Chief Abudu Akodu was from the West — a wealthy cocoa farmer with a large following of rural people who formed his IPC because a prophet predicted he would become the next president of Sofalia.

Prof. Mrs. Mildred was originally from Cyprus. Her husband, Professor Amumu, a renowned nuclear scientist, had been nominated to represent the North-West constituency but detested politics. Instead, he offered his wife, who had excellent social skills, studied human anthropology, and served as Minister of Information, Culture, and National Orientation for several years. But her husband's tribe did not consider her a serious candidate and threw their support behind Kanyi's CMC party.

Things looked promising for Kanyi, but unfounded rumours about his personal life kept resurfacing. He thought he would settle the marriage matter by marrying his long-time girlfriend, Princess Amenika, the beautiful, curvaceous princess of Kepeland. But things went awry.

He believed she was within reach, having welcomed him during several visits to his mansion in Calanana. Kanyi instructed his social media team to leak a story that he and the princess were finally exchanging marriage vows just after the elections. She would be sworn in on the same day as him as the First Lady of Sofalia.

But the Princess was not thrilled. She let him indulge her by introducing her to other high-ranking government officials as the next First Lady. However, at night, she rejected his touches. She declined Kanyi's engagement ring, stating she had decided to move on.

"Why?" was all Kanyi could ask.

"Kanyi, did you ask me why?"

"Yes, because you know I've been waiting for you all these years."

"Liar. You were busy waiting for me among many women worldwide. You waited among women of all shapes and colours."

"Believe me, First Lady, you and you alone were what I waited for. I was hoping you wouldn't listen to Sofalia's rumour media. They even accuse me of being gay. Imagine. Me? Gay?"

"Sweet talker, you."

"No, it's not just a sweet talk. Even my mother thinks there's something not quite right with me. But all this nonsense will stop once we are married and start having children."

"Kids? Kids already?" She laughed.

Kanyi knelt beside the bed, holding out a diamond ring. "Will you marry me, Amenika?" he asked.

She looked at him and snickered. He thrust the ring into her hand. She took it and held it up to the light.

"No, Kanyi, I will not marry you." It was an emphatic no.

"Will you not even consider my engagement ring?" Senator Kanyi asked.

Holding the ring to the light, Amenika said, "As to taste in fashion and jewels, you are second to none. Wow, this is the star among diamonds — the very pink star diamond engagement ring. A sixty-carat diamond is a rare treasure!" She slipped it onto her finger, admired it, then: Pfft. She removed it and handed it back.

"Senator, I can't take your ring now. It is too late."

"So, there is someone else?" Kanyi asked in a subdued voice.

"Yes, Senator, someone entered my heart and has locked it against all intrusion."

"Now that hurts, Princess. I am not intruding on you. I am entitled to you. We are from Kepe."

"Oh, that, Kepe? Yes, indeed, but Senator, the world has changed. Everybody is now from Kepe, and Kepe is everywhere."

"But Amenika, you are not just anybody. You are the Crown Princess."

"Very well, and I shall remain the Crown Princess of Kepe even when I marry my beloved Matteo Mantegazza."

Kanyi stood up, disgust dripping from his voice: "Matteo Mantegazza!" He rolled the name. "Please, don't trust these Italians. You cannot throw away genuine, tested, trusted love to become a mafioso — or reject being Sofalia's First Lady to marry a gigolo from Milan."

"Distinguished Senator, I must object. Please do not insult me. He is charming. While he may not be as wealthy as you, his family is respectable. He also works hard with his hands. He owns the Matteo Mantegazza fashion line, the leading brand for women today."

"Amenika, please, I am sorry. Tell me you will consider."

Amenika gazed at the diamond resting on the bed, worth at least seventy million dollars. She turned her attention back to Kanyi.

"Senator Kanyi Mulaake, if my father, the Most Royal Highness, the Apu of Kepeland, had not been appointed the highest traditional ruler in Sofalia — with the constitutional court deferring to him on all election matters — I might have believed your act. But handing over even a hundred million dollar ring means nothing to you. One kidnap victim can fetch you all this in a few hours.

"If I had not read your Bible — Robert Greene's *Forty-Eight Laws of Power* — I might not have realised you wanted to use me. But I read those sinister books. They teach the politics of hatred. You don't love me. You love nothing. Not even your mother. You are a user, not a lover. But yes, we are from Kepe."

She stood over his kneeling body, assured and dominant.

"Yes, we have been lovers for years. I did not mind that I was a royal and you a commoner. I admired your drive to get an education and become civilised; that was your selling point. But you carry too much baggage. Admit it — you have integrity issues. Declutter yours and come back when you are ready.

"I will consider your proposal, Distinguished Senator. But in your current form, we are not compatible. Declutter."

She pressed the engagement ring back into Kanyi's palm. "Here is your sixty-carat star of diamonds — while we wait."

Kanyi clung to her frame as he slowly rose to his feet. "Amenika, you've made me see myself through different eyes. Thank you. Thank you. But what about Matteo Mantegazza? I hope he will do nothing foolish while we wait."

"Like?"

"Like eloping with the princess to Cancun."

"He will also wait for me. He has always waited. After all, we will not wait too long — the elections will be over in three months."

"And you will be the most beautiful First Lady," Kanyi quipped.

They embraced and went to bed, each lying at the farthest edge of the king-size Posturepedic bed.

29

TIME OF LITTLE JEHOVAH

Prof. Mabel Gado expressed her gratitude to her former boss, Senator Kanyi. The acting Vice Chancellor, Prof. Udenku Addendum, presented her with the appointment letter for her new role as Vice Chancellor of the University of Calanana. The presidency had announced her appointment three days earlier.

She looked at the letter, smiling broadly, and said:

"The Eagle has landed!"

The struggle for the vice-chancellorship lasted six months of intense lobbying and campaigning. Gado was not rated among the five best candidates. For one thing, she was a woman. She had written a book about the large mammals in the Sofalian Senate, including their feeding and mating habits. Although she considered the book a formidable academic achievement, her colleagues mocked her behind her back, nicknaming her simply "Large Mammal."

Others derided her discipline and claimed she was not a mainstream dietetics professional. Rival candidates sneered that she was merely a cook for the senators. She had only recently been promoted to professorial rank. Finally, unable to bear the insults any longer, she took her campaign to her boss. Kanyi suggested calling the pro-chancellor, which is precisely what he did.

On learning of her appointment, Gado hurried to the senator's residence. Since her face granted her access to all the rooms, she soon encountered him in his dressing room. He struggled with the button on his trousers, which he couldn't reach. He turned to her in embarrassment.

"Prof, it's been a while."

"Yes, Senator. I serve on five university committees now — been busy."

"When you become vice-chancellor, it will mean less and less of our seeing."

"Well, that is why I am here today. I just received the letter from the council appointing me Vice Chancellor of the Federal University of Calanana!"

"So, the Pro-Chancellor kept his word."

"Yes, Senator. And he didn't attempt to molest me or anything. Thank you, thank you. My friends who left for America and Canada will now respect me for refusing also to run away from the Sofalian experience. Through this appointment, they understand that the glass ceiling for female academics has been broken forever. Please don't say that I won't see you again; you will be the president and a visitor to my university. My dear boss, I am confident you will be an exceptional president of Sofalia."

"Not many women see things this way."

"They can think whatever they want. You are the most gentlemanly of gentlemen. For all the years I worked for you, you did not own me, disrespect me, or abuse me."

"Professor, you were an excellent staff member. You treated yourself with great dignity in our house and will make a great VC."

"And when president, I will be your Minister of Health. Together, you and I will make Sofalia the healthiest country in the world."

"Do you know what I call that?"

"Yes, I know, Senator. You call it greed, but I call it opportunity. In this country, it is not what you know but who you know. I don't need to lobby anybody. You are my passport to whatever is desirable here in Sofalia."

"A vice-chancellor bears greater responsibility than a minister of health. She acts as the guardian of our country's most valuable national resource: youth. Youth is an essential resource and the most treasured driver of our nation's development and productivity."

"Yes, Senator. I am neither ungrateful nor greedy. The ivory tower is not what it seems. It no longer reflects society's ideals. Instead, it mirrors our society's worst vices. Professors are mostly focused on money, and the VC's office has become their only hope for a proper job, which keeps my office in constant turmoil."

"So, go there and make the change."

"And you, too, be a good president and change agent. Stand for justice and the downtrodden. Our country is in the agonies of death: corruption, tribalism, and foreign interference are our undoing."

"Professor, you have no idea; this country is more complex than you think. The people who control it are far removed. They are resolved to have their way. I have so many enemies."

"Many enemies, Senator, indicate you have taken a stand and are a person of convictions."

"You can't imagine that even among the principalities and powers, they pray against my victory."

"But Senator, I would hate to be your enemy. Do your enemies ever triumph?"

She helped him put on a tuxedo, but the waistline vanished under a voluminous shirt and potbelly, leaving the coat open.

"My boss, you will need another nutritionist soon. Your waistline is under threat."

"I know, Professor, but the campaign tours are very unhealthy. Everywhere we stop, eating their food is the first sign of allegiance and loyalty."

"In most Sofalian cultures, refusing food offered is seen as disrespectful. Therefore, small portions are advised."

"Okay, Professor. Thank you for stopping by and please join us in praying for this election. I have a funny premonition."

"Cast all doubt aside; you will be president."

Kanyi descended to the dining hall, where his parents had just finished supper and were weary of waiting. Baba Kanyi was the first to speak.

"Son, we have organised a Thanksgiving service in your honour in Kepe as part of your campaign. Please, don't disappoint us."

"Daddy, I can't come now, but when I win, we shall return to Kepe for the celebration."

Mama Kanyi, who had been quiet, spoke. *"Kanyi, e nefa good to be president, and no first lady."*

"Mama, please don't listen to them. I will be married. I have proposed to Amenika, the King's daughter. We will marry after the elections, before the swearing-in ceremony."

"Okay, I go happy well," replied Mama Kanyi. Then, lowering her voice in a menacing, conspiratorial manner: *"Otherwise, wetin dem say no good."*

"Mama," he interrupted, "if I had listened to what they've been saying all along, I wouldn't be where I am today. Let them talk. First, they branded me a thief. I was six years old, and one crazy pastor said I was possessed and needed to be exorcised. Then they said I wasn't educated enough or intelligent enough to speak English and do business. I spoke the best English and outsmarted the most intelligent white people. Then they said I would die in poverty. See for yourself; poverty is the one dying in my presence."

"Okayoo," said the mother in resignation, opening her palms and pulling her hands apart, knowing she could never win an argument with her son. She left the house.

As dusk approached, a new band of musicians assembled at the swimming pool. They had become popular with their latest hit song, *"If our victory pains you, take boiling water and die."* As the talking drums accentuated the words, dancers contorted their bodies, lowering themselves to the ground, mimicking death.

Kanyi surveyed them before heading to his convoy. He whispered to the lead driver, who then ordered the convoy to remain stationary. The lead driver retrieved the new vehicle — the bulletproof G-Wagon. The senator carried two hundred thousand dollars in cash and his military-issued magnum pistol in a compact black leather bag. Minutes later, they arrived at the thirty-six-storey Intercontinental Hotel, Calanana. A side lift took Kanyi to the Penthouse.

There was a young boy, barely twenty-one years old. Little Jehovah, they called him. People came from East and West to pay homage to this new religious sensation. On one side of the three-seater lay the Christian Bible and the Torah; on the other side, the Koran, the Hadith, and the Bhagavad Gita. The senator brushed aside two soldiers, jokingly remarking that Sofalian taxpayers were joyfully paying for their expensive stay at the Intercontinental, keeping watch over the man of God.

Little Jehovah had memorised not only the Bible, the Koran, and the Torah, but also the sacred texts of Hinduism and Buddhism. He presented this eclectic canon to new disciples — among them, Senator Kanyi Mulaake.

Kanyi was asked to sit in the sitting room, while Little Jehovah prayed in the bedroom. The senator left his rank and power outside the door. He removed his shoes and cap, squatted on the floor, and faced the entrance to the prayer chamber.

He purged his mind and focused on Little Jehovah's "radiant light." He imagined the holy man speaking face-to-face with the Almighty, like an elder brother with his junior. Nothing Jehovah asked was ever refused. He was rumoured to be God's younger brother — same mother, same father.

Little Jehovah at prayer was an ordeal no mortal could survive, they said. The glory of the Almighty descended, and matter dissolved into non-matter. Witnesses claimed he levitated a foot above the ground before dissolving into vapour. When this happened, he prophesied.

His origins were hazy. Born in India, he had been missing for fifteen years. Some claimed he spent them in a Pakistani prison for inciting Buddhists against Muslims. Others insisted he had been caught up into the Seventh Heaven to study at the feet of God and the Guardians of the Universe. In his own brief biography, he preferred the second story. There, he said, he was consecrated with authority over all earthly events. He condemned the world's religions as frauds and taught that there was only one true faith: the exclusive worship of Little Jehovah.

As his numinous energy filled Kanyi's mind, the senator drifted into sleep. He had fasted for three days on Little Jehovah's command, abstaining from sex, food, and drink. Today, the third day, he came in a tuxedo, as if attending a royal homage. Yet his dreams were filled with ballots and polling booths.

The bells on Little Jehovah's ankles jingled as he entered. Kanyi opened his eyes slowly and bowed to the ground.

"Allah-u-Abha," said Little Jehovah, borrowing from the Baha'i greeting.

"Allah-u-Abha, God is the greatest," Kanyi replied.

"The Almighty Jehovah has decreed you will be president of Sofalia," the holy man announced with assurance. "Not only president of Sofalia, but also of the United States of Africa. Your prayers have found favour."

"Amen," Kanyi whispered, eyes shut.

Jehovah continued: "Your rule will not end until you die in the saddle, an old man. But only if you obey His commandments. There are three."

"The first: Build Jehovah a temple in New York, in the centre of Manhattan — the largest holy shrine on earth."

"Your word is my command, master," Kanyi replied, though visions of zoning laws and New York mayors flickered in his mind.

"The second: Before the election, you will go to the streets of Calanana and marry an Atsan beggar for a day."

Kanyi blinked. "Your Holiness, pardon me, I don't understand."

"Very well. The day before the election, you will make love to a mad woman on the streets."

"But there are no beggars in Calanana. The streets are clean. Yet, if you say so, there must be."

"Yes, there are. Jehovah will send her."

"And the third commandment: Bury seven virgins at three in the morning on the morning of the election."

"Your Holiness, how will I know they are virgins?"

"I, Little Jehovah, will enter them and declare."

Without waiting for a response, he jingled back into his chamber.

The protocol officer emerged, thanking Kanyi for the half-million dollars credited to Jehovah's offshore account. He advised the senator to begin delivering virgins one by one from the next day. He also requested additional funds to extend Jehovah's stay in the penthouse, which, he explained, gave his master "special cosmic radiation."

"No problem," Kanyi answered. "Wisdom will sort reception tomorrow. And something extra for you. This project is for all of us."

As he left, dazed, Kanyi glanced down from the thirty-sixth floor at the blue Atlantic. He swore he would be the first Chribudslam president — Christian, Buddhist, Muslim, all fused — uniting secular and spiritual powers within himself.

But the idea of burying seven virgins gnawed at him. In Sofalia, politicians were rumoured to sacrifice one or two virgins. The current president, HE Kila Kama, was said to have buried three. Seven was unprecedented. Grotesque. Yet in the senator's mind, the virgins were like Thanksgiving turkeys: expendable offerings from the overpopulated Atsan poor.

"The enchantments of power are irresistible," he later said. "Like the charms of beautiful women. Power is beauty, and beauty is power. That is all I know and need to know."

And what after the presidency? He already knew. He would sell religion to the masses. Hope was the best commodity. The return on investment was unmatched. He would crown himself Minor Jehovah, transform Sofalia into a syncretic theocracy, and seize every church, mosque, and shrine. Above all, he hungered for Paradise — the glittering Church of Paradise, jewel of Calanana. And after that, perhaps his cosmic radiation would begin to challenge Little Jehovah.

30

G8 SUMMIT

Senator Kanyi was surrounded by the press at Nick Agyo International Airport, Calanana. He had widely publicised his overseas tours to consult with Sofalia's allies on the forthcoming elections. He considered it essential to establish his foreign-relations credentials. He had already declined an open debate with the other candidates, insisting it was beneath him to share the same stage. The polls placed him at a comfortable seventy per cent lead.

Politics was big business, and presidential elections were its most lucrative venture. For Kanyi, it was less about ideology than outspending opponents dollar for dollar. But he had little to fear; none of his rivals could match his war chest. He had several potential running mates but leaned toward Aminu Tenge-Tenge, the corrupt billionaire governor of Abulum Province. Tenge-Tenge had been siphoning offshore crude oil and selling it through an international racket of buccaneers. He promised to funnel a large portion of the provincial budget — about thirty billion dollars annually — into Kanyi's campaign. For Kanyi, it was a return on investment safer than the stock market.

Sofalia was ruled mainly by the Chop-Me-Chop (CMC) party and the military. The generals were no longer guardians of the state but shareholders in its spoils. Their retired peers and widows still enjoyed official perks. Their children inherited bank shares, oil wells, and utilities — electricity, water, and telecoms. These were "passive incomes" from castles lining the coast, their vaults stuffed with foreign cash.

They owned nearly all banks. Even when the national economy collapsed, they reported record profits. In Sofalia, the joke went, "Other nations own armies; here the army owns the nation."

Senator Kanyi was their protégé, their reliable investment. They had backed his businesses, and now his presidency. He was their dividend, the poster child of Sofalia's "stable democracy," useful to Western allies as proof that neo-liberalism had taken root in Africa.

The day before, Kanyi had unveiled his new private jet: the Airbus A380 "Flying Palace." Outfitted with conference rooms, situation rooms, a cinema hall, and even swimming pools, it was protected by missile-defence systems. The manufacturers had told him only three others existed: one, "Heaven-Mail," owned by His Holiness Godswill of the Paradise Church, another by a Saudi billionaire, and one by a Russian oligarch.

Godswill's aircraft, he knew, was reserved for ferrying prayers. Letters and petitions from Paradise followers were flown upward, released to angelic couriers at the Pearly Gates, and hand-delivered into Heaven's Throne Room. To Kanyi, this was competition: the overlap of politics and religion.

His own "Flying Palace" was monstrous and elegant, intimidating yet dazzling. It would carry him to the G8 summit in Muskoka, Canada, where leaders of Western nations and China were eager to meet Africa's newest strongman. They saw in him a promise: expanded trade and a revival of empire's golden age.

When his convoy reached the departure wing, journalists swarmed him. A CNN correspondent thrust a microphone toward his face.

"I am Amantuur from CNN, Senator. What message will you carry to the G8, given the closeness to your election?"

Kanyi smiled broadly.

"Excellent question, young lady, excellent question. I intend to request their help in our forthcoming elections. Our elections are too expensive. I will ask them for a loan. It will be repaid in full, from the Sofalian treasury within the first month of my administration."

There was stunned silence from the embarrassed journalists.

Kanyi squinted, scanning the forest of microphones, before pointing at a brightly dressed woman. Her hair was plastered flat on both sides of her head, elongating her small face. She had large brown eyes, flat cheeks, and dark blue lipstick smudged across her lips and eyelids.

Ying Jang of Xinhua News Agency stepped forward.

"Mr. Senator, you will be elected Sofalian president, all things being equal, in three weeks. How will your presidency benefit China?"

"Zhu ni hao," Kanyi replied, deploying the only three words he knew in Mandarin. "Hello, good day — that is a fundamental question. As you see, I am heading to the G8. I will meet the Chinese Premier, who will tell me everything I need to know. But let me put it on record: before China befriended Africa, the West was shy and coy, killing us with their so-called aid. Then came China — like bulls in a china shop! There is no stopping them. Every Sofalian village will soon have a little Chinese enclave. We are all Chinese now."

Loud, awkward laughter rippled across the press corps.

The next question came from Ahine Akiki Jr., a squat young reporter with an oily, pimply face framed by an afro halo.

"Distinguished Senator, congratulations on your new purchase of the Airbus A380, the world's largest private jet. This brings your fleet to four. But let me ask, sir: does it trouble you that individuals like yourself are so rich while Sofalia remains so poor?"

There was silence. Then Kanyi smiled.

"I was a billionaire before I came to serve this country, and I will be a billionaire after serving. Sofalia should be proud that one of its sons sits among the world's big boys. I deserve a national honour for my enterprise. Does it worry me? No. Why should it? Even Jesus told Judas, the thief, that the poor will always be with us. Poverty is a mindset. My rags-to-riches story shows Sofalians are poor by choice. I will use my expertise to help them build wealth. I am a self-made man."

At that point, the Chief of Protocol discreetly muted the microphone. He always did when the senator launched into the "self-made man" refrain, which invariably led to boastful detours. Even so, the journalists scribbled furiously.

"Gentlemen of the press," the Chief announced, "Q&A is concluded. Please see the Director of Media for your transport fare. And thank you for your favourable reporting this morning."

The senator's entourage numbered nearly fifty — party stalwarts, women supporters, loyal senators, and spiritual advisers. Many had been promised ministerial or ambassadorial appointments. They were motivated, fired up, already dreaming of palace offices.

Flying on the Airbus 380 was more than travel; it was an initiation rite into Kanyi's kitchen cabinet. His personal marabout, a mystic from Mali, accompanied him, dictating what he should eat, with whom he should speak, and whom to avoid for fear of "spiritual pollution."

The absurdity of Sofalian delegations abroad was not new. Years earlier, under President El Hadi Kobani, the entire UN delegation had been delayed two extra days when the president's prayer leader, a marabout from Senegal who spoke only Arabic, had gone missing in New York. The police had detained the marabout in handcuffs for indecent exposure at a Manhattan water fountain where he attempted ritual ablution.

Kanyi's entourage arrived in Toronto two days before the Muskoka summit. They lodged in the city centre and immediately spent over a million dollars on jewellery, perfumes, clothes, and walking canes. By dawn, several major stores closed temporarily to restock.

Meanwhile, Little Jehovah — travelling on his own private jet — insisted on the penthouse suite of the sixty-storey Intercontinental Hotel Toronto, claiming the "spiritual vibrations" there were essential.

Witnesses reported that during an outdoor massage on the sky terrace, he and his masseur suddenly levitated two feet above the skyline, terrifying onlookers. But those on their mindless shopping binge heard it only as unconfirmed rumours.

Back in Sofalia, state-controlled media went into overdrive:

• "Senator Kanyi receives a hero's welcome abroad!" • "Sofalia's leading candidate endorsed by the West!" • "Kanyi insists Sofalia must join the G8!"

In truth, Kanyi and his delegation were luxuriating in Toronto — and privately admitted they had no idea where Muskoka even was on the Canadian map. Still, they looked forward to "business" the following day, as aides consulted Google Maps in panic.

31

TIME OF QUEEN AKEMBER

Barkin Banka was a ruthless monster who feared women. This was why, despite his immense power and wealth as the acting head of the Sofalian Liberation Action Power (SLAP), he never married. After Gungun's sudden disappearance, many whispered that the great warlord was dead. Barkin Banka knew otherwise. Gungun could not die — it was impossible. He had seen his master ascend into the sky in a Chinese helicopter, and he believed, with religious conviction, that he would see him return. The sound of the departing rotors still roared inside his skull, like a permanent drumbeat, reminding him that the master would resurrect.

In Gungun's absence, Barkin Banka maintained loyalty by reporting daily to Gungun's wife, Queen Akember. She insisted on transparency: he was to account for every dollar, every rifle, every bullet. Though she did not command the battlefield directly, she was the de facto leader of SLAP, emerging from her hidden fortress, the Binda Cave, whenever it pleased her.

Barkin Banka had no taste for politics, strategy, or generosity. He believed money was useless except for buying weapons and paying for kidnappings. Under his brutal stewardship, SLAP became less an army than a slave colony. Thousands of hostages — traditional rulers, businesspeople, farmers, students — were forced into mining the caves to exhaustion. He disdained "charity" as weakness, though Akember often diverted funds as she saw fit.

He also lived by one central rule: no sex. Once, in his youth, he had tried it. The act had left his body convulsed, his eyes had gone blind, and his mouth had emitted guttural pig-squeals he could never forget. From that day forward, he obeyed the injunction of the medicine man who gave him the sacred Bante shield: sex would drain a warrior's spirit. Instead, he let his sub-commanders glut themselves on sexual slaves, while he stayed "pure."

Gungun, however, was the opposite. He had turned sex itself into ritual: climax was followed by the pistol shot; a victim's eyes obliterated. No woman survived seeing Gungun naked. He absorbed power from virgins, patterning himself after the legendary Queen Aminat of Zanzan, who bedded men and discarded their corpses at dawn.

But when Gungun met Akember — a stunning university dropout with ruthless instincts — he declared her his equal, his rib. She was merciless, beautiful, and deadly. Now that he was gone, she ruled in his name. Barkin Banka, despite his size and savagery, was content to serve her as second-in-command. Yet he trembled: she wanted to be both leader and second-in-command. She did not trust a misogynist who cloaked cowardice in loyalty.

Queen Akember trained daily, mastering pistols, rifles, grenades, and knives with frightening precision. She moved like a predator, a shadow among insurgents. Barkin Banka once stumbled upon her at dawn.

By the stream, her skirt, blouse, and sandals lay folded on the rock. Curious, he waited. The water's surface rippled, then churned. Half an hour passed before a hand broke through, clutching a gasping tilapia. Then the head of a woman rose — voluptuous, radiant, unearthly.

For a moment, Barkin Banka believed he was witnessing Mami Wata herself, the feared spirit of the waters. She emerged nude, her papaya-shaped breasts trembling, her waist narrow, her hips wide, her skin glistening with divine sheen. She recited incantations with closed eyes, hips swaying like waves.

Barkin Banka froze, weaponless, struck as though lightning had pinned him to the earth. His throat was dry. Taboo. Abomination. He dared not gaze too long, yet he could not look away. Terror overtook him, and he collapsed to the ground, covering his face with his palms. He felt her presence advancing toward him — and then stopping.

"Barkin Banka," she called out, her voice echoing like iron striking stone. "Why are you hiding your face? You already saw my nakedness. It is too late. Get up and face me. *Like my husband, like Queen Akember, you see my nakedness — and die.* Keep your ugly face on the ground until I dress."

After several minutes, she emerged fully clothed, retrieving the pistol hidden beneath her folded garments. With deliberate precision, she aimed it at his skull.

"Raise your head," she ordered.

Barkin Banka turned slowly, cradling his face in his palms. His voice cracked.

"My Queen and Commander, this was a mistake. I was not spying. Forgive me."

"For violating me?" she pressed.

"No, Queen. God is my witness. I did not."

"Yes — you did."

"No, I haven't. God knows."

"The devil knows you did, pig."

"Please, forgive me. I beg. I did not violate you."

"Oh yes, but you did. The moment your eyes touched my body, you imprinted me into your mind. Your brain has stored a million photographs of me, encoded forever, ready for your filthy pleasure whenever you choose."

"Queen, please. It was not my intention. I wish I could go blind."

"We will see to that soon."

"You mean — you would blind me?"

"Yes. I will dig my fingernails into your sockets, pluck out your eyes, and throw them into the pond."

"But Queen, how can I serve you blind? I served your husband, and I have served you faithfully."

"You have served enough with eyes. Now you will serve with faith, *blind allegiance.*"

He trembled. He had seen her kill with bare hands too often to doubt her threat.

She moved with sudden speed. Before he could breathe, her thighs locked around his neck, her hands pressing down on his skull. His air choked. His vision darkened. So this was how he would die — smothered between a woman's legs.

But just as quickly, she released him. He gasped, stunned.

"Listen to me, deadwood," she spat. "You are already a corpse. You feel nothing, fear nothing. Death would be a gift. No — you shall live, but as my slave. My husband was soft; that is why they captured him. I am not soft. I am the most ruthless killing machine Africa has birthed. From today, you belong to me."

The secret bound them thereafter. Akember's naked form haunted Barkin's nights. He dreamed of her body pressing against his, torturing him. Once, in desperation, he abducted thirty girls from the Government Girls' Secondary School at Mandep, executing twenty-nine and sparing only Mariam, who resembled Akember.

Mariam became his captive — fed, sheltered, placed on his bed while he lay on a rock slab outside. Yet after a month, the Queen's image burned sharper than ever. Terrified of the strange kinship between Mariam and Akember, he released the girl in secret.

When Mariam resurfaced, the Sofalian army claimed credit, parading her before cameras as a victory. She smiled faintly, whispering only to her friend Umami: "The place was paradise."

From then, Akember's dominion was uncontested. She convinced Barkin that his power was broken — that by seeing her naked, by imagining her in his dreams, he had violated his spiritual vows and lost his protective medicine.

Thus, she made him her slave for life. SLAP's money, mines, and all were now hers. And with them, she vowed vengeance. Senator Kanyi Mulaake, she swore, would suffer for Gungun's downfall.

32

THE KANYI OVERREACH

At Muskoka, the Canadian Prime Minister had little difficulty convincing the other G8 members to extend an invitation to Senator Kanyi Mulaake. Sofalia was viewed as a rising African power, strategically too essential to ignore. Besides, Kanyi was the frontrunner in his country's elections, and his address might hint at Sofalia's future direction — how the West could predict and profit from it. The members knew he was here as spectacle, not as equal.

Western oil executives lobbied hard, urging their governments to cut deals with the incoming president. They wanted Kanyi accessible at the summit's sidelines. His presence immediately boosted Muskoka's economy. Holiday cottages filled with his entourage; he bought one outright for three million dollars, paying triple its value. Nobody complained.

At midnight on his first night, Kanyi gathered managing directors of the largest oil companies. He reassured them: the new petroleum law that had just passed the Senate was "for show." The outgoing president would never sign it. Once in power, Kanyi would restart the process and guarantee the long-standing arrangement: Sofalia's crude would continue to be refined abroad and sold back at premium prices.

He told them politics was the highest form of business and promised his government would be their most profitable investment since colonial times. If Sofalia had only remained colonised longer, he lamented, his people would not be "dying of ignorance." The executives pledged vast sums toward his election expenses.

On the second day, Kanyi was scheduled to speak. He arrived in a perfectly tailored dark-blue Zegna suit, a white shirt, and a black bow tie. On his wrist glittered the Graff Diamonds "Hallucination" watch — worth fifty-five million dollars. On his feet, Moon Star shoes.

Kanyi had everything: boyish good looks, Oxford diction, Westernised inflexions, and a smile that was not quite a smile — more an arrogant display of charm. Life had been generous. He belonged not just to Sofalia's elite but to the global super-elite: a man who shopped at Rodeo Drive, Fifth Avenue, and Paris boutiques, invested in art and real estate, and spoke the language of power. His invitation to the G8 was no coincidence; it was a deliberate move into the world's ruling class.

This elite controlled the United Nations, the IMF, the WTO, and central banks. Kanyi believed he was ready to join them.

During a tea break, the Head of the European Commission, Henrich Verwoerd, pulled him aside.

"Hello, Mr. President," Verwoerd greeted.

"Hello, Mr. Verwoerd," Kanyi replied smoothly.

"I'm the Head of the European Commission to the G8. And you?"

"Senator Kanyi. Kanyi Mulaake."

"Which country, if you don't mind my asking?" Verwoerd crushed his hand in a bone-cracking shake, eyes probing for weakness.

"Sofalia," Kanyi said evenly.

"In East Africa, isn't it? Where were those American hostages buried? Yes, yes — Black Hawk Down."

"No, sir. West Africa. A democratic republic, once British."

"Ah, yes. So sorry. Then South Africa?"

"No, sir. Sofalia. West Africa."

"Ah, of course. My apologies, Mr. President."

"I am a Senator. But next time we meet, it will be as President."

"Well, Mr. Klinis, it was lovely meeting you."

"Kanyi," he corrected coldly. "Kanyi Mulaake."

"And what are you doing here, Mr. Kanyi?"

"I'm addressing the summit in ten minutes."

"Really? How extraordinary. But addressing the summit about what?"

Kanyi cast him a tolerant, whimsical glance. *Ignorant racist bigot,* he muttered inwardly as he walked away.

He entered the Lake Ontario Hall and was guided to the podium. The vast room was nearly empty. Many delegates had decided the Sofalian senator's slot was beneath them — an interruption to shopping or siesta. To them, Kanyi, with his diamond watch and borrowed mannerisms, was not a rising statesman but a gaudy distraction, a caricature.

The organisers carefully prepared the podium: a clean glass, a water bottle, and microphones aligned like weapons. The PA system crackled, and the master of ceremonies announced:

"Ladies and Gentlemen, our next speaker is Mr. Kanyi from the Federal Republic of Sofalia. Mr. Kanyi is a leading African entrepreneur listed in Forbes as the world's eighty-seventh wealthiest. He is a senator and the leading presidential candidate in the forthcoming elections. Mr. Kanyi — the floor is yours."

Despite his trademark swagger, Kanyi's heart pounded with stage fright. He had memorised his lines, but as he approached the lectern, his mind went blank. He stared into the hall. Fewer than twenty people, and the high table was empty. None of the G8 leaders had bothered to attend.

He glanced toward the press gallery. Packed. A wall of cameras and microphones pointed at him like bayonets. His lips were dry. For thirty agonising seconds, he stood frozen. Then, his voice broke through:

"God is great!"

The hall echoed. He pressed on:

"Your Excellencies, ladies and gentlemen of the G8, and your spouses, I thank you for this honour bestowed upon me, my country

Sofalia, and by extension, Africa. I have been informed that I am the first private-sector individual to address this body since its inception. I thank the Government of Canada for the warm welcome."

He paused. Still, the seats remained empty. His own delegation was absent, despite the hefty per diem. Rage surged through him. He decided: *If they won't hear me, the world will.*

He squared his shoulders, stared into the cameras, and declared:

"God is great, but the men and women He created are not so great. I stand here fully conscious of my identity as a black man from Sofalia. I speak for the voiceless, the objectified, the oppressed of the world. I stand before those who control humanity's fortunes — and misfortunes."

The press gallery stirred. His words were live across the globe. Kanyi's confidence returned.

"We live in the best of times — for some. Advances in medicine, science, and technology have created a paradise for a few. But for most — especially in the global South — it is the worst of times. Poverty and disease turn life into hell.

"The G8 presides over obscene inequality. One per cent owns more than the other ninety-nine combined. God Himself is outraged. He sends His rain to sinners and saints alike — yet you, the richest, hoard His blessings."

He leaned forward, voice rising:

"You hide behind neo-imperialism and market forces. You reward greed and punish humility. You perpetuate injustice while calling it order. The Almighty has given humanity knowledge to eradicate poverty — yet you choose profit over dignity."

Then came his fatal flourish:

"In Sofalia, we redistribute wealth. We give the wretched the power to exploit their resources — gold, diamonds, titanium. Yes, we take billions in not-so-decent ways: through robberies, through kidnappings. But we do so to survive a system designed to keep us broken.

"And now, I hold out my hand to the West. Return to us the

billions our leaders stole and hid in your banks. Send us not away empty."

The journalists leaned forward, unsure if they had just heard a global confession or a manifesto.

His voice thundered to the finish:

"As I return to Africa, let my presence bring hope. Let us march toward a world of justice, dignity, and respect where humanity may finally say with one voice: God is great!"

He looked up — and blinked. The hall was suddenly full. Delegates stood, clapping, cheering, hands raised in ovation. Cameras flashed. Leaders queued to shake his hand. He smiled, half-believing his own myth. He wondered if the applause and handshaking was not more theatre for the cameras than genuine respect.

That evening, Kanyi flew back to Sofalia in triumph. He had one more week before elections. The chairman of the electoral commission had quietly assured him of victory — millions already wired into their Belize accounts. All Kanyi had to do now was remain alive until election day.

33

THE AGREEMENT

Everything has a beginning and an end. Every insurgency has an expiry date, when the fever has run its course and the fire burns to ash. Sofalia's SLAP insurgency had mutated so many times it should have died a natural death. But it did not. It refused to die, because it made sense to those who profited from it. Insurgencies, like epidemics, thrive until the profiteers stop feeding them.

At first, it dressed itself as an Islamic jihad. The world believed its bombs and beheadings were the work of global Islamists. But it revealed its hypocrisy when it bombed mosques and kidnapped Muslim families alongside Christians.

Next, it rebranded as international banditry — a protection racket for camels, cows, and goat herders across Africa. That too collapsed under its contradictions. The Sofalian army, drawn from every tribe and faith, fought it while secretly arming it. The same hand that struck it also fed it. SLAP's weapons came from the world's most powerful nations — often from both sides of the same U.N. table.

The insurgency was both an enigma and an open book: a puzzle to diplomats, but an economic machine to its beneficiaries. For the government, it justified bloated, unaccountable security budgets. For foreign nations, it meant arms contracts and black-market weapons sales. For global corporations, it provided cheap, enslaved labour to mine Sofalia's gold, diamonds, and titanium.

Traditional rulers played their part. Each was assigned territory, his palace doubling as an armoury. They ruled like warlords. The middle class vanished. Those who once drove cars now trudged barefoot.

Sofalia was no longer a failed state — it was something worse: a marketplace of collapse. The Atsan raised vigilantes to defend themselves against the central government's failure. President Kila Kama and his senators were businessmen in robes, taxing citizens into slavery. Entry into cities required government-issued passes stamped:

This pass permits the bearer, (name), a registered property of the state, to enter Calanana for a period (stated) to serve as domestic slave of Oga (name stated).

Foreign nations, rather than recoil, salivated. Collapse was investment. Not only arms dealers and the IMF, but also universities. The University of Calanana was overpopulated with unemployed intellectuals, "humanities graduates" deemed dangerous to global order for producing too many ideas.

The international community bought shares in Sofalia's insurgency. They divided the country into three classes:

• The Ogas: politicians, business elites, clergy. • The Processing Class: civil servants turned siphoners of public funds. • The Atsan: impoverished peasants bound under Queen Aisha, who was unseen but obeyed.

The twist of Sofalia's fate: its most feared leaders were women. Queen Akember, widow of Gungun, and Queen Aisha, leader of the Atsan. Both products of the University of Sofalia, both ruthless, both indispensable. They controlled kidnapping as industry.

An ambassador from a U.N. Security Council state met them privately, helped launder their funds offshore, secured Western medical treatment, and ensured international immunity.

When President Kama sought U.N. help, he was rebuffed. The

General Assembly told him to negotiate — "like every other West African president."

But elections loomed. Senator Kanyi Mulaake's rise threatened Sofalia's delicate architecture of chaos. In Washington, U.S. Secretary of State Field Marshal Martin Cornell summoned Ambassador Abigail Maloney to a closed-door briefing.

Inside, she found Cornell and Lt. Gen. Lois McBride bent over war maps.

Cornell opened:

"Madam Ambassador, forgive the sudden recall. You've met General McBride, Joint Chiefs of Staff. We've studied your cables. The U.S. cannot afford Sofalia's total collapse. Too much is at stake."

He pointed to the map of Sofalia.

"Sofalia is our vulture. Nobody keeps a vulture as a pet, yet vultures keep the ecosystem clean. They eat the carrion that would spread disease. Sofalia devours its own carcasses — corruption, greed, insurgency — and spares us the stench. They are ugly, yes, but useful. Sofalia is not a failed state; it is carrion management.

"Like vultures, Sofalians can digest toxins — anthrax, rabies, corruption, tribalism — without dying. Their stomachs are built for it. In fact, their numbers are increasing. And they speak better English than most of our population."

"They arrive here highly skilled in their professions and require minimal adjustments," the Secretary of State went on, tracing his finger across the Sofalia map. "Their ethnicity represents the most educated group in the U.S. We need them here. Sofalia does not. That country thrives on self-perpetuating corruption and tribal racism. We give them opportunities. Sofalia gives them decay.

"But the dam is about to break. The next election is the dam."

He looked up.

"The U.S. military and the CIA have outlined three scenarios."

Scenario One:

"We take no action. Kanyi wins, becomes president, and manages affairs as he knows how. He is a convicted felon, a graduate of Miami-

Dade Correctional Centre, a willing fool. And whenever the United States chooses, we give him the Noriega treatment."

Ambassador Maloney and Gen. McBride smiled knowingly. It was a smile that said: *we've done this before.*

"But that," Cornell continued, "is less effective these days. The U.S. can no longer play global cowboy without consequences. The world still smoulders from Panama."

Scenario Two:

"Expose him. Leak his scandals, his offshore accounts, his theft of Sofalia's gold and titanium, his collusion with President Kila Kama to bleed the Central Bank. And the darkest of them all — his ritual of seven virgins buried alive. Such revelations would enrage the masses, and the army might topple him. Chaos would consume Kanyi, the president, and half the system with them."

The ambassador and general exchanged a glance.

Scenario Three:

"Seize control of the electoral commission's command-and-control. We have already intercepted the Belize bribes. The chairman and four commissioners are under sealed U.S. indictments. Their plea bargain allows us to feed them alternative results. They will announce Derib, the candidate expected to finish third, as the winner."

Cornell shook his head. "But Victor Derib is a Moscow man. Patrice Lumumba University. Ph.D. on *How to Delink the U.S. from Africa.* Elect him, and we gift the Kremlin Sofalia's gold. Suicide."

He leaned back. "We are not fools. We are not drunkards."

The room fell into silence. The ambassador and general lowered their heads, weary.

Cornell's voice hardened.

Scenario Four:

"The only real option. Outsource. Since Somalia, our doctrine has been no American boots in Africa's chaos zones. We will hand Sofalia to an ally — a friendly nation to do our work. They will be our bearded Sierra Nevada vulture, restoring equilibrium to Sofalian politics."

He jabbed at the map again.

"Ambassador Maloney, your role is to bring together the insurgent leader, Queen Akember Gungun, and the Atsan queen, Queen Aisha. Between them is one man they despise — Kanyi. Both women were entangled with him. Both command the country.

"Aisha rules the masses. Akember controls the guns. One is the river. The other is the teeth of the tiger. Bring them together. Our ally will reveal himself in Sofalia. And then — we reset the balance."

34

TWO QUEENS, ONE THRONE

The sun gleamed over Binda Hills, the mountain range straddling Sofalia and the Benin Republic. The sky was vast and cloud-scarce, the air tense with anticipation. At the foot of the mountain, the High Command of the Gungun insurgency gathered in formation. For them, receiving yet another international visitor was proof of their growing stature.

At the centre stood Queen Akember, encircled by twelve armed guards. Ammunition belts criss-crossed their chests. Two carried ground-to-air missile launchers.

Today's visitor was not the British ambassador, Sir James Pickering, though he often visited here. It was Queen Aisha of the Atsan — a legend in her own right.

A helicopter appeared, circling above the cave mouth before settling on a rough helipad. Dust and dead leaves swirled like a storm as its rotors slowed. Armed escorts fanned out. Then Aisha emerged — tall, commanding, in fatigues, with her commander Awus at her side. Soldiers hauled out metal trunks behind her.

Akember advanced to meet her. Though they had never met, each woman's reputation preceded her: one ruled Sofalia's forests, the other its plains. Their embrace was brief but heavy with history.

"My sister," Akember said. "At last, we meet."

"Yes," Aisha replied. "And under unusual circumstances. The ambassador promised you would come alone. Strange, isn't it? Strangers uniting us."

Akember smiled faintly. "Welcome, Queen of the Atsan. Welcome home."

The two queens clasped hands as martial music filled the cave. Guards marched in a parade, their rifles glinting under theatre lights rigged across the cavern walls.

Life inside Binda Cave was complete. Over seven thousand fighters lived and ate there, fed by kidnapped labour who farmed, fished, and herded in exchange for life. For those unlucky enough not to be "adopted," shallow graves outside told their story.

After the parade, there was a banquet: jollof rice, pounded yams, catfish stew, grass-cutter meat, with discipline evident in every gesture: stewards cleared plates quietly, while the commanders ate with controlled precision.

When the last course ended, Aisha leaned toward her hostess.

"You are a world-class insurgent, Akember. Had Charles Taylor known your strategies, he would still sit in Liberia's palace. Instead, he rots in The Hague."

Akember smirked. "He misunderstood his people. Liberia became a farce. Sofalia must never follow."

"Amen. We will make mistakes, but we must never become Nigeria or Liberia."

Akember rose, floodlights painting sharp lines on her face. She addressed both Aisha and the assembled command:

"Today is historic. Ironically, it was the international community that had to unite us. Still more ironic is that we — the despised women of Sofalia — now command armies. Do you remember our university days? When professors lectured us by day, and politicians dragged us into limousines by night? When we were 'entertainment' for ministers and senators?"

Her voice hardened.

"They thought we were toys. Instead, they created warriors. The very men who bought us drinks, fed us lies, and left us broken now tremble at our names. They rule a corpse of a state. We rule its living body."

The hall fell silent. The two queens looked at each other — not as rivals, but as rulers measuring the weight of shared power.

"Coming from poor backgrounds," Akember began, her voice echoing against the cavern walls, "we gritted our teeth and offered our bodies for their games. Ministers, senators, Ogas. They threw crumbs of stolen money at us — money kept in bedrooms, not schools, not hospitals, not roads. We were their trophies, their ornaments. Some of us dropped out. Some, like you, my sister, persevered and graduated.

"But look what their betrayal built: a democracy of parasites. A government of Ogas, by Ogas, for Ogas. They chose predation over production. When hunger grew too loud, they invented the insurgency — to mask their crimes, to siphon their budgets, to keep chaos profitable."

Her eyes swept the cave, catching the gaze of commanders and foot soldiers alike.

"At the start, they used us to mine their minerals. They funded us to burn mosques and churches, to ignite sectarian fire, to spread their poisonous propaganda. We were pawns in their lies.

"And my husband — my Gungun." Her voice faltered. For a moment, she reached into her handbag, drew out a handkerchief, and pressed it against her face. When she spoke again, her tone was steel.

"He lives in a German hospice, paralysed from the neck down. A talking head. A man once feared across Africa, reduced to muttering Bible verses like a penitent priest. They drained his strength, brainwashed his courage, made him a husk. And who betrayed him? Senator Kanyi Mulaake."

Her fists clenched.

"I swore to my beloved talking head that I, Akember, would avenge him. And tomorrow, when Kanyi is humiliated at the polls, when he is denied the throne he covets, I will stand vindicated. I don't want him killed — no. Death would be mercy. I want him broken, alive, stripped of the only thing he values: power."

She straightened, her eyes burning.

"Listen well. I was raised a Catholic girl. I dreamed of teaching children and of raising a family. But fate tore me away from my parents and my faith. My first blood was my best friend Kuyila — a classmate. Then my father. And after them, countless others. At first, killing thrilled the boys. Pulling a trigger was their drug. Rape, drugs, kidnapping — they called it glory. But it was emptiness. They deserve pity, not worship. Forgiveness, not endless war. Our youths need rehabilitation, not graves."

Her voice rose, gaining momentum.

"So, hear me, my sister. Hear me, my commanders. Our plan is simple. Tomorrow, Sofalia's sham democracy falls. Kanyi will not be declared president. What the public expects will not happen. Instead, we will end this war. This insurgency, born of betrayal and greed, will surrender its weapons."

Murmurs rippled through the cave. Then voices rose — first in shouts, then in chants:

"Amnesty! Amnesty! Amnesty!"

Akember raised her hand, and the hall quieted.

"Yes — amnesty. Clemency for our fighters. We are tired of sleeping in the bush. Tired of killing strangers. Tired of dying nameless deaths for Ogas who never bleed."

She turned to Queen Aisha, her eyes searching.

"Tomorrow, we drain the swamp. We end Sofalia's parody of democracy. Not for titles — not for crowns — but to end Kanyi. To end the Ogacracy. To give our people a chance at real democracy, a people's democracy."

The applause was deafening, echoing against the stone walls. Fighters banged rifles against the floor in rhythm.

Standing apart, Queen Aisha watched. She let the roar wash over her, a flicker of a smile crossing her face. To many, her pale skin made her appear ghostly, mistaken for foreign and half-mythical. But to the Atsan, she was flesh, blood, and command. She had lived among them since the streets, leading their hunger, shaping their rage.

For years, the state had hunted her shadow. But the harder they searched, the more she became a symbol. Not a woman, but an idea — the whisper that Sofalia's poor could fight back.

Now she had been summoned to receive the instruments of surrender from Akember herself. She had not expected such a confession, such a theatre of vengeance. But the moment demanded a response.

She rose slowly, her fatigue plain, her shoulders bare of rank. The chants dimmed as thousands turned to listen.

"My beloved sister, Queen Akember — thank you for your warm hospitality to me, my chief of staff Comrade Awus, and my delegation. Thank you for that fierce, honest welcome.

"I agree — it is an irony that foreigners brought us together to begin mending our broken country.

"My sister, though I lead the impoverished masses, I cannot accept the instruments of surrender on behalf of our fighters. That belongs to the state — to the government of Sofalia — and to the law that still claims to bind us.

"Our sovereignty has been stolen. A crumbling government has devalued human life, hollowed out public institutions, and normalised violence. They created the conditions that made us necessary. They mined our people as they mined our wealth.

"They used us — to dig their minerals, to light sectarian fires, and to entertain their nights. When we rose, they called us monsters. When we struck back, they called it madness. This is why we filled the vacuum: to keep our people alive when the state abandoned them."

She paused, her voice dropping.

"Yet listen: killing became a drug for our young — a cheap thrill offered to the hopeless. Rape, kidnapping, violence — these are not glory; they are sickness. Our youths deserve rehabilitation and purpose, not graves.

"So tomorrow, we will stop the theatre. We will deny the sham its

crowning. Kanyi will not be declared president. This insurgency —
born of betrayal and profit — must end on our terms. We will
demand amnesty and reintegration for those who lay down arms."

A roar rose from the ranks, and the cave answered with a chant:
"AMNESTY! AMNESTY! AMNESTY!"

"My sister," Aisha said, looking across at Akember, "we are not
here for trophies or titles. We seek a people's republic — not another
Oga's shrunken court. Join me, not as a subject, but as a co-builder. If
we fail, a military coup will sweep through, cleansing nothing but
replacing one set of predators with another.

"So I raise a toast — to those who refused to accept the status quo,
to the outcasts who fought, and to the day after tomorrow when
Sofalia begins again.

"May you live long, my sister, and may we witness not only the
end of an old order but the slow, stubborn birth of something new."

35

THE PRISONER'S DEFENCE

I am Senator Kanyi Mulaake. At this stage, I must tell you, the reader, the truth about what happened on Election Day in Sofalia, the twenty-fifth of June 2015. The famous Nigerian businessman Moshood Abiola once said, "You cannot shave a man's head in his absence." That is why I speak for myself — before others narrate my downfall for their own purposes.

It was worse than you could ever imagine. On that day, democracy faced its darkest hour in Sofalia. Citizens queued patiently under the scorching sun, clutching ballot papers, ready for change — the inevitable change whose winds had swept through our beloved nation.

The voting was peaceful, transparent, and credible. Both local and international observers hailed it as fair and orderly, an election that finally reflected the will of the people. From the capital Calanana to the most remote corners of Kasar, Ijato, Nune, Ihuu, and Gbagir, the result was the same: the people chose the Chop-Me-Chop (CMC) Party. They chose me.

That morning, I travelled to Kepe and voted at my polling station in Otom, accompanied by my parents. After we cast our ballots, we watched thousands of others patiently doing the same. I did not fly in luxury but in the Sofalian Air Force helicopter No. 1 — a symbol of respect for me, the incoming president. Across the nation, everything suggested redemption at last. But destiny had other plans.

By the time I returned to Nick Agyo International Airport, the atmosphere was surreal. Staff had deserted posts to vote, and the silence was heavy with expectation. I had no cause for fear: Dr. Kila Kama, the lame-duck president, was my friend. I had promised to appoint his son as Sofalia's UN representative and guaranteed five per cent of our Internally Generated Revenue — approximately fifty billion dollars annually — into his offshore accounts. The Central Bank was even to build him a two billion dollar palace-library in Kyado Village, designed by the grandson of Kenzo Tange. With such arrangements, betrayal seemed unthinkable.

The Armed Forces chiefs had already pledged loyalty. I reassured them their perks would continue. The business elite — the most treacherous creatures in Sofalia — remained silent but expectant. They fund all sides, hedge bets, then blackmail whoever wins. Yet no one dared claim they financed me.

When I arrived at my thirty-six-storey campaign office in Calanana, the streets were flooded with supporters — youths dancing, singing in my T-shirts, many of whom were not even registered to vote. The building's command wing was alive with plasma screens connected to offices nationwide and to the election commission itself. Our tech experts monitored tallies as they came in.

By three in the afternoon, I had not eaten. Princess Amenika — radiant, coy, playing her part as incoming First Lady — signalled for food. My chef wheeled in a table. We shared brunch quietly as we watched the screens.

Then it came. Breaking News on Sofalia TV: "Any moment now, the Chairman of the Commission will announce the winner of the presidential election. It is a landslide. Senator Kanyi Mulaake has scored nearly seventy per cent of the vote."

The room exploded with jubilation. Champagne corks popped, journalists snapped pictures, and my phones rang incessantly —

even the private line known only to my parents and the president. My heart swelled. Then I answered.

It was my mother. Her voice trembled:

"My son, Kanyi, dem kidnap me."

Then my mother screamed: *"Dem beat me. Dem wan kili me. No, doam, Kanyi. No doam. Let them kili me."*

Rage tore through me. I could hear them slapping her, then a gunshot. I screamed into the phone. "In the name of God, leave my poor mother alone. I will give you anything — any amount."

A cold voice answered: "Hello, Senator Kanyi. We've got your mother. Five men are ready to rape her and execute her. We will cut off her head and send it to you."

I almost fainted. My mother — the woman who gave me life — was held at their mercy. I begged, "How much? Tell me the sum."

"Everything," she said.

"Please, don't touch my mum. Request any amount in any currency. I will pay." I pleaded. "Please, Akember, please."

She corrected me. "Don't call me Akember. My proper title is Her Majesty, Queen Akember Gungun."

"Okay. Your Majesty. Please, spare her. Kill me instead." I kept crying. "I didn't betray Gungun. My mother has done nothing."

Another voice cut in: "The men are undressing your mother now. The rape will start; then we will shoot her. You can collect her head in a sack on No. 1 Kanyi Mulaake Street."

"Please, no," I begged. "She hasn't harmed you."

"She hasn't harmed us. Her son has. He stole husbands from wives and fathers from children."

A name in the voice made me hesitate. I tried again. "Aishatu — is that you? Please, forgive me."

"No. I am Queen Aisha," the voice declared. "You will do as we command."

A laugh escaped me — disbelief that Aishatu, the mad street girl, now led a guerrilla movement. I had searched for her after Little Jehovah's demand that I sleep with a mad beggar as penance. I wanted it to be her. I could not find her, and now she had my mother.

"Senator, are you there?" Aishatu snapped.

"Yes. Anything. Please, tell me what you want," I said.

Her demand was blunt: write a signed withdrawal letter to the Electoral Commission, announce it during a live press conference, and state that you are withdrawing for family reasons.

I begged to speak to my mother. Aishatu put the line through. My mother said, in a strangled voice, *"My pikin, Kanyi, let me be — let it be."*

What followed broke me: I resigned. I wrote the letter, prepared a press statement, and bowed out — the only candidate left standing had already been under siege by claims of my dominance. The commission's chairman and his colleagues, compromised and paid, were ready. They announced my withdrawal.

Afterwards, my mother was returned home — alive, physically unharmed. We embraced and prayed, kneeling in a state of grateful shock. For her, no crown was worth this price. She wanted nothing but life.

This is what happened. Two women — a queen and a madwoman — destroyed me, democracy, and the bright future I had believed was mine.

36

GUILTY OR NOT GUILTY?

I am Senator Kanyi Mulaake. At this stage, I want to tell you, the reader, the truth about what happened on Election Day in Sofalia in 2015. The Nigerian businessman Moshood Abiola famously said, "You cannot shave a man's head in his absence." That is why I ask for your attention: let me speak before others tarnish my name.

It was worse than you imagine — worse than you could ever imagine. On the twenty-fifth of June 2015, democracy in Sofalia faced its darkest hour. Citizens stood under the scorching sun in long queues with their ballot papers, ready to vote for change. They cast their votes peacefully, affirming their faith in electoral democracy. Observers described the process as calm, transparent, and credible — reflecting the will of the people.

I ask you: where did I go wrong? What would have been Sofalia's fate without me? How did I become a "high-risk factor" for the international community plotting my downfall? Why am I at the International Court of Justice in The Hague while my accomplices laugh in freedom, even in government? Why do I languish in a lonely cell because of two unstable women — one a prostitute, the other a madwoman?

My lawyers tell me I am detained here because I committed

crimes against humanity. They say I assassinated opponents, kidnapped people, trafficked arms, committed slavery, and led one of the world's most feared terror groups. They even took me to a morgue to identify the skeletons of seven girls they claim I buried alive.

I have been indicted for these crimes. The new government has seized my Sofalian assets, frozen my overseas accounts, confiscated my aircraft and yacht in Greece, and auctioned them off. My defence is now pro bono.

This is why I insist you hear evidence from my lips before this kangaroo court that disproportionately jails and executes influential men of colour from Africa and poor nations. At the end, decide whether I should be freed to return to Kepe to live with my people, marry the princess, and raise grandchildren for my mother, or go to the gallows.

My parents were only children. I was born in Kepe. My mother's parents were fishermen; my father, although literate, had only a primary school education. Both were devout Christians who believed in God and witches alike. My mother was said to have been betrothed to a sea creature who seized her womb and killed my only sister, Ambura, at birth. I was born after months of fasting and prayers, the answer to their vigils.

At seven, I was accused of demonic possession for envying my classmate Dan Kwado, whose lunch box overflowed with meat while mine held only yams. One day, the aroma overcame me; I took a piece of meat. I confessed, but the crime was already in my stomach. I was suspended from school for "stealing."

My father, believing in discipline, handed me over to Prophetess Dekpenen to exorcise demons. Many children died under her. I was not prepared to die, especially that kind of death. On the fifteenth of January 1978, before dawn and the rain, I fled Kepe. I was seven years old. I had no food, no shoes, no money. I ended up in Calanana as an anonymous soul, raising myself on the streets, scavenging from garbage cans.

Hunger, loneliness, and fear drove me to the ocean's edge many times. I wanted to sink beneath the waves. Often, the water threw me back. My swimming saved me from drowning.

At thirteen, I decided I would not die poor. I would be unique, never inferior. I would build myself. At that time, I discovered the power of the English language. It became my passport to the world, my best decision. The English language gave me reach and legitimacy. I practised Larry King Jr.'s diction from TV until I spoke like him.

I denounce all these charges as malicious, deliberate attempts by my enemies in Sofalia and abroad to undermine me. This court tries me under a shameful system of double standards. Tell me: what politician in the US, USSR, Saudi Arabia, or China does not live in privilege? When nations invade others, kill people, and destroy families with bombs under the pretext of saving them, are they brought here for judgment?

Assassinations and genocide by states are tolerated, much like the actions of powerful politicians who eliminate opponents before they are eliminated themselves. If I killed, it was self-defence. If I failed, I would be dead.

I plead not guilty to kidnapping, gun-running, slavery, blood diamonds, and terrorism. The actual true cause of these charges isn't Senator Kanyi Mulaake; it's the new world order — globalisation.

The rise of insurgency in Africa is tied to globalisation's adverse effects on individuals and societies. These effects ignite civil conflicts now branded as crimes against humanity. Globalisation penetrates societies, erodes morals, and exposes vulnerable nations to insecurity without protection.

I refuse to take responsibility for the crimes of globalisation.

The International Court of Justice must recognise that globalisation is the new colonisation in Sofalia. Just as the British refused to admit guilt for the atrocities of imperial rule, why should we, the Ogas of Sofalia — the new imperial rulers — now be compelled to confess under a double moral standard?

Globalisation transformed our government into a corporation. We, the elite, became entrepreneurs and shareholders; our citizens turned into customers. We increased taxes until they broke, yet we still demanded repayment so we could service foreign loans and keep the market afloat. We mastered the doctrines of globalisation and plunged headlong into wealth creation. I invested in precious stones. I employed people, paid them wages, and gave them livelihoods. If they wasted their earnings on drink or beat their spouses, why should I be to blame? I am not a slave driver. If this court is searching for the greatest criminal against humanity, look to globalisation itself.

Globalisation bred tensions, spawning insurgencies like Gungun's. We embraced free enterprise, yet I stand accused of "terrorism." When we privatised state assets, welfare collapsed. Competition grew fierce, even within families. Why is it a crime that I treated an insurgency as a business? Globalisation assigned value to everything — resources, relationships, even blood. Would it not have been foolish of me not to seize the chance to build wealth and live well? The culprit is globalisation, not Senator Kanyi Mulaake.

Yes, I ran for president. I ran because of our nation's poor leadership, and because bandits, warlords, and criminals had hijacked the state. Each time they kidnapped citizens, the government itself paid ransom. Paying bandits became official policy, creating more bandits. The Sofalian State was terrorism's biggest sponsor. And now you accuse me of "leading" insurgents? No. If anyone is guilty, it is the government that created those conditions. I am not your scapegoat.

Then comes the vilest accusation: that I raped and buried seven virgins alive. This cuts deepest. Human life is sacred. Religion is central to all men; when they lack God, they fashion gods out of wood and clay. Of all charges against me, this one unsettles me most. It was a tragedy, yes. But no witness links me to it. I neither raped nor buried anyone. No evidence exists. Yet the horror of it terrifies me.

I grew up mourning my only sister, Ambura, who died of preventable causes. I learned to respect women, to believe in their equality. My mother is my idol, my anchor, the woman I love most. How could I, of all men, have sanctioned harm to daughters?

On the very day of my stolen election, Amenika — the Princess of

Kepe — and I dreamed of raising two daughters in the Sofalian State House. We would give them the finest education and all the love in the world. Those murdered girls, too, had fathers. Fathers who wanted to protect their daughters, as I would protect mine.

If I am guilty of anything, it is of being trapped in Sofalia's corrupt values. Bernard Shaw once said, "We must reform society before we can reform ourselves. Personal righteousness is impossible in an unrighteous environment." Tell me: how can one man be righteous when his whole nation is corrupt?

In Sofalia, the Church itself is a business empire. It did not promote righteousness but iniquity. Politicians wore religion like a mask, echoing Machiavelli: a prince must appear devout to impress the people. That was our downfall.

Yes, I sought guidance from men like Little Jehovah, who ought to be on trial alongside me here. He dictated those rituals. Yet he still roams free, revered as a prophet. I take responsibility for my failings, but I will not carry the sins of false holy men.

If this tribunal chooses to hang me for these girls' deaths, then let me be hanged. My life has been a wound; your sentence would be its salt. I do not ask for pity. I am neither bitter nor angry. Life is a tragedy and beauty entwined. I built my paradise, and it became my hell.

Now, in this cell, I am shaped by fire. I no longer need medicine for my asthma. I no longer crave wealth, fame, or power. I only desire the joy of sitting with my family and thanking God that I found Him here, behind bars. If I die, I will die in paradise.

Thank you for being so patient.

THE END

ABOUT THE AUTHOR

Iyorwuese Hagher is a professor of Theatre for Development, a novelist, a poet, and a playwright. He was Nigeria's Ambassador to Mexico and High Commissioner to Canada. Hagher is one of the world's most politically exposed creative writers. He was a Senator, a cabinet minister, and a member of Nigeria's constitutional conference.

He lives in Dayton, Ohio, with his wife, Nancy.

ALSO BY IYORWUESE HAGHER

The Conquest of Azenga

Corruption in Africa: Fifteen Plays

A Day in Mexico and Other Poems

Nigeria After the Nightmare

The Kwagh-hir Theater: A Weapon for Social Action

Diverse but Not Broken: National Wake Up Calls for Nigeria

The English Language and Its Discontents

Leadership: Leading Africa Out of Chaos